ODD'S END

ODD'S END

Tim Wynne-Jones

McCLELLAND AND STEWART

The Canadian Publishers
McClelland and Stewart Limited
25 Hollinger Road
Toronto M4B 3G2

Published simultaneously in the United States
by Little, Brown and Company, Inc., and in
the United Kingdom by André Deutsch Ltd.

CANADIAN CATALOGUING IN PUBLICATION DATA

Wynne-Jones, Tim.
  Odd's end
ISBN 0-7710-9052-8
I. Title.
PS8595.Y66032   C813'.54   C80-094454-2
PR9199.3.W96032

Printed and bound in the United States of America

To my mother and father

ODD'S END

BARN

SHOP

LOFT

SHED

STUDIO

LAUNDRY

PANTRY

KITCHEN

UP

DINING ROOM

COURTYARD

LIVING ROOM

FP

STUDY

THE OLD COTTAGE
VESTIBULE

FP

South Wing

West
Wing

Upstairs

CHILDREN'S
ROOM

BATH

BATH

MASTER BEDROOM

SPARE
ROOM

Author's Note

To the ragged coastline of Nova Scotia's south shore I have surreptitiously added a peninsula or two and imagined several small towns where it seemed appropriate to do so. Likewise, I have added imaginary works to the *oeuvres* of several real, living artists. This is done with great respect to the artists named. The characters in the story are fictional, though close friends might notice a reflection here and there.

Finally, the events in the story are totally fictitious. I know of no similar incident.

The Initiation

The problem with yard lights is that they go out. Mary Close
had grown up in the city where the lights never went out. A
yard light just wasn't the same – one small, solitary bulb and
when that went, nothing. What was the use? Mary wasn't at
all sure she even liked yard lights. She couldn't decide which
was less comforting: one light or no light at all. She sometimes thought the former. If trouble doesn't know you're
there, it won't bother you. You become invisible. She had
learned since she had moved to the country that you do
what country people do, and she had conformed. Of course,
if the bulb burned out when you were at home, that was one
thing. But if it went out when you were on your way home,
that was quite another. Nobody ever changed a bulb before
it burned out, that would be nonsense.

She knew the light was a courtesy, a candle in the window
to lost wayfarers or motorists in trouble. But since her house
was alone on an otherwise deserted road, and a dead end, no
less, such creatures were mercifully few and far between.
True, there was the occasional sightseer, a beach party that
had lost their way and could have no idea they were trespassing since she had not put up a No Trespassing sign. But
that only happened once in a while, and it had never happened at night. Sometimes when it was very dark, like
tonight, it was not difficult for a mind of quick invention to

people the dark with trespassers. No doubt the light was a deterrent to criminals. Better the devil you know et cetera, and to see was to know, so they say, and yet . . . .

There was another complaint with yard lights. They had the annoying habit of casting shadows. With a strong wind off the sea the trees that circled Odd's End on three sides conspired with the light to produce outlandish shadow plays. And since the light standard itself waved like a sapling, the shadows darted around the courtyard like grotesque, noiseless children at tag – damned scary. At least in the dark there were no shadows. The one time Mary found a yard light indispensable, however, was when returning to Odd's End late at night alone. She had religiously switched it on that very afternoon at three, with the sun still high in the May sky. She had felt the fool she always felt in doing so. Now, as she turned off the little-used Peninsula Road onto the seldom-used Park Road, she remembered just how frightening it could be to arrive home, but for that solitary light. The light at the end of the tunnel.

She geared down as she turned off the asphalt. The Park Road was little more than a trail; it was deeply rutted and just wide enough for the truck to pass. The underbrush was thicker at the top of the road and at places closed in, rustling and scraping against the sides of the vehicle. After a moment there was a clearing where the Rood Manor stood – decrepit old thing – shuttered, abandoned; slated for renovation by the provincial tourist office but not this year. A road curved off to the right to the outhouses connected with the Grange, and another circled the overgrown lawns until it dropped down into the forest. Mary guided the truck down this second route; a bend and the massive house was lost to view in the matted darkness. The Park Road bounced and swerved and fell almost a mile to the sea and Odd's End.

Shortly Mary would see the light flickering its indecipherable code through the trees. The woods thinned out towards the sea. "The sea was the end," they said hereabouts.

By now, she thought. That should have been the turn, but then in seven years she had never actually managed to count the turns in the twisting descent. After another couple of turns, however, she began to fret. The light *had* gone out. Her mind began to manufacture an assortment of scenarios – the gang of drunken beach bums in dune buggies, the maniac escaped from Springhill, the pirate ghost. She had played all these scenarios a thousand times. Out of the darkness, she constructed awesome sets and desperate players. She was not a nervous type by nature. She could not tolerate ninnies, especially the female of the species. It had been her decision to move out here, to live in isolation. But if she was not nervous, she was, at least, cautious. Glancing at the truck's clock she realized that Malcolm would be less than half an hour behind her. She maneuvered the truck through another long turn and her growing anxiety was dispersed. There was the light after all. Or was it? The relief was short-lived – the light was from the house, from inside the house, from the west wing which had been obscured from view at first. She was still too far away to be able to discern any movement within. Stupid! It must be Malcolm. He dismissed his class early – if not a typical event it was not unknown to happen, especially this late in the term. In another moment this cheery notion was also dispelled, for suddenly all the lights went off. This, at last, was truly disturbing. She slowed down the truck to a crawl and locked both doors. She would reconnoiter and wait in the truck. If it seemed prudent, she could turn around in the courtyard. She would wait and see.

And so she did. She sat staring at the dark house, but not entirely dark, as she discovered to her discomfort – candles had been lit and dimly illuminated the dining room. Odd's End sat around a large courtyard on three sides. The bulk of the house formed the south wing to her left where she sat at the head of the courtyard. At the back of the yard was the west wing, the first floor of which was all glass. To her right

11

was a corner of her studio; the shed and the stables, presently used as a garage, formed the north wing. The dining room was in the west wing where the candles now flickered. After twenty minutes, that was the only movement she had seen. As eerie as the scene was, she found herself feeling distinctly foolish. For one thing, there were no trees in the front of the house, only the road, reduced to a sandy path, and beyond that the dunes, the beach, and finally the sea. The oppressive darkness of the park opened to the sky; the darkness was neither as impenetrable nor as frightening. For another thing she was simply growing impatient. Perhaps it was a surprise party, although she could not think of an occasion warranting one. If so, the hidden guests must be laughing themselves silly at her expense. If the scene was eerie, it could not be considered really frightening, not after twenty minutes. She was feeling very much like a ninny.

At last she saw through the trees the lights of the Fiat, heralding Malcolm's arrival. She waited a moment more but her impatience got the better of her. If it was nothing she couldn't bear the thought of Malcolm laughing at her. She would leave the truck's engine running, just to be safe. She jumped from the cab and began to cross the courtyard. She could hear the unmistakable groan of the car now; Malcolm always took the road much faster than she did. By the time he reached the house, she was at the French doors. She heard him shout something, the meaning of which was lost in the noise from the idling truck. She didn't turn around. As she opened the doors, the aroma reached her. She entered and stared at the dimly-lit table in amazement. Malcolm's voice reached her again. She spun around to greet him with a wry grin.

"You devil!" she cried.

Malcolm looked back over his shoulder but hugged her affectionately. Having kissed her, he looked beyond her into the ill-lit room, squinting. Curiosity, surprise? It was to be a charade. Fine; two could play.

"I am sorry but I seem to have lost my way. Is this the Dalrymple Estate?" she exclaimed theatrically.

Malcolm looked quizzical for an instant. "My God. Is it really Chetwind?"

"Sir Reginald!"

"Zenobia!"

They embraced again stiffly. Malcolm pulled away suddenly and scowled at the truck, still idling at the foot of the courtyard.

"You might quell that grumbling monster of yours, Zen darling."

"Anything for you, Reggy," she said passionately.

Without further ado, Mary ran back across the courtyard, stopping briefly to curtsy.

Malcolm applauded. "Bravo," he called after her, but nonetheless he noted what a bizarre image she made, curtsying deeply in the headlights of an idling truck. For that matter, how odd of him to be clapping; an audience of one. He went upstairs to change.

The table had not been set, it had been staged. Mary's seldom-used family silver had been polished until it gleamed and the family crystal shone. The serving platters were bright with distorted reflections, all pink and gold: the Alençon lace place mats, English porcelain, vermeil flatware. From a tall cut-glass vase, calla lilies stood like tropical birds hovering in attendance over the exotic stage. Malcolm was greeted on his return by a long-stemmed glass of Pouilly-Fuissé and a kiss which tasted the same—he guessed the vintage. They stood together for a moment, staring at the familiar table in its unfamiliar dress. Malcolm had changed into shorts and a T-shirt. He felt ridiculous, as if he should have put on evening clothes instead. Mary looked at her own jeans and cotton shirt. She felt insignificant, out of place in her own home. The table was inviting, certainly, but also oddly repellent in its grandeur. Damn it, it was the table that was inappropriate, not her. Her presentiments were interrupted.

"So the family heirlooms have come out of the closet," said Malcolm. The spell was momentarily broken. They sat down.

"To haunt us, no doubt," rejoined Mary.

Malcolm began to serve the salad. He suddenly laughed a knowing laugh.

"How did you remember?" he said.

"Remember what?"

"That it was one hundred and eighty-four days before our anniversary."

Mary thought a moment. "Sixty-two, sixty-three days before my birthday." They toasted each other.

"Happy Unbirthday, my love."

"Happy Unanniversary, darling." She raised her glass again, ceremoniously.

"Universary," he corrected.

When the toast was accomplished, Malcolm excused himself and disappeared into the living room. When he returned, he was followed by the scratched but still mellifluous voice of vintage Bobby Short: "I Like the Likes of You." He found Mary with a crease in her brow, lost in thought. Finally she spoke.

"What I can't figure out is where you parked the Fiat."

Malcolm looked distracted. "The Fiat?"

"I mean, where could you park it so that I wouldn't see you but that was close enough for you to sneak back past me in order to make your 'entrance'?"

Malcolm looked piercingly at the tip of his knife, which he held poised before his nose.

"The Fiat, yes, of course! A fiendish plot; poor cretin, he never had a chance!"

Mary waited until he had finished this curious and inconsequential outburst and then barreled on enthusiastically.

"At the long turn, the old logging road, right?"

Malcolm looked perplexed momentarily, but then he winked knowingly. Mary frowned. The game was to continue.

"What I find more amazing than where I might have secreted the car is that you have coddled the eggs. It is, after all, the correct thing to do, but we have always settled for raw." When Mary merely looked down at her plate and back to Malcolm he continued uncertainly. "Caesar hails you?" The pun was lame – he knew it. When she didn't speak, he added, "It *is* a compliment, or meant to be."

Mary didn't answer immediately. She felt uneasy, the odd sense of repellency she had felt when they first sat down now returned so that the salad seemed unpalatable, and not because the eggs were coddled.

"Malcolm, you can't seriously believe that I am responsible for this?"

Her husband looked around him and then, putting his finger to his lips, he whispered, "Don't worry, I won't tell a soul."

She was becoming unreasonably annoyed; their scenes did not usually go on, but then he had gone to enormous lengths with this meal. She could at least play her part. But which part? Good, old, reliable Zenobia Chetwind.

"You won't leave me over the eggs, will you? I couldn't bear it. Not again."

Malcolm only grinned. His mouth was full; a piece of romaine had stuck to his lip and she watched it intently, waiting for his reply, or the reply of Reginald, the Beast or somebody, it didn't much matter who. But none came. Her voice dropped out of character, and she spoke peevishly.

"You didn't have to make me wait so long."

Malcolm carefully unfolded a linen napkin nestled in a porcelain bowl. A thin stream of smoke arose. "Whoever it was that coddled the eggs and cleaned the silver also found the time to bake croissants, unless the bakery in Steep Cove has changed owners." This was said in a tone that implied complicity, or at least sympathy, with whatever game he supposed was afoot.

Mary responded with an impatient edge to her voice.

"Malcolm, stop it! I had nothing to do with this, and you know it. Besides, I resent the implications; I have never made a croissant that didn't taste like a boomerang!" With this startling comment, she again dug into her salad. Malcolm was momentarily speechless. Mary was obviously not about to be taunted. Somehow he had spoiled the celebration. But what celebration? It occurred to him that his comment about the croissants had somehow been misinterpreted.

"Sweetheart, I'm sorry, this is all lovely."

Mary slammed her fork down on the table. It was a petulant gesture, but she was tired, and the joke had gone on long enough. She also had that uncanny sensation that it wasn't very funny; that it was too elaborate to be funny.

Malcolm was stunned. He looked to the living room as if an answer might be expected from that quarter. "You Make Me Feel So Young" was not the correct answer. When he spoke again his tone held not the slightest hint of derision.

"You really think *I* did all this?"

She nodded expectantly. Malcolm lifted the lid on the nearest chafing dish. A delicate aroma of fish, tarragon, and lemon perfumed the air. It was his answer, his exhibit for the defense. He replaced the lid and looked at Mary as if to say his sorties into the kitchen could never hope to produce such an aroma.

Mary suddenly perked up. "Maybe it's my mother."

Malcolm shook his head. "No," he said confidently, "it's fish."

Mary glared.

"Mary, I was at my lecture until nine. I've got sixteen witnesses who will swear that they were soundly bored by 'The Author-based Theory of Literary Interpretation' – I'm trying out my paper on them – until at least nine o'clock." He paused, and there was suddenly a mischievous grin on his face, replaced as quickly by a look of mock severity. He boomed, "And where were *you* on the night of, that is to say, the night in question?" His face had wrinkled into the improbable caricature of a bewigged attorney.

"Lower West Pubnico," she threw back at him.

"Your Honor! Contempt of court."

"At an auction with Kevin." She laughed in spite of herself.

"Tell that to the judge, lady," Malcolm persisted.

"My Lud ...." But it was no use. She didn't feel like improvising any more. This was not an appropriate time.

Malcolm waited for her to finish. When she did not, he opened a second bottle of wine from the cooler beside his chair. The cooler: last time he had seen it, it was in the shed, broken. He contemplated it a moment.

"Don't you see, my chuck," he said grandly, "that we must eschew theory and base everything, *everything*, on observation and subsequent experimentation. Give me empiricism, or give me death!" He banged the table loudly with his fist. A curl of blond hair fell idiotically over one eye, and he attempted to blow it away.

"Theoretically, my dear, something must not exist and yet it does. Take this cooler, for instance. Theoretically it is broken, in a heap in the basement, laden with dust, all wrapped about in cobwebs. So much for theory!"

"Take this dinner," murmured Mary, under her breath, "please!"

"What was that?"

She gave him her "if-looks-could-kill" glare and dug her fork violently into a crouton.

Malcolm stood up suddenly and a little woozily.

"Logic. That is all. Logic."

The impromptu performance over, he sat again. They looked at each other. Each was looking for the telltale glint in the eye; each was waiting for the mask to drop, the knowing smile, so that the last laugh could be laughed, and the abortive meal could resume as merrily as the feast deserved. Nothing happened.

"You would have seen the Fiat if I had parked it on the logging road." It seemed an inane thing to say at that moment, but it had the ring of sincerity.

Mary bit her lip. When she spoke, the testiness was gone. She asked meekly, "You did none of this?"

Malcolm shook his head. "You?"

"No."

"Mrs. Rapsey?" The disbelief with which Malcolm imbued the reference to their cleaning lady lightened the mood momentarily. Meanwhile, the record had stopped. The silence was charged with expectancy. Malcolm continued.

"For instance, you can't tell me what is in this tureen?"

"I haven't looked."

"Or any of these chafing dishes?"

"I thought it was supposed to be a surprise."

Malcolm raised one eyebrow at the note of irony in her voice.

"Surprise," he murmured. The silence rushed in on them again. He was baffled and as ill at ease as Mary. Not knowing what else to do, he lifted the lid on the tureen and peered inside.

"Vichyssoise," he said. "Shouldn't we have served this first?"

She opened a narrow dish. Eggplant, and what she suspected might be truffles.

"Truffles."

It became a bizarre game, played without the banter of parlor games but in deadly earnest. Malcolm would uncover a dish. Endive, chestnuts in wine sauce, another unrecognizable fish, snails in a bed of parsley, green fettucini, roasted pheasant – the air was thick with intoxicating smells. They were surrounded by more food than they could ever hope to eat; surrounded and helpless.

"Why do I feel like Goldilocks?" asked Mary. No answer was forthcoming.

Finally there was only one dish unexposed. The monstrous serving platter. It was a piece of Grande Baroque, sensuously patterned, deeply chased. Malcolm reached for the gold handle. Mary gasped and Malcolm snatched back his hand as though his fingers were burned. Mary said nothing but her eyes did. It was not going to be a turkey, in fact it was not going to be anything recognizable. Or worse still, it might be all too recognizable—something familiar. Something one didn't eat. That was what Malcolm read in her eyes. When he reached out again for the lid she turned away.

What was exposed was indeed extraordinary—grotesque but simultaneously beautiful. It was a large ham glacé, at least the shape was that of a ham but the color, an incredible mustard yellow, was not. The aspic was as hard and smooth as polished porcelain. An intricate pattern of pimiento and sliced olives swirled over the surface like something out of Islam—the elaborately jeweled cover of a Koran, perhaps. It was impossible to imagine eating such a thing, but then it was impossible to imagine eating any of the food without knowing who had made it, why it was there, or whether it was all just a sensational mistake.

"Why do I feel like Goldilocks?" repeated Mary, a little louder.

Before Malcolm could respond, the timer on the stove went off. An air-raid siren could not have been more startling. Neither moved for a moment while the timer went on dinging. Finally Mary lifted herself from her chair. She walked stealthily into the kitchen, looking back over her shoulder to Malcolm for support. There were no walls dividing the two rooms. Two oak pews stood to either side of the entranceway. The stove was directly across the floor. It was like some strange religious ritual—the stove like an altar and she a reluctant initiate to the rites. She did not open the oven door directly. Having turned off the bell she moved aside, crouching behind the wooden counter. What might that door trigger? Was this the punch line, perfectly timed? But her curiosity got the better of her. It was not a bomb. Or at least it did not go off. She turned around to Malcolm with a look of desperation on her face that made him leap to his feet.

"What is it?"

She could scarcely talk. "I think it's a coconut soufflé."

1

I believe I have found a home! You can have no idea how monumental a struggle it has been. What is a home to you? Have you found the ideal home? Think back. The home of your earliest childhood – that was a home, but after that? A succession of walk-ups, bed-sitters, duplexes, splits, and condominia. The average soul never has the opportunity, as the pious sage advises, to make his home where he finds it. Rather, his home is where his job finds him, and what his pocketbook can afford. From the outset you must realize what "home" means to me. I have invested in my search all the fervor of Galahad seeking the Grail, or, more appropriately, Odysseus searching for Ithaca. And there have been Odyssean adventures: monsters, sirens, animated rocks – gods for and gods against. I am getting old; I limp a bit when it rains and my hair is no longer a color, only a shade. But I am there, almost.

Like Odysseus, my voyage has been cyclical, though it did not begin here. I speak of a greater cycle; you see, I contend that to find one's true home, as distinct from the cots and the kitchenettes one merely puts up with, is to find one's way back upstream to that first home with its lofty ceilings and blackest cellar. That first home safe under the heart in the amniotic oblivion of one's "proper dark."

Real estate. The meaning of real estate is lost to most.

There is only one real estate. It is not simply a possession – a home isn't – it cannot really be bought. It is the manifestation of a man. In its decor can be found the reflection of his sensibilities: its windows are his eyes, its portals are his mouth. A home speaks of a man. Its walls are his ears. A home, by my exacting standards, must be the heart and soul of the inhabitant – the nautilus, the turtle shell. I doubt if any two people can, for that reason, live in true harmony under the same roof. Appropriately, I have remained a single man.

Do you begin to grasp it? It is the belief, the hypothesis, that has dominated my life. To find the perfect home, to carve out of the world a place that is me. Man is, after all, despite his desperate rationality, still a creature responding to the territorial urges of a creature. A wolf, stalking out the limits of his realm. I am different from my fellow creatures only in the tenacity with which I have tracked down my goal. I am different only in that there could be no compromise. But that makes me very different.

How long has it been? Thirty years. I set off as a boy with no other motive in life. You cannot imagine that, can you? Then neither will you be capable of imagining how I must feel at this moment. You say, but wait, if you have searched so long, Mr. X (you may call me that, people do), with only one goal, is it merely one home you have dreamed? And how can you be sure this is it, the one among millions? If I had dreamed this house, I could have built it. Certainly I know all there is to know about domestic architecture, and money is no object. I have never had any trouble laying my hands on money. Could Galahad have made himself the Chalice? Never! Dreams do not translate into gold nor into bricks and timber. Which is to say that to dream of my home was in no way to create it. A child is born of a woman. If he never knows his mother, he can still be sure that she exists, and no matter what form he dreams she may take, he will recognize her when they meet at last. But then, of course, there is Oedipus, you argue. All I can say concerning that unfortunate wretch is that putting out his eyes was only a belated recognition of their blindness. Mind you, he wasn't looking for his mother. Answering a tricky riddle did not make him a seer. My eyes see all too clearly. It was my premise that such a house already existed, even as I began my search. A house that would be my sense of place.

The Japanese, they know. They identify the first utterance of a baby, *ma*, not as mother, as westerners insist, but as place; and truly, does it not make sense that a human's first word should do more than merely identify a machine? Surely that is all a mother is. No. The human recognizes himself existing in space. "Ma," he says.

The accident of my birth, for I had no say in the matter, took place in Ohio—Dayton, Ohio. I will not bore you with the story of my childhood except for telling you of my home—the home in which I was born. The Crows, it was called, and a magnificent house it was. I remember its always being dark, with dark wood, and dimly lit. For me it was a house of hiding places: the laundry chute, the narrow winding servants' stairs, a room over the study, reached from the landing through a door three feet high, cupboards built under the eaves. It possessed the full score of architectural idiosyncrasies that all old houses have: places for a little boy to hide his tin soldiers, and for a solitary child to hide himself. Curled up in the storage closet I could feel the pulse of the house—the dark, warm heart of the crow.

I would watch the world from the attic window, looking down like a prince over his kingdom on the broad expanse of South Mahone Drive. The attic window was like a window in the elms which towered the length of South Mahone. I could watch the little people on their porches, in their gardens, in their bedrooms, unaware of my presence. The Crow's Nest, I called it, my attic window. It was set deep and there was a wide ledge. I could sit in an old wicker basket there, armed with an eyeglass that had belonged to my grandfather, and watch the world go on about its curious business. I was a retiring child, always happier to watch than to participate. I learned the art of "joining in" much later but only because I found that it could enhance what I had learned from observation. Truly, I did not join in in spirit because I did not share with others. I only gathered useful information. Even as a youth, it was the judicious participation of the private eye. In those lazy summers of childhood I learned the virtue of patience, of silent waiting.

We lost The Crows. My father's business collapsed. The fool, I never forgave him. It makes little difference to me that it was not his fault (it was the Depression). I could not understand that then, but understanding it now, I still will not forgive him; a man must fight, but not him—we lost The Crows! We moved to a bungalow in a new suburb, which did not even offer the comfort of going upstairs to bed, let alone an attic from which to spy. So, I would bicycle across town to South Mahone to carry on my observations there. For six years I did that. Watching strangers coming in and out the door that was my door. I never once saw a face in the attic. One day I climbed in through a basement window and explored the house again. In the attic, by the window, unmolested, I found my wicker basket, now too small for my adolescent frame.

Six years from the day we had left, The Crows was burnt to the ground. If I could not live there, should anyone?

I left Dayton shortly thereafter. I had a half-cocked idea of finding another house like The Crows. My search was purposeful, not the meaningless peregrinations of an adolescent, but it was undisciplined and my exact goal was unclear. In my youthful naïveté, I expected to find a substitute. I wasn't prepared for what would happen. I found houses in the older part of Cleveland that were very similar to my birthplace. Later in Portland, Iowa City, St. Louis. It seemed an outrage. I even discovered a house in Florida, of all places, that was not unlike The Crows. I considered that these houses were masquerading. I had hoped to find a house like

The Crows, not hundreds of houses like it! This complicated my search; indeed, it undermined the very reason for my search. I was a confused boy.

When I look back, I can understand. Another young man might be attracted to a pretty face. He mistakes personality for character, and in any case, he is too distracted by bright eyes to care. He is satisfied to be amused by an engaging persona. Similarly, I confused outward appearance with inner character. And just like a young man who finds that the prettiest face he has ever seen can be found on any street, in any magazine, I became angry with the familiarity of the once-held-beautiful façade. I became contemptuous of what I considered to be fraudulent duplicity. It was all classically Freudian. But I am digressing – a psychologist at heart.

The Crows was razed yet again in my mind. But its image was firmly entrenched in my active imagination. I began to reconsider my goal. I was looking for that something which had everything to do with The Crows and yet was not The Crows. I began to search for its phoenix, its soul incarnate, its essential property. I realized the futility of searching for that place which had been snatched from under me like a rug and wanted in its place only that earliest sense of place. *Ma*. My search took on holy proportions. It became a kind of pilgrimage. With religious conviction I accepted the existence of such a place – a heaven on earth, if you will.

In Almora in the Himalayas, I briefly found something like it – heaven, I mean – in the cloistered gardens of Ishwaribhavan, "abode of the divine." But too much else was alien to me and after several months I moved on. A year later I lived in the abandoned clay hut of a potter on Shishu, in the out islands of Japan. It was a humble place, smelling of seaweed and fire. Its single room looked out in all directions. It was as if that room was merely the vestibule at the center of four halls that stretched off into space to the horizon.

Let me tell you something strange: I do not like to travel. I have never liked to travel, ironic but true. I would rather watch others move while I observe in silence and stillness. Be that as it may, my complicated search has taken me the world over. Despite my reluctance, there has been nothing in my life but this. This search. Deep into the fjords of Norway; deep in her woods I have burrowed under the moss-covered timbers of a thirteenth-century stave church, listening. Listening to the rhythmic creakings of its carved pillars and beams as the edifice settled into a mountain storm. In the dry shadows below the storm, I have traced with my fingers the grotesque wooden jaws of beasts and monsters and the tortured vegetal tracery of wooden vines. I came to know that church, that house, with my hands. Like Braille, its walls spoke a silent language. All my homes have spoken to me in their way. The mad, echoing walls of the Cistercian abbey in the south of France spoke proudly of its faith. Listen, it said, only the hearing attains the truth – and I listened. What some learn from wise, old men I have learned more deeply from wise, far older houses.

You mustn't think, however, that I am only attracted to ruins. True, I do like the deserted, but now and then it is inevitable that I should see a home that potentially meets my requirements and is other than deserted. I am not one for sharing. As I said earlier, to share a home is to reduce the experience of it. There was a time when I was content with surreptitious occupancy. Sneaking in and out of people's homes. Stealing an hour here, an evening there, perhaps taking a little something upon my departure as a memento. It is a fleeting pleasure. My needs grew more complex and such pussyfooting palled. To know whether a home is the right home requires living in it, purely and simply; an uninterrupted stay, no matter how brief. When a home seems particularly suitable to my needs, I must stay longer in order to make very sure. In this consequence my plans become most complex. In my impulsive youth I would sometimes settle for nothing less than immediate occupancy, but as you might imagine, the tenants suffered. I have learned how to take my time, to wait and to plan. And so for the time being, I have taken lodgings in a town nearby the house I have found. The rooming house is called the Sea Winds. It was an unusual step for me to take for I shy away from such establishments. There is an implicit social obligation to one's fellow guests and, of course, to the proprietor, in this case an elderly spinster named Deirdre Tinker. People are too curious. I prefer anonymity, but my decision to board was not uncalculated. I needed a headquarters from which to mount my campaign. You see the house I have found, the house of my dreams, is occupied; for the time being, at least. But that does not present me with much of a problem; I have years of experience in such matters.

2

"Could it be K.C.?"

"K.C. is in South America as far as I know."

"But it could be K.C., couldn't it? It's the kind of thing he would dream up."

"No, Edmonton; I think someone told me he was in Edmonton."

"Malcolm!"

Malcolm shook his head and crossed his arms defiantly. "*Nyet.*"

Reluctantly Mary stroked the name from her list.

"What about your Aunt Celia?"

Malcolm groaned. "She's in Venice."

"But Celia is nutty, you've always said ...."

"Yes, nutty, but in Venice. Living out her golden years pinching the neat little bottoms of gondoliers, not prowling around the South Shore, springing elaborate feasts on unsuspecting nephews."

Mary sighed and vigorously crossed out the name. She perused the list, scratching the back of her head with her pencil. Malcolm was fidgeting impatiently. "This is getting us nowhere."

"But we have to do something."

"You seem to forget, my love, I am a professor and have dedicated my life to doing quite the opposite."

"You're impossible."

"I hate to be so archetypically phlegmatic but why don't we just wait?"

"Until someone writes a paper?"

"Touché. No, not quite that long, but until the culprit or culprits arrive at the front door in red ribbons, or parachute into the courtyard and reveal their identity and the purpose behind this culinary outrage."

Mary was not really listening; she was thinking out loud. "It isn't Mom. She has no sense of humor."

"I hope you are referring to your own mom."

"Your mom is dead!"

"Yes, I know." Malcolm winked.

Mary frowned at him and went on with her inquiry. "And it's not Pip because I talked to her on the phone only yesterday in Toronto. You know, it just could be Kevin and Tom."

"I thought Tom was away in Digby on some long-term engagement, or 'gig,' as he insists on calling it, at the Pines or somewhere like that."

"He gets time off now and then. And the first thing Kevin does when he comes here is to chastise me for the state of my silverware. He even sat down and polished it once."

"Why?"

"Why does he polish my silver?"

"No, nincompoop, why would he, or they, have done it? There has to be a motive, you know."

"I don't know why."

Malcolm clicked his tongue in disgust. He folded his hands behind his head and leaned back. Mary was lost in thought, slouched in her chair, and then suddenly there was a gleam in her eyes. "Tom worked in some shishipooh restaurant in Montreal. I bet they cooked it up between the two of them!"

"And I have come up with a motive," said Malcolm grandly. Mary looked at him with surprise. "Yesterday marked the fifteenth anniversary since you painted the dean's office puce."

"We never painted the dean's office puce."

"Well, then taupe."

Mary sat up with a start. "Of course! You've got it! It must be the anniversary of some silly event from art school."

"Graduation?"

Mary frowned. "No. I can't think of anything in particular, but Kevin always remembers stuff like that."

"Good. Now may I go back to work?"

A smirk appeared on Mary's face. She jumped up and ran to the phone and the next moment was on the line to CNCP:

"A telegram to Mr. Kevin Brain, c/o Hope Springs Eternal Antiques, Lunenburg. Thanks for the memories stop Feast a delight stop Wish you were here to wash dishes stop Love Reggy and Zenobia."

The phone rang two hours later. Mary answered in the kitchen and Malcolm listened in surreptitiously on the extension in his study. It quickly became obvious that if Kevin had anything to do with the mysterious banquet he was not prepared to let on. He and Mary went over her list of friends again but to no avail.

"Maybe it's Malcolm," Kevin suggested at last. "Senility setting in early."

Mary snickered and Malcolm made his presence known with a loud cough. Kevin chortled with glee.

"Now, now, kiddies," Malcolm said. "I admit I'm an old sobersides but I'm not quite falling asleep in my soup."

Kevin managed an apology of sorts between giggles. Mary cackled away in the background and the whole conversation deteriorated to mock indignation on Malcolm's side and laughter from the other two.

When Kevin finally hung up, Malcolm spoke before Mary was off the line.

"So we now adopt strategy number two."

"What's that?"

"We wait."

"Whatever you say ... old sobersides."

Malcolm could hear her giggling as she hung up.

3

Odd's End. What an odd house. Even before I learned the real significance of the name, I did not question its aptness. At its best the house is eclectic, clinging to no recognizable style or period – vernacular, an architect would call it; indeed, and in several tongues at once! The eclecticism, I would later find, is matched on the interior. It is most certainly like no other house in this part of the world.

The most prominent feature is the yard open to the sea. The house sits around the courtyard on three sides. At one time, there was just the cottage in the southeast corner and in the northeast the stable. But successive owners have joined these two early structures in stages around the courtyard.

The cottage is not more than twenty-feet square inside and is over a hundred years old. It is, as I would find later, Odd's End proper. The rest of the house has merely adopted the cognomen. The walls are thick, a foot thick in places, and made of fieldstone and stucco. There is one enormous central oak door, diagonally planked and studded with black round-headed nails. Its lintel butts with the plate of the roof. There is no overhang. The cedar-shingled roof is steeply pitched. Flanking the door on either side are deeply set diamond-paned windows. Extending out from the back of this humble cottage, the house grows in successive stages. The first addition has walls of stone and plaster and is

31

perhaps nearly as old as the cottage itself. The windows, however, are tall in proportion to the walls and they are mullioned. Beyond that, the walls are of brick, whitewashed in harmony with the older house. The third addition constitutes the living room and was built in the thirties of this century. The windows are tall and narrow. On the northern face, two peaked stained-glass windows, expropriated from a chapel I expect, have been placed.

Then there is the west wing, not twenty years old. The entire first level is glass, floor to ceiling, with French doors in the very center opening out onto the yard. A free-standing staircase leads to the second-floor sleeping quarters. The five large windows of the second floor are identically curtained in lace. White lace.

My first impression of Odd's End was that it was a house of opposites. Its façade was both male and female, a rural temple to both Hermes and Aphrodite. Godhead demands as much, I decided; neither sexed nor sexless. Lace curtains behind a rugged weathered face. This sense of opposing principles could be found elsewhere. The whiteness of its whitewashed walls, almost Mediterranean in their brightness, ground for the figured blackness of its deep-set windows. The house is muscled and four-square and yet is at once supine, disposed as for a lover: the sea perhaps, waiting to rush into the courtyard and crash against the glassy west wall, against the tall and elegant French doors. In my mind's eye, the grass-covered dunes become a hot and fragrant *mons veneris*. I built a monument for the house, an archway amidst the soft grasses. It didn't last, however, because I built it out of sand.

Last fall, for four weeks my destination was always the same. I watched the inhabitants come and go and I felt like nothing so much as a small boy in Dayton, Ohio, watching strangers infest the home of his birth. But I was no longer an impulsive lad. I have become a patient man. A stubborn man. I entertained myself at first with window-shopping while the tenants were out. Nothing I saw disappointed me; far from it. I was drawn like a moth to the proverbial flame.

There is a studio occupying the northwest corner of the house. It is the most recent addition, connected to the west wing by a corridor off which there is a pantry and a laundry room. The studio is also connected to the old shed and through it to the stable which forms the extremity of the north wing. I could see into the studio, in fact its north wall is glass.

A studio that is empty of art is a very empty place. This studio contained only large, flat crates, obviously holding canvases, which were stacked against the walls on every side. There were ten in all, some as large as sixteen by ten feet. On my original visit last fall, those crates were not opened and neither had the artist begun any new work; there were not even any sketches lying about. My curiosity was piqued. A lull in the creative process or a crisis of some other kind? I suspected that the crates were just back from a show, and a show is always an end of sorts for a painter. But it was strange that nothing else was in progress. Either the artist was on the verge of something monumental or washed up. I know quite a lot about art; I am a connoisseur of other people's art. For obvious reasons, I have never collected. My memory far outstrips most collections. I fancy most the arts that can be appreciated alone: painting, poetry, recorded music. So much is lost in a crowd. Art cannot be shared any more than a home can. Painting is the supreme decoration, whether illusionistic or concrete; whether it pretends to be something it is not, a landscape, shall we say, or whether it is what it appears to be, a mass of colors and lines. The effect of art in a home is a study I am eminently qualified to discuss. I have seen so much good art in so many beautiful homes and have had the time to study it without the hindrance of the owner at my shoulder boring me with details of the "value" or the history of the painting's ownership. The very last thing I am concerned with is the ownership. My own appreciation transcends ownership. A painting can sap a room of life or imbue it with sunshine. It can quiet a room, deaden a room; it can sing or scream, fade into the wallpaper or command. It is naturally something that concerns me greatly, painting. I am glad that Odd's End has been in the hands of a painter, but last fall I had no idea what kind of painter. I would find out. Patience.

4

"What are you thinking?"

Malcolm stirred from his reveries with a start. Mary was leaning against the bookcase; he had not heard her enter the study.

"Don't tell me, let me guess. You were thinking of how much fun it would be to stop working on your paper and come and play croquet with me. Am I right?"

Malcolm suddenly looked very solemn. "Not croquet. Not since you insist on using hedgehogs and ostriches."

"Flamingoes!"

"Not in the original manuscript."

"Well, if not croquet, what?"

"Actually, my love, I was thinking about the child. I've decided she can't stay after all."

Mary's knees buckled and she fell to the floor in a heap. She spoke in a tormented whisper.

"One mistake, Reggy, one horrible mistake. Can't you forget? Must I go on forever in the shadow of that wretched evening?"

Malcolm rose to his full height and loomed villainously, as best as he could, above his wife, now writhing on the floor.

"It's no use, Zenobia, whoever you are. I shall not, this time, change my mind."

"Oh, Reggy, one more chance, please, one more chance. You can cut off both her arms, if you like; she'll never steal again. I promise."

"Yuck!"

Mary grinned. "I thought it quite novel."

"Novel? It's revolting. Cutting off both her arms!"

Mary had unwound herself and was kneeling on the floor. "The best melodrama always has a bit of gore to spice things up; it's always off stage, of course."

"Melodrama?" Malcolm imbued the word with disgust. "What we, that is to say, what *I* am enacting is not melodrama. It is 'Theater.' What are you doing now?"

Mary had passed him and was staring distractedly at the wooden *ange gardien*, which hung on the wall above Malcolm's desk.

"St. Michael is crooked."

"I hadn't noticed."

"You wouldn't notice him if he fell on your nose." She straightened the figure and stepped back a step. "I could have sworn he had more of a lance than that."

Malcolm had taken his seat again and he looked up at the saint. He was trying to remember when he had last looked at it. He stroked his chin thoughtfully.

"Come to think of it, didn't the dragon have more of a tail?"

Malcolm shook his head. "Damned if I know."

Mary was still absorbed by her observation.

Malcolm continued. "To listen to you the house would seem to be positively humming with change. If it's not one thing it's—"

"Listen!"

Malcolm was stopped in mid-sentence. He did as he was told. There was nothing. Mary smiled mysteriously and left the room.

Malcolm watched her leave. He shook his head and looked up pensively at St. Michael, half expecting him to

move, to say something. Was she right? Was he so inatten-
tive? Mary was in the kitchen, singing out of key. That, at
least, was in character. In so many other ways she seemed
unusually preoccupied, restless; for several days she had
spent little time in her studio. He leaned back in his chair, it
creaked comfortably; he stared at the wooden angel.

Come to think of it, Mary had been restless ever since the
dinner party, or whatever it was. The dinner party that
nobody threw or at least that nobody was willing to take
credit for. They expected from day to day an explanation
from one another, from someone, and then, when there was
no explanation, it just seemed preposterous and worth
forgetting. They hadn't phoned the police. A mysterious
gourmet dinner, while discomforting, was not the stuff of
criminal harassment. It was too comical really, a practical
joke, although it had not seemed so at the time.

And what of the other little crimes; could he put any stock
in them? Mary was not prepared to take the case to the
authorities. How do you say that the plants on the kitchen
window have been switched around, or that there are more
grapefruits in the fridge than you had bought, more coffee in
the coffee bin? To claim that someone was giving you free
groceries and you wanted it stopped was inviting the worst
kind of incredulity.

Malcolm reached up and felt the top of St. Michael's lance.
When he examined his finger there was the finest sheen of
sawdust.

5

The history of Odd's End turned out to be as fascinating and unique as the house itself. The name – and the story behind it – have indeed become something of a local legend. Bits and pieces of it were told to me by various people, and, of course, some of it I learned myself from old records.

Jeremy Odd had been the park warden of the Rood Estate from 1836 to 1851, a tenure that exactly coincided with Emrett Rood's stay in the New World. Rood had, for political and financial reasons and perhaps because of a perverse streak, moved his entire estate from Scotland. The move included his trusted park warden. The estate was large, the entire Fourth Peninsula – 1,000 acres or so – and the "park," for it wasn't a park at all, consisted of that woodland stretching along the north shore and around the tip of the Fourth, like a giant stole around the fertile neck and shoulders of the peninsula. Some of the woodland is densely undergrown; the responsibility could have been ominous for Odd since he was charged with maintaining the lot, but, as it turned out, it was really a remarkably easy task. There were, after all, not many people about. Sparse fishing communities and boat builders up the coast, closer to Halifax, but little in the way of determined poachers. Perhaps Odd grew restive with nothing much to do but scare off the occasional Micmac squatter or perhaps he tasted the heady freedom of the New

World where many of his countrymen were already starting new lives on their own property without landlords or overseers. He didn't write about it; one can only imagine. In any case, it seems he became quite a headstrong individual. There are reprimands listed in Rood's diary. Jeremy began to think of the "park" as his own. Not such a crazy idea really. Carried away by this notion, he one day shot Rood's adolescent son, who was hunting rabbits. It might have been an overzealous mistake but it ruined everything. If Jeremy had been living in a cloud-cuckoo-land, he fell out of it with a thud. It seems he returned to his sturdy little cottage and hanged himself. The end. Rood, who wasn't at all that stable to begin with, as far as I could tell, went round the bend and left for the Old World again, leaving everything. Local lore tells how Jeremy's wife stayed on and gave birth to a son. And there are Odds in the Steep Cove Cemetery as late as the 1890s – although not Jeremy, of course. The epilogue is fascinating. The Grange was gutted by fire, although its stone shell has survived. The arable land fell into disuse but was eventually taken over by settlers. There is probably a distant Rood somewhere who could put forward quite a good legal battle for the property; the property never changed hands on paper, but then you can't really take away property from someone who has lived on it and farmed it for a hundred years plus – the inalienable rights of possession, etc. Apocryphal as it may be, it is a pleasing story. Malcolm and Mary know the story; everyone on the peninsula knows the story. They joke about ghosts, I have overheard them.

But the story has a moral. The cottage was originally called the Rood Cottage. It was an extension of the estate, as were the Rood stables, greenhouses, milk sheds, smokehouse, *et al*. But through Jeremy Odd's sensational murder/ suicide it has become known as Odd's End. His name has overtaken his master's. Through an extraordinary act he took possession of that which was really his anyway. A wonderful story. It lends the house extraordinary appeal.

The Closes enter the house through the French doors, which open onto the courtyard. But I was determined to enter it for the first time through the old oak door into the original cabin, wishing to experience the house as it has grown through time. It is one of those acts that many would consider mere caprice, but for me it is no more capricious than the wine taster swilling his wine around in his cheeks, tasting it to the full, learning about it, savoring it.

When I was quite sure that Odd's End suited my requirements, I was anxious to explore its innermost recesses, yet I was cautious. I watched the comings and goings of its inhabitants for two weeks before I made my move. I wanted time to explore in peace.

One morning in the early fall, when both the occupants were clearly off for the day, I entered the house. There are any number of ways to break into a house, but it is important not to leave any traces. I always carry with me a length of fine wire and, in a soft leather pouch, a series of slim steel picks designed for just such occasions. They were lifted from a nosy detective some years ago.

The door open, I entered the original cottage. It was clearly the vestibule. The walls were discreetly papered in red flowers on a pale gray ground – Bursley, I think. Most of the wall to the left was taken up by an enormous fireplace. One could roast a whole pig across its breadth (or perhaps a deer, purloined from the master's park?). It was now unused. Heavy iron dogs stood on guard on the slate hearth. A large brass vessel full of chrysanthemums sat on the mantel. They were desiccated and ready to be thrown out; I loathe mums, an ignominious flower. The room was dominated by a large circular table decorated with Chinese scenes, lacquered black and gold. Upon it sat a witch bowl half-filled with water. Roses floated on the surface but they had withered and the water was discolored and smelled faintly bad. In fact, the room seemed musty and abandoned. Perhaps the cleaning lady considers the room done with, since it is not used. She seems only vaguely competent, Mrs. Rapsey; I have watched her. She lives in Steep Cove and comes over every Tuesday. A little dotty, I've heard, but a hard worker.

To the right of the door was another oak door, opening into what was probably once a kitchen. It was a narrow room, better suited to its present lot as a closet and clothes storage area. There were shelves for gloves and hats, a box for boots, and a thick wooden clothes rack, dangerously bowed from the weight of winter coats and plastic storage bags. Beside the closet door in the vestibule was an odd sculpture, which I had thought to be Chinese from the window. It was, in fact, contemporary; a black box on a pedestal painted in a shiny black to match the lacquered surface of the table. A small brass plate on the stand identified it as *The Floating Bridge for Izanagi and Izanami (M. and M.) from A. Urquhart, 1970.* To say that the box opens is to miss the point: by an elaborate set of small gold hinges, the cubic form breaks up into irregular chunks of matter – plaster, I suppose – revealing an interior of smoky pink and pale azure, the paint rubbed into the plastered surface. When entirely open, the cubic shape all but disappears and in its place is a forty-inch hinged chain of "floating" parts – the floating bridge of Japanese mythology. There was other artwork in the room. Above this box was a grouping of Hokusai and Hiroshige wood-block prints, the inevitable processions of Japanese nobility, a rainstorm, the sea. Elsewhere a small drawing by Alfred Kubin, full of grotesque phantasms, and a canvas by Le Sidaner, dreamy in pale gold and rusts. Two women without facial features in an evoked landscape. Family money put to unusually good uses. Mary's parents, the Carlton Drapers, N.Y., N.Y., notable collectors of chinoiserie. But Mary, being her own woman, has concentrated her attention elsewhere.

The house was a strange marriage of disparate styles, but it was to prove more eclectic still and vastly to my liking. I delight in the niceties of fine furnishing and, I might add, I

41

have spent a lifetime examining the most beautiful homes in the world. Odd's End is not, by a decorator's standards, a most beautiful home. It is not a showplace, which is not to say that it is without art. Far from it—but it is artless in its artfulness. With that ambiguous conceit, let us go on.

Two black bamboo chairs inlaid with ivory and seated in black wicker flanked the doorway on the farthest wall of the first room. These double doors led into a room probably added to the house in the 1860s by Thomas Odd, Jeremy's son, when his own family had outgrown the original cottage. Above the exposed rough-hewn lintel was a rifle, a breech-loading Snyder-Enfield, old, but dutifully cleaned and oiled. Possibly in working condition. It looked dangerous. Perhaps it was the very rifle with which Jeremy disposed of the young Rood. One can only imagine.

If Mrs. Rapsey had forgotten the vestibule she was obviously not allowed to touch anything in the study and never has. It looked at first as though the police had conducted a frenzied search for incriminating evidence, but gradually one realized that there was an order. The parquet floors were sparkling and the copious bookshelves were dusted, but every other available surface was strewn with papers. It was the comforting clutter (squalor?) of the scholar. Various projects or papers occupied different "stations" in the room. There were, in all, three desks: a heavy bureau in figured maple with its writing surface folded out for use; an escritoire with one long, narrow drawer, shaped and carved standards, and fitted with a red leather top; and, along the entire northern wall a monstrous Victorian pedestal table. The latter, built for a library, made it difficult to imagine how it was moved into a house in the country. It was fully five feet wide and sixteen feet long and must have weighed a ton. The cupboard doors were veneered in sabicu, and at four points they were flanked by demure caryatids. Like the other surfaces in this, the vortex of Malcolm's world of letters, this one was piled high with paper and had also become the home for various periodicals from the college, some, I noticed, disastrously overdue. On a pedestal sat the omnipotent *Compact O.E.D.*, the *Oxford English*, volumes A-O, opened provocatively at *epibasal – episcopalian*. The west wall seemed constructed of books, floor to ceiling and above the doorway. There was, no doubt, some order but it was not alphabetical nor did it seem to be by subject. How difficult it would be to disturb this system of cataloging; ironically it is foolproof!

There were two windows on the south wall and two on the north overlooking the courtyard. On the east wall, more books, but only up to the dado. Above hang several framed letters and drawings and above the escritoire, a French Canadian *ange gardien*: St. Michael and his dragon, but with much of the polychrome gone and quite a lot of the dragon too. The saint was rather effeminate, not unlike Malcolm facially. He hung above the typewriter looking down triumphantly; the saint I mean. The letters were rare and valuable: one from Symons to Mallarmé on the nature of decadence and one from Ernest Dowson to someone named simply "Bee." I love to read other people's mail, even the mail of dead men. The drawings I had seen before in France. They were, surprisingly, the originals of Virgil Burnett's illustrations for the obscure *Le Rêve Lointain*, by the equally obscure Saint-Pol Roux. The ink drawings were classically figured and dramatically poised, elegant and surrealistic at the same time. The figures were luscious, full-bodied and ambiguously sexed. Once again I was faced with the hermaphrodite; how strong my impression of this house's own androgyny. Here again manifest in ink. They were images befitting a literary sensibility.

But there was work to be done. The typewriter – a useful instrument, but prone to idiosyncrasy. This one was no exception – three times out of ten the lower case *y* failed, and the image typed was red instead of black. A simple enough discovery, but very useful indeed. And the drawer, stuffed with letters and bills. Amidst the jumble, some interesting finds. Two postcards from Mary in New York, gallery hopping and "cooling off." Cooling off from a bad spell? "Good to see Mom and Dad. Not mad with you any more, hon. Yours..." Everywhere there were these signs of a difficult marriage which makes my job so much easier. Mary's signature on the card was the merest of *m*'s. A diagonal slash with a burp midway, more like a representation of a bird in flight than an initial. Easily copied after only a few attempts.

Sitting at the desk in a rather shabby but comfortable captain's chair I surveyed the room. There would only have to be slight alterations.

But I am forgetting myself; perhaps you have misunderstood all along. You have assumed that I wish the Closes to move, lock, stock, and barrel? Never! Just themselves with what clothes they happen to have on. When I have talked of a home, a perfect home, I have meant the home *as it is*. The site it occupies, the structure, the furnishings; chattels, they are called. Oh, little details can be altered, but the whole remains. Now do you understand how difficult my task has been? More so than you expected – to find not just a shell, but a living, breathing home in whatever incarnation it has come to assume. And Odd's End is that home; sitting here now I can feel it. Where the tastes of the Closes differ from my own I will adapt – I adapt very easily. A regular chameleon.

Through the deep-set doors on the west wall, I found the living room. This addition was made in the early part of the century by a retiring merchant from Mahone Bay, so says my landlady, Miss Tinker. There had been great plans but the man died.

It was an impressive space divided by furniture groupings into three distinct areas. Immediately to my right upon entering the room was the corner that is blind to the outside due to the stained-glass windows. Outside the glass is opaque, lifeless, but inside, the eye of God, turning light into a technicolor extravaganza. These two slim pointed arch windows are of St. Mark and St. Luke, the one with his flying lion and the other his flying ox. The latter is appropriately the patron of the artist. I found myself wondering whether the *ange gardien* and now these evangelists were the manifestation of faith or merely of acquisitiveness. This corner was like a little sanctuary although there were no icons or other signs of a religious nature. There was one oversized, heavy birch chair, clothed in royal blue, its arm rests warm and worn birch-yellow. Arms inviting one to enter rather than simply perch. There was a tall brass reading lamp and surrounding the chair, plants in Ch'ien lung porcelain urns on the floor; suspended from the cross-timbered ceiling, philodendron, fig and various palms, tall and broad leaved. Sitting in the chair, some of them dwarfed me. I am six feet tall and yet I had the strongest desire to curl up in that chair in that hidden nook. The scale of things: the giant plants, the ceiling fourteen feet above, and the whole, bathed in colored light, made me feel like a child again. There was the elemental security of the corner, with the saints at one's back and the wall of transparent green leaves. The rug here was thick and already sun warm and on the wall was a tiny Samuel Palmer landscape, gold and sepia, tinted yellow by varnish. This added to the illusion, for the tiny painting was at hand; from the chair I could have reached out and touched it, and yet it was so distant, so visionary. In this corner a person could let the world go by; the pendulum of a grandfather clock across the room told me that time was going by too but in its grandeur it did not tell time so much as register the pulse of this strange and nearly perfect house. Looking at it more closely, I saw it had a second face, a docile moon on a painted dial rose from behind eleven o'clock and set behind two o'clock, registering yet another time – that of the heavens. That could be changed; little things can be changed.

There was the clock and beside it on the wall, a late Turner sketch, a seascape in his familiar gray-blue. It was a dim and moody twilight. Under the painting there were two Chinese Chippendales and between them, four nesting tables, papier-mâché quarletto inlaid with mother-of-pearl floral wreaths. A single piece of eighteenth-century blue pottery sat on the topmost surface. The room went from sublime to sublime across polished floors of pine boards, plugged rather than nailed. The sublime of stained glass and rush-seated Chippendale side chairs and a Feraghan rug to the sublime of 1960 New York abstraction, huge hand-painted pillows and Corbusier chairs. Everywhere it was bathed in dappled light from the four large windows on the southern wall. Between the windows there were two enormous canvases, sister and brother; a Frankenthaler in orange and crimson. Oil paint diluted and stained into the canvas in the shape of a tentacled Martian land mass with violent red rivers subdued by open passages of raw, ungessoed canvas. On the same wall separated by a window was a Rothko. It was of the same color: it might have been called "two openings in orange over red." But it was a dense work, deeper in texture, not striking like its sister, but absorbing. There was one other large painting in the room on the opposite wall: also in orange and red tending to violent pink, like crazy clouds against the sun. It was signed in a feathery orange stroke, Montgomery. Above the stereo to the left of the fireplace there was a doodle by Hans Hofmann, a small Soutine and an early hieroglyph in crayon by Pollock. These paintings led me to suspect what I would find in Mary's studio. Brought up wealthy, a teen-ager in Manhattan in the sixties with the Saturday trips with mother and father to the lofts in Greenwich Village. Hobnobbing, making contacts. I expected to find a dedicated abstract expressionist; action painters, they call themselves.

The stereo was good. The records: only the usual classics, with an emphasis on lieder; a large number of spoken word recordings and a large selection of medieval and Renaissance. The preponderance of the records, however, were jazz. Vintage recordings of Robert Johnson, Bessie Smith, King Oliver through Billie Holiday, Lee Wiley and Art Tatum, Goodman, Gillespie, Parker, M.J.Q., Monk, and Mingus. There were some representatives of the later *avant-garde*, Coltrane and Coleman, but the jackets suggested they had seen little use.

How much can be told of people by their possessions! The Closes, I learned, are refined, their tastes are subtle. I intend to appeal to that in them. My campaign will catch and hold their attention on an intellectual plane; simple scare tactics would be wasted.

Every household has its palladium, the gift of Athena, the idol that guarantees its security. The Greeks knew they could not hope to capture Troy without first destroying its idol. The task fell on Odysseus and Diomedes, but they were tricked into stealing a forgery. They had obviously not done enough groundwork: observation, research. I will not be so tricked.

These artifacts represented the Close palladia; stealing them would not be enough, but disrupting their power to render security, that is something else. Think how dependent you are on those visual clues, the sum total of which you call home. To alter, transform or otherwise displace those clues ... what extraordinary results can be gained!

But let us return to the living room. The fireplace was large and the stone hearth was warm red brick. Before the fireplace there was one sumptuous davenport, deeply padded and covered in unbleached linen canvas. It was, mercifully, alone. No matching group, no modular setting. The Corbu chairs, a side table in tiger maple and walnut and a bizarre rocker of strapped brass shaped like an arabesque. To the right of the fireplace was a nook, and by itself in that nook another box sculpture, this by the enigmatic American surrealist, Joseph Cornell. It was strangely out of place but then even into the life of an abstract expressionist a little mystery must fall. A little mystery; the work was called *Homage to a Secret*. It was a simple narrow box hanging low

47

on the wall. In it there were fifteen compartments, each of them, but one, containing a star, a five-and-dime sheriff's badge; and on the glass cover is painted a silhouette. One asks oneself, where is the last star?

The west wing I was already quite familiar with since its first floor is made entirely of glass, a box filled with sun. An enterprising interior designer of independent means built this addition. Artists leaving Halifax for the beauty and quiet of the country immediately gravitate to the South Shore, the scenic lighthouse route. They have snapped up old barns and farmhouses, even lighthouses, whatever seemed novel, and turned them into studios or luxurious "primitive" retreats. The interior designer was not liked in Mahone Bay, I have come to find out, and the bumpy Park Road was too much for his springless Lotus Super Seven. He had only been in the new house a year before he sold it to a lawyer who was the tenant prior to the Close family.

To the right of the entrance from the living room, I encountered an informal grouping of four wicker chairs, painted white and fitted with bright primary-colored cushions. There was a low, glass-topped table between them. Underfoot, a large straw mat. To the left of the entranceway from the living room was the dining area. There was the sense that it was separated from the rest of the wing although there were no walls. The predominant impression was that of bright colors against black. The black absorbed the light which permeated and warmed the rest of the room so that the dining area seemed cooler and more formal. On the floor, a black oriental rug—an antique Star Kazak with bright squares, again of primary colors. The table was contemporary: long, solid and mahogany. Likewise the eight chairs. Against the wall was a black chest, six feet long and three feet high. It was painted with rampant and comical unicorns, tulips and distelfinks, the recognizable iconography of Pennsylvania Deutsch. All around its border stretched a line of German rendered in spidery Fraktur.

Above the chest and exactly as wide was an impressive black canvas by Ron Shuebrook, an east-coast artist whose work was included in the *Artscanada* issue which featured Mary. This minimal work with its scarcely perceived figurative patterning etched into the monochrome surface seemed to be an intellectual response to the whimsical primitive work at its feet. It whispered while the painted characters on the chest neighed and chirped but the response was not a patronizing one – there was a complicit agreement. The Shuebrook was sophisticated; it made one laugh at the spindly-legged unicorns and the stylized polka-dotted flowers but they in turn made one laugh at the self-conscious "art" of the canvas. Like a balloon above the dimwit cartoon character which says, "Wittgenstein was right," or something to that effect. I laughed. I had interpreted the work to my own amusement. I am not one to be swayed by the opinions of anyone else; I can amuse myself. Living alone one learns.

From the room I left the grandfather clock struck ten. It was time for coffee.

Although my life style has demanded the sublimation of my desire to write or paint into that of the critic and keen observer, it has in no way dulled my imagination or my appetite. My creativity reaches its peak in cooking. A cook without a kitchen is difficult for you to imagine? Think of Hemingway's *A Movable Feast*. Who do you think prepared it? More jokes. It is the weather, I suppose. This room had made me light-headed. I have enjoyed and suffered the kitchens of countless homes. I have baked beetles wrapped in gum leaves on a thatched houseboat in Kashmir and I have boiled eel for catigau d'Anguille in a Provençal chateau. The chef had to be tied up in the pantry and to keep him quiet I was forced to give him a bottle of one of his master's precious wines.

I daresay I have experienced all forms of cooking the world over and I have distilled from that a sixth sense about kitchens. Many cooks are merely fixtures in their own kitchens. Disorient them and they are nothing. They lack the power to improvise. They work from recipes which they alter in this way or that and rename. They are like those tiresome musicians who cannot play without a book before them. The gourmet transcends his resources. He makes his kitchen an extension of himself, geared exclusively to his style and the sometimes complicated strategy involved in manifesting that style. I have learned to read a kitchen, to decipher the implicit structure imposed by the resident cook.

I sat in the corner of one of the two pews which ingeniously created the entranceway to the kitchen. I could, in a moment, determine its potential and its limitations. I oriented myself immediately.

This kitchen was spacious and full of light. Apart from some small features it was quite typically North American – functional, clean, but not as antiseptic as some. At the far end there was a tall apothecary chest whose fifty small drawers had been put to use as an elaborate spice cabinet. The range of spices was telling: it was wide with a particularly impressive range of pepper, ancho, serrano, hontaka, and so on. But still more impressive was the range of herbs growing along the wide window ledge. Tarragon, chives, basil, chervil, fennel, to name a few. And on the counter by the stove: Madeira, brandy, and sherry not hidden away in the liquor cabinet but here in the kitchen where they can be put to better use. The garlic was hanging *en plein air*, the way it should be. The salt was sea salt, there were dried mushrooms and salt pork – absolute necessities. There were perhaps too many gadgets, a common misconception in North America, but I could overlook that. In this kitchen, I first thought of my opening gambit, the first little surprise for my host and hostess; I looked forward to it immensely; it was to be a party. Although I did not make an appearance in person, I was there in spirit. Turbot à L'Espagnole, aubergines en gigot, châtaignes au lard; something from Brillat-Savarin, something from Chevalier, something from

Escoffier. It was really too much, even vulgar, but it made the impression I desired.

But before I planned the menu, I took time for my coffee, and this too, like so much else I do, was a ritual, one I have learned from the Bedouin. I had brought with me the required implements. Like myself, that proud race are nomads; the coffee break takes on a new meaningfulness to a nomad. The raw beans must be roasted in a long-handled pan, and then allowed to cool in a special box. Then they must be pounded in a mortar and brewed with cardamom in three successive pots. It is an involving, time-consuming process and is used especially upon the arrival of guests. Nothing is said during the ritual: it is a time for the guest to come to know his host and vice versa. Finally the heady scent filled the sun-hot room. The perfume was an offering to this house. The liquid was for me, to sip in the wicker chair looking out over the courtyard to the sand dunes and the strip of sea. I had stood, only the day before, on the other side of the glass looking in, imagining this incident taking place.

6

Climbing the stairs for the first time held all the excitement a younger man might have felt when finally led upstairs by a lady friend. I had seen the second story from a glassless window in the stable loft but actually mounting the stairs had about it the bouquet of consummation.

To the left of the landing was a spacious black-and-white tiled washroom complete with wicker chair and potted palm. Through a second door a corridor led to the master bedroom, through a dressing room lined on either side by mirrored closets. The master bedroom took up the remainder of the upper story facing the sea. It was a decidedly feminine room. The deep-set windows each boasted a window seat with white canvas cushions. The lace curtains were caught in the draft and billowed first in and then out through the partially opened windows, breathing softly. The bed was butternut with a crocheted bedspread, and a bedstead fitted in silk brocade. From the same warm wood was made the bow-fronted regency commode presenting to the room its breast of drawers. One was open and from it hung the white corner of a slip, perfumed. When I was young I was an experienced explorer of women's drawers and vanities, rifling through the lingerie for secrets, replacing the neatly folded clothes when the rifling was over. Now such things hold little surprise or mystery. Against another wall there was a canvas and leather-bound steamer trunk and by one of the windows two basket chairs with cushions covered in chintz. Between them stood a small round table upon which a chess game sat – in progress. The white king could be put in check in two moves by moving only one black pawn. I wondered if they would notice. Upon the walls were a suite of four etchings by David Hockney – visions of Grimm's fairy tales: a lady in a tower, a man curled up in first an egg, then a fish, and finally the lady in the tower. On the same wall there was a ladder leading into the attic. It was only a crawl space lighted by small hexagonal windows facing north and south. I have an affinity for hiding places; it was a useful discovery.

The bed was unmade. Mary sleeps on the window side. I had watched them prepare for bed for several nights. They sleep naked: he is tall and pale, sunken-chested youngish-looking, blond; she is an attractive slim thing, small-breasted, still tanned from the previous summer. Her hair is dark and manageably short, almost business-like. Her eyes are large and a beautiful deep green. At some point I would like to engage those eyes face to face. Ah, but you must not think that I have ulterior motives; you suspect that I am no better than a voyeur. Hah! I am no more titillated by my quarry in their bedroom than in their kitchen. I must observe; it is all just research. I am as unmoved as a doctor, and besides, my occupation leaves little room for dalliance.

Across the hall I discovered two more rooms, spare rooms only, I expected, and found that to be true in one case but in the other – an extraordinary surprise! A child's room. On the low, quilted bed and across the yellow dresser dolls and teddy bears of all shapes and sizes. There was a rocking horse and all along a shelf the length of one wall, toy trucks. A child? Has there been a child? Was there to be a child? Either circumstance could have drastically changed my plans. But no, I think not. They were all antiques, all of them. And finally I saw it. The most extraordinary toy of all.

Standing on a blanket box, an incredibly beautiful dolls' house. To be small enough to live in a house like this, to sleep in the tiny bed, to rock on the hobby-horse, back and forth, back and forth ....

Elsie, that was the name they were calling. She lay on the gravel below the window; below that most beautiful window with its carefully constructed view, every detail like a painting. Elsie, Elsie, where are you? They were calling all over the manor; their voices echoed through the manor, through my head over and over. And then someone screamed horribly. Elsie!

Distantly a grandfather clock struck four. Strikes four! It is not last fall, it is now. How many times have I watched and waited like that first time; how many times have I entered and re-entered these rooms. I have lost all track of time. Back in the master bedroom I throw the windows wide open. The smell and sound of the sea and the sea birds and the hot spring sun laden with balsam fills the room. A bracing salt air swoops through the window, waking me. It is as if I have been asleep, forgotten myself. I don't like these spells. Sitting on the side of the bed I try to reorient myself. From here the sea fills one-third of the window, the sky two-thirds. The land is lost to view. I feel myself again.

Beside me on the bookcase I notice Simone de Beauvoir's *Memoirs of a Dutiful Daughter* and waiting under it is the second volume in the series, *The Prime of Life*. Both are Penguin paperbacks. It is a book I know well. *The Prime of Life*. Some insistent memory makes me thumb through it – and there it is: "... she was said to have practiced various disgusting perversions with her lover, being addicted not only to masochism and algolagnia but to coprophagy as well." It was that word – *algolagnia*; I have never found a definition. The sentence is guaranteed to send one off to the nearest dictionary, but to no avail. Perhaps this too can be put to good use. Nothing must be wasted. I will see what I can do.

And the studio. I have already recounted my frustration at finding a studio empty of anything so much as a sketch. And it remained empty until one day early in October I arrived to find the window draped in funereal black. I thought perhaps they were having a wake, but the curtains stayed. I could not understand what she could be doing, blocking out all that northern light.

The paintings she began then are well advanced now, and they are extraordinary. I make regular trips to the studio; as I have said I appreciate art. When I am attracted to a piece of art, I am compelled to study it until I know why. Not only does it draw more carefully than any other artifact the personality of its creator but it says something about me. My very attraction to the painting indicates that the work has something to divulge to me about myself. I will stay at a painting until I have come to understand precisely what. I am a patient man. I do not care to understand the painting. Why should I care to understand a painting? Myself—that is what I care about! I engage in an intense reflection intended to suck the meaning from the canvas. It leaves me drained and simultaneously it seems to drain the painting of life, for upon understanding, the painting seems to me to be anemic, lifeless. I suppose that is why I do not collect art. It is, after all, materially worthless, and when it is stripped of meaning—empty. I am like a new man for the experience—revived, like a vampire, by the blood of the painting.

Some of the canvases are completed and in their stretchers stored in racks the length of one wall. Several, obviously unfinished, lean against other walls; while one, twelve feet by six feet, sits on an easel fixed to the floor and to the exposed joists of the ceiling. Around it are cluttered tables piled high with acrylic paint in tins and bottles but also with an assortment of enamel paints, all in striking but somehow unwholesome colors: greenish-orange, a dead blue-brown, a color not quite chartreuse, a color too bright for rust. And amidst these on the floor and the table, bags of plaster, blocks of wax, pails of gravel, a bag of asphalt. All of these materials have found their way onto the canvas in broad sweeps across the surface, in blotched and ragged relief. Between these expressive areas of powerful, even ugly work, passages of surprising sensitivity, fine, delicate brushwork like graffiti scrawled across the harsh ground. Somehow a balance had been struck. The delicate tracery holds its own. It is based on real imagery. I turn off the lights and flick on a slide projector behind and above me on a wall bracket. On the canvas appears the image that Mary was painting: several old women on a busy street corner talking, oblivious to the noise all around them. The angle of the projector elongates the image, distorting their bodies. Parts of the image disappear altogether where the passages of tar soak up the projected light. Mary has simply painted over the projected images, but with a tremendous freedom of detail seldom realized by so-called "photorealists." The projected slides provided her with an elaborate paint-by-numbers. That is why the windows are draped. The dense and expressive background somehow captures the noise and dirt of the street – the anonymity. The old women are figured against this backdrop, frail and almost inconspicuous and yet holding their own. Somehow she has achieved the difficult task of keeping out even the slightest hint of maudlin sentimentality. In other of the canvases, Mary has doped the surface with photographic emulsion on top of the heavy ground and then developed black and white images by projecting them onto the doped canvas. The "real" images fall across the canvases in bizarre patterns. One struck me particularly. For many minutes I could not move from in front of it. There is one figure, a solitary figure, so projected as to be only scarcely recognizable as human at all. A huge grayish-green shadow on a ground of bleached-yellow and dirty-brown stain. It is like a shadow left on the beach, engraved in the sand by some solar photographic trick. The shadow is long, the sun low on the horizon and the world tilted cockeyed. I have lingered over it.

I feel I know these paintings well, intimately. I appreciate the ingenuity with which the idea has been made manifest. I must match that ingenuity in my own campaign. In my own way, I too am an artist.

7

Malcolm came out onto the courtyard, dragging a wicker chair. He huddled in it dressed in a bulky sweater against the early morning chill. Distractedly he peeled a grapefruit and ate the sections like an orange. He spit the seeds as far as he could; he seemed absorbed by the task. He squinted out past the dunes at the sun hanging above the sea. It had been a sleepless night.

After a while he gathered a rake, a trowel, and a hoe from the shed behind the stable and dragged them to a patch of loamy ground at the northeast corner of the stable which was to serve as a garden. He set to work in a desultory manner, half-asleep, hacking at the ground without enthusiasm or strategy. He stooped every now and then and picking up a stone, he tossed it over his shoulder. After a few minutes he began to put more muscle into his work, and before very much longer he was swinging the hoe with great vigor. His action was not effective in any practical way. He was angry. Dirt was flying in all directions.

After fifteen minutes the garden was pockmarked like a miniature battlefield, and Malcolm's temper seemed to be flagging. By the time Mary came from the house, he was working at a reasonable pace trying to straighten out the damage he had inflicted. She came slowly across the yard and leaned for a moment against the corner of the stable before approaching. Malcolm did not look up. She stood for several more moments at the edge of the plot with her hands in her back pockets, looking at her sneakers, kicking at a tuft of coarse grass.

"That was Kevin. He's down at the Pines visiting Tom."

Malcolm did not reply at first, then he muttered a curt "That's nice."

There was another pause.

"Tom received one of those letters. Like the one Kevin got."

Malcolm did not look up, but he did stop raking.

Mary went on. "It was unsigned. It was typed on your typewriter."

"Listen! I've had about enough of this! I do not send your friends anonymous letters, least of all vile and threatening letters. What do you take me for, for Christ's sake?"

It was Mary's turn to look away. Malcolm, however, was not finished. "You're the one at home all day!"

Mary's voice was even when she spoke. She ignored the implication. "Mal, I'm not saying that you did type them, but someone did." She paused and when he didn't reply she went on. "I just don't want to see Kevin hurt like this."

The statement made Malcolm livid with rage. "Did you actually say what I thought you said? You don't want to see Kevin hurt—was that it? What about me? Do you give a shit about me? Do you care whether I'm hurt?"

Mary was fighting back tears. She had spoken impulsively. "Of course I do. I didn't mean it that way. Oh, what's the use!"

"Mary, for a week you've been giving me these furtive looks every time I turn around and then out of the blue I'm writing obscenities to your gay friends. Do you wonder why I'm mad, hurt? There must be more than one typewriter that makes goddamn red y's. Maybe it's a feature of that model. Did you think of that? And in any case, don't you think I might have been able to produce prose without those little red y's? Especially incriminating little red y's."

59

Mary hesitated for just a moment, and then from the pocket of her pullover she produced a package of plain drugstore envelopes.

"I found these shoved in the back of your writing desk."

Malcolm reached out slowly and took the crumpled package from her hand. He looked blankly at it and then at Mary; realizing that he was gaping, he snapped his mouth shut.

"You have been rifling my drawers?"

"Not rifling, I just ... looked."

"I haven't the foggiest notion where these envelopes came from, but I can assure you I know nothing about them or those blasted letters. Amen!"

With that Malcolm handed her back the package and made a feeble attempt to work. Mary watched him; unconsciously she stepped back out of the range of his hoe.

"I thought maybe you didn't like me spending so much time with Kevin."

"Give me a break!" he answered, without looking up from his work.

Mary put her hands deep into her sweater pockets. She spoke without looking at him. "I don't know what is going on. I don't believe you did it, but when I found those envelopes ... Mal, Kevin doesn't think it's you, if it makes you feel any better. There have been so many things happening lately, I don't know what to think any more."

Malcolm looked away, up the coast. His eyes followed a sea gull scouting the shoreline. He watched it as it plunged down into the surf and flew away again with something glittering in its beak.

"So many things have happened lately," he said at last. He had regained his composure, but his voice still sounded piqued.

He turned to Mary. "What motive have I got?"

Mary shrugged her shoulders, "I don't know; does a person always have to have motives?"

"It seems logical."

"But none of this is logical; it's mad."

"Well, there are really only three people with access, ready access, to my desk: you, me, and Celia Rapsey – pick one."

"Mrs. Rapsey?"

"Oh God, Mary, I was kidding! I doubt if Mrs. Rapsey can even spell; and although I'll grant you she is a certified rustic, I don't think she's mad. Do you think it's because we don't pay her enough?"

"She can cook."

"Coquilles Saint-Jacques? I doubt it."

"I know, Mal, but she is the only other person who has access to the house."

"Except you, of course," Malcolm said. "I repeat. Who is to say you aren't responsible for all of this? What could Celia Rapsey possibly hope to gain?"

"What could I hope to gain?"

There was another pause and Mary spoke. There was a crack in her voice. "You do really think it could be me, don't you?"

Malcolm looked at her. He obviously didn't, entirely, not yet. He slowly pulled her to him. No sooner had her head touched his chest than she burst into tears. She stopped almost at once. She didn't want to be cradled, and she seemed annoyed at having cried. She stabbed at her tears with her finger.

"Remember Joanne Woodward in *The Three Faces of Eve*? Maybe one of us is Eve or Sybil or something horrible like that," she said.

"Ahah! That would explain all those dresses in my closet."

"What?"

"Only kidding."

"Don't kid, okay?"

"Okay. Promise."

"Can we have some coffee now?"

"Please."

8

I like a home of large proportions. This Odd's End is not palatial but there is a commanding sense of size. My cottage on Shishu was enormous in imagined size, if you will permit me a conceit. Yet I can remember with disgust a certain castle on the Loire where the decor was so vulgar it denied the very grandeur of its scale. That castle was a perfect example of sheer, stupid size stunted by the petty perception of the small mind. I despise the small mind.

I inhabit and I learn. I learned from the almond-scented breeze that blew in the window of my thatched windmill in Mykonos. I have learned the perfect coolness of a mud-brick Yakh chal in Persia. And for one exotic year I even put up with teaming humanity to live in Banani, a village hugging the Baniagara Cliffs in Mali. The village was built from cliff debris looking like so much broken crockery. Those strange little warrens like jugs and pill boxes with conical thatched hats were the home of the Dogons. I learned from these people something I had known all along – that no one owns his house; it belongs to no one and therefore to everyone. It is a lesson I have learned exceedingly well.

For twenty years I roamed the "other world," the East and Europe, stopping in forgotten corners and backwaters and, more often than not, hurrying through its populated sectors. I have grown intolerant with society and its laws, especially those regarding ownership; I have very definite ideas on the subject. But even in the city one can find from time to time a spot to be perfectly alone. On the rue Boutarel, on the Isle St. Louis in the heart of Paris. There I lived for several weeks quite alone, exquisitely alone, with a view from one window of Notre Dame and from another down into a deeply-shaded courtyard. When it rained I would open all the windows; the courtyard was like a room of rain. I love the rain, despite the discomfort it can prove to a man leading my precarious existence. All my greatest discoveries have been made in the rain. Rue Boutarel; in the end a tragedy. How did he introduce himself? M. Bertrand. A fat little financier, soaking wet and stinking of attar of roses. Arriving home like that in the middle of the night, a week earlier than planned and having the unmitigated gall to ask me what my plans were and what was I doing in his apartment. I could have explained but would he have understood?

I made my way to England in rather a hurry, unfortunate really, for I had always wanted to see the coast of Brittany. That was eight years ago. I had a yen for the sea and decided to explore the coast of Britain, having reached the conclusion that, like an aging sailor, I must have the sea lapping at my door. I was planning to circumambulate the country beginning, in my perverse way, at the end – Land's End. Penzance, The Lizard, Plymouth Sound, Exmouth and all the other "mouths" emptying into the English Channel. In Sussex I discovered an exquisite seventeenth-century manor house, Owlfence Hall. It was a bizarre concoction at once grand, even extravagant, and yet charming, with intimate niches. Its magic stretched out beyond the roof into the park, a man-made landscape, a design of lakes with vast oaks and beeches, so that every window framed a painting – the view constructed precisely by hand to please the eye.

I fell in love with Owlfence as I had never done before. It spurred me on to create my most brilliant and complex plan, a plan guaranteed to win me the house of my dreams. Never before had I planned so patiently; I like to think of Owlfence as the beginning of my mature style. One by one I got rid of the house staff in one way or another, and domestics are hard to find! Slowly but inexorably I drove that household into despair so that living there became intolerable. Her ladyship moved to London, a lazy son went off to the Continent. Day by day the house became more and more my own; room by room. And then ... in a moment of giddy extravagance I threw it all away. In another week or two they would all have fled like rats from a sinking ship but in a trice I lost it, overthrown by a chambermaid – Elsie. Elsie.

She had no business being in the library, it was not her usual practice to be in the library. God how she screamed, screamed her fool head off. Everything happened very fast after that. It would be no use going into it. Once again I was on the run. Luckily I had picked up a few items of value monetarily and I was able to leave England for the New World, my old new world. I had learned much; not least the value of sticking to one's plans, not mere patience but infinite patience, silent waiting.

The New World would be a new start; the search took on a new light. America was no longer familiar to me. I saw her through middle-aged eyes. I had to admit to myself I was beginning to feel old, and a little desperate. Owlfence had profoundly altered me; however, I did not lose sight of my objective. I began in New England where I had left off exploring the shore. I remembered having read, "I want my house to be like the sea wind, all quivering with gulls," a French poet – an exquisite vision. Here was a sea wind as fine as that in England and just as old, and here were gulls as noisy, as omnivorous as any. All the building materials were at hand.

It was the old ocean I wanted at my front stoop, not the new one in the West. The Maritime seaboard. I felt I was narrowing the search – The Crows born again as Sea Gull. Yes. I felt better about Rhode Island than Massachusetts and better still about Maine – more rugged, less spoilt, less populated. I began to focus in on my target. I would dream of it at night and wake refreshed and ready to go on.

I suspect I was going through a change of life. I was still strong, road-strong and weathered, but how long would it be until the slower footstep and arthritic joint? – all that rain gathered behind my knee, in my elbow, between my fingers. Ahhh, you are thinking middle-aged compromise. Well, you are wrong. When you have experienced what I have experienced there is no such thing as compromise. Besides, I have no dependents, no one to compromise to.

Ogunquit attracted me but only for a while, a truly perfect little spot, with certain exceptions; people *will* interfere. You would think an old man would get a little respect. I came out of it all with some money, funds for my continued search. I find money tiresome but it does come in handy. Were I a common thief I could be as rich as Croesus with my intelligence and experience, but I take only what I need and then a little more. The search goes on.

Late last August I stepped off the Bar Harbor ferry at Yarmouth, Nova Scotia. It was my first trip to the land of the Loyalists. How could I have known it would be so perfect. How could I have known – a man who had meditated in the Himalayas, slept on the stone floors of Romanesque abbeys and the silk couches of dukes – that my destiny would be here in such a humble country.

It always astonishes me to look back on the profound moments in my life and to realize how differently things might have turned out. I never think of how things might have been better had I done something differently, taken the other road – I have an elaborate internal defense mechanism against that kind of reasoning – but I can't help thinking that with all the myriad decisions that a traveler must make, I made the right one. The signs I followed, any one of which, had it been missed, would have led me away, led me here instead. Despite my faith in my quest and my wholehearted commitment I cannot say that I felt inexorably drawn to this improbable destination. I simply followed my instincts. And what are instincts? I suppose they are nothing more than a species of highly refined knowledge, the mind tuned to the body's needs.

Would I not have to stop, if only for a while, in a town bearing the name Mahone Bay? I am not overly superstitious but neither am I such a fool as to ignore a significant name from my past. In a quest like mine one must read all the signs. Mahone Bay. They call it "Ma-hone," not "Man" the way we did in Dayton, but it's all the same.

I read the landscape like the geomancers of China. I look for patterns, for the happy coincidence. The Maritimes landscape had already revealed itself to me as both vulnerable and powerful. It was old, scraped down, and gave up its signs easily to my trained eye. I read it as one reads the skeleton of an aged, emaciated body. The mystery of the landscape can be divined like the heavens. One looks for the living strength from the land. The air, salty and pine-laden, had the fragrance of hidden power. Somewhere, somewhere near, I sensed I might find that power bubbling to the surface. I have come to know that I could not hope to find the right home unless it was in the right place. A simple enough idea, overlooked by most – but then how little choice most people ever have! A location somewhere near, sheltered from the wind and bounded by water – "Fengshui," wind and water. Already I had felt on this South Shore a unity with the land and the weather. It is prone to violent moods. The sea is wild but sheltering, tranquil coves are like mirrors in a rough cupped hand. Everywhere I sensed the delicate poignancy of *déjà vu*.

Having found Mahone Bay I eventually found Raven's Bluff, another reference, albeit oblique, to my childhood. Raven's Bluff sits at the highest point of the rounded spine of the Fourth Peninsula. It is no more than a huddled gathering of weathered gray frame houses, but standing there one can see the length of the peninsula; any traveler on the road or ship on the sea. Raven's Bluff was like the Crow's Nest of my childhood. I knew I was closing in. Somewhere nearby – it had to be. The end of the road. The Peninsula Road circles back two miles beyond Raven's Bluff, dropping down along the South Shore through Steep Cove and then back up along the coast. Where it turns there is a road leading off into the woods, to an enormous deserted grange. Following that, the road winds down through a woodland: fragrant balsam, tamarack, yellow birch and clumps of what they call Acadian Red Spruce. And then, Odd's End. The end of the road.

Having found it, I backtracked. I dug in at the Sea Winds guesthouse to plan my campaign.

It is fifteen miles from Mahone Bay to Odd's End. Sometimes I walked or borrowed the bicycle from the guesthouse. How glorious those fall days were, with my head teeming with ideas, all dedicated to one end. I was like an adolescent in love.

I would stay with the northern shore of the Fourth Peninsula. The coast has been gouged and rutted by glacial action and then over millions of years all the edges had been softened, rounded by the pounding sea. The rock is pockmarked with tidal pools. To my left the sea and to my right woods of hardy spruce, larch, and pine. What a vital perfume – salt and pine and the turbulent air. Beyond the trees, the sloping shoulders of the great whale-like drumlin which constitutes the peninsula. Its spine is rich with deposited soil, and it is there along the spine that the farms huddle. The sloping shoulders are meadow land yellow with buttercups – they were at that time of year. The meadows give way to hearty stands of trees – a fringe around the bald peninsula and beyond that, the shore.

Here and there I would discover those tidy little coves with pebbled beaches – pockets of calm. It was no wonder this coast was notorious for pirates and rum runners. It is dotted with natural harbors – hiding places to stash gold or tin soldiers. My childhood still lives in me. I imagine the peninsula a huge household. Under its thatched roof are these rooms, little, calm rooms containing the sea.

Some days when it was damp, and the fog hung over the bay, I could understand the vivid stories that abound in the region of ghost ships appearing in the harbor and then vanishing again. One could easily construct material forms out of the dense slabs of still, gray air. It was a haunting shore, a characteristic that appealed to me immensely.

My destination, bright or rainy, was always the same— Odd's End. I found I could approach it from the north by way of a long strip of sandy beach, without being seen. The dunes rose like a sloping wall before the house. It was the geomantic equation manifest; sheltered from the wind, bounded by water. Fengshui. The beach was always deserted. Short of the long and somewhat grueling route along the peninsula, the only other approach was down the Park Road. There were no signs to ward off trespassers—I was glad of that. But apparently tourists seldom found their way past the Grange—I was glad of that also.

Convincing someone to move, to give it all up and go, requires a large effort. I faced the challenge with enthusiasm; it is the only game in town, as they say. I have told you, albeit briefly, of former campaigns only to indicate to you how all is lost in this game if one loses one's patience, acts rashly. Mind you, I am not above drastic measures, I play this game for keeps. I allow for tenants' reluctance, it is only natural, but my prodding increases as their reluctance does, directly. I have a certain bent towards psychology; one cannot simply pop people over the head. The joys of such a victory are short-lived; a day or two almost, and then the house is crawling with coppers. No, the idea is more subtle. My tenants should never know quite how to fight back. I remain invisible; who can they fight if they see no one?

I build myself a perch in the flies and gently tug at invisible strings. Day to day life is altered slowly, unnoticeably until one morning my puppet-victims awake to find their happy home intolerable. The job is twice as easy when there is a couple, for reasons that will soon become obvious.

9

Mary Close didn't move. For one full minute her eyes did not blink. She sat back on her stool, and afraid to lift her gaze from the painting for even a fraction of a second, she reached behind her, groping in the dark until she found the string that switched on the overhead light. The light bleached out the image thrown on the canvas by the projector; the trance was broken. She got up and notched the projector's switch from light to fan, pressing her palm against its hot side until it had cooled, and finally, several minutes later, turned it off. She looked around her at the seven large canvases: four complete, three within days of completion. Soon they would be carefully packed and shipped off to Toronto. How soon? she wondered. How much longer could she go on? She looked at the black curtain across the north wall blocking out the light, that wonderful northern light the studio had been designed to capture, and she spoke to herself a little soliloquy she had repeated several times in the past few days: Outside the sun is shining brightly; I am sitting here in the dark. Perhaps Mary doesn't have both oars in the water or is not playing with a full deck!

My painting is painting itself. It's no use pretending it is Malcolm having a little joke. His hand shakes so violently it is only good for brushing his teeth and besides he is color-blind. And who else could it be? Assuming someone had access to the house, he would have to work in a darkened room with a noisy projector going, over which he would be hard-pressed to hear the approach of someone from the house. Technically it was possible; she was at the boring stage of her work where it was just a question of matching paint to colored light and applying it to the canvas where the pattern fell. But it was altogether too audacious to imagine.

She pushed the hair from her forehead and pressed her hand against her mouth; it smelled strongly of turpentine. She closed her eyes, but it was no use, the image buzzed behind her eyelids. She was too nervous to work any more; restless again. Malcolm had said that just the other night; she was restless. Her nerves were on edge.

Malcolm would be home soon; she wasn't sure whether she dared tell him about this new development. He was so flippant about it all.

"The way I see it, Zenobia, it's either you or me, and since it isn't me, then by deduction it must be you." He clowned about it, which in itself worried her, and the clown always pointed a finger at her.

"If you insist that logic is solely concerned with induction, rather than demonstration, and the business of induction is to arrive at causes, then let me suggest the cause—you're nuts."

It wasn't that he was callous really, but he couldn't take it seriously; what she found creepy, he found fascinating; inexplicable but harmless. "So far!" she had thrown back at him belligerently. He didn't spend all day in the house with all its audible frights: creaking, bumping, squeaking. He hadn't thought it so funny when she accused him! He refused to accept it but could offer no other explanation. And that was that.

She spent too much time alone and the thought of its being one of them was scary enough. If Malcolm was mad then to live alone with him in isolation was madness. But more horrifying still was the idea that she was mad and didn't know it. It was an idea that kept insinuating its way into her consciousness. But why did he insist it was one of them or a friend having one over on them? His answer was again flippant but not without a certain plausibility. "Why suspect a stranger when you can suspect a friend?" Some friend! Mary didn't like to think it was anyone she knew, least of all herself.

She remembered hearing of an otherwise gentle woman, who, having been rudely awakened, murdered her husband, strangled him without ever knowing she was doing it. Mary comforted herself, "I am neither gentle nor strong enough," she said out loud to her assembled paintings. It was odd to hear her own voice in that dimly-lit room. "A voice screaming all around you that was once your own voice": that was how Beckett had put it. She wasn't screaming. It had never seemed odd before; she had always been in the habit of talking to herself. Sometimes she sang; sometimes she remembered scenes from plays she had acted in; sometimes she pretended she was being interviewed by Dick Cavett: "Well, Dick, I think the retrospective at MOMA had been quite successful and of course the new book by Ashton had told me things about myself I had never known before now." Suddenly it seemed silly – worse, it seemed perverse. She tried to hear in her voice another voice trying to get out. Sybil or Eve, one of those multiple persons, people, whatever. The thought startled her and only made matters worse.

The telephone rang and Mary ran down the corridor to the kitchen to answer it. It was Malcolm phoning from Mahone Bay. He was on his way home. When she spoke she heard no other voice but her own. Yes, she had saved his supper and she had not eaten herself. Malcolm replied in a very poor impression of Groucho Marx, "Good. If anyone is going to eat you, I would rather it was me." There was no one in that voice but Malcolm, she thought.

Half an hour and he would be home. It was nice of him to phone and yet the idea of his stopping fifteen miles away to say he was on his way and the concern in his voice . . .

She slipped on a heavy sweater and walked out into the yard. The wind was picking up again and the sky was overcast. It was eight o'clock, but looking back she could still see the sun. It was a fiery red. The house was back-lit; the windows in the west wing seemed on fire.

She loved Odd's End. There was a time she would not have dreamed of living in the country – a nice place to visit, but, for a city girl, not a place to live. How would she live without all the excitement, she had thought, without being where things were happening when they happened? And then, as she had become more secure with her work, she realized that if something was happening she would hear about it soon enough. She began to realize that anything worth knowing would eventually make itself known, and her isolation was far from complete. All the periodicals she cared about came monthly in the mail, and when she wasn't painting, she could pop down to New York for as long as she wanted or needed. In the last couple of years she had found that if the frequency of her trips was not decreasing, the duration was. She really liked being at Odd's End. It was home.

Now the sun was behind the trees. The underbelly of the massive cloud bank was red and dirty gold. The sea reflected in that eerie light looked purple and sometimes as red as blood. The stucco walls of the house were yellow in this light; the shadows were crisply outlined and long, reaching out towards her across the court. A de Chirico painting. The sea gulls were shrieking, the forest birds chirping madly, the way they always did at nightfall, as if they had no memory of the solar cycle and this night was the end of everything. Mary realized she was frightened. The wind off the dunes, usually invigorating, now chilled her, and she did not look forward to the storm the way she normally did. Storms had been one of the best things about Odd's End; she had never seen anything so beautiful as a storm roaring down the bay, building up the water into huge whitecaps. To go inside and feel the house settle into the storm – it had always been thrilling. Now the prospect did not please her even remotely. All she wanted right now was for Malcolm to reach her before the storm, before the nightfall was complete. Lord knows Malcolm wasn't much protection against the "forces of evil" but he was another human, and she felt terribly alone. Alone and not alone.

She didn't want to return to the house. And she was aware of feeling ridiculous for not wanting to. She wandered instead across the sandy road and climbed up onto the dunes. Her bare feet sank in the sand – it was already cool. From here she would be able to see the car coming down the road. The wind met her with its full force. It was howling, competing with the gulls, and behind it the sea roared at high tide. Caught off balance by the force of the wind and the instability of her footing she involuntarily sat down in the grass. Amidst the long grass the noise was muffled again. It was comforting, like falling into a small room, a playpen.

What if every event that had occurred in the last two weeks was unrelated? What if each thing was a coincidence? Hadn't she read in *Scientific American* that statistically it could be shown that a lot more coincidences happen to us than we perceive? It didn't seem to make sense now, but it had been quite convincing when she had read it. If enough independent phenomena are studied, correlations will be found. Statisticians called it the "fallacy of the enumeration of favorable circumstances." Favorable, hah! Perhaps she was in for a heavier than normal slate of coincidences.

Odd's End was now in shadows. It had all happened suddenly. The clouds had shifted, a gray film had been drawn across the house – a pall, she thought to herself, and immediately regretted having thought so. Why did nature conspire with the events of one's life? Why was a storm transforming the house into a mausoleum? Why did the house, which moments ago had been radiant, now seem sucked dry?

The car's horn reached her like thunder. She hadn't even noticed the lights. Malcolm was home. She clambered down the hill to meet him.

"Our house is haunted, you say. I suppose it makes as much sense as anything else." Malcolm crunched on an ice cube and then let it slither down his tongue back into his drink. Mary swirled her drink around, her eyes were a little glassy. She was smiling. Malcolm continued.

"Don't think for a moment I will confuse that smile with enlightenment or your silence for contemplation." There was no reply but he hadn't really expected one. "No, that is not the smile of a Zen master in satori, it is the smile of a drunk, that is what it is." His own consonants were blurred around the edges.

Mary slouched down further in the couch. Her voice was thick. "This smile is four giblets deep. Gimlets, I mean."

Malcolm leaned over and kissed the top of her head. It was a precipitous move. He fell over, landing beside her on the couch and upsetting her drink as he did so. Mary sucked at her arm where it was wet. In the silence, the storm that had broken could be heard, subsiding now, moving inland. The wind shook the trees sending little showers of rain against the windows. Thunder would roll, long and distant rumbling, and the Modern Jazz Quartet stretched out into "Django." The cool soothing ring of the xylophone was salubrious. Mary finally spoke.

"Yes."

"What yes?"

"Yes, we, that is to say, us is haunted."

"Ohhh." There was another long pause as Malcolm reconstructed the conversation they had been having earlier, several drinks back.

74

"What do you suppose he wants?"

"The house, of course. What else?" Mary answered without apparent concern. "To himself," she added.

"Why didn't he let us know before the last mortgage payment?" No reply. "In fact why didn't he let us know before we moved in? I assume he was here when we moved in."

"That would be typical," replied Mary. "I think ghosts come with old houses."

"It's not in the contract."

"Shall we take the ghost to court?"

"He'd get off on a habeas corpus." Malcolm chuckled at his own joke. Mary only smiled. The record finished and skipped for a moment before turning itself off.

"Maybe he only wants a room."

"And board?"

"No." Mary seemed pensive; drunk and pensive. "I mean maybe he – *it* – only wants the old part of the house. What for instance could *it* want with all these additions?"

"Aren't you forgetting that my study is in the old part of the house? And besides, he seems to be spending most of his time in your studio, if I am to understand what you are telling me."

"It, I mean he, which *is* right? Anyway, Ghost couldn't be interested in my studio; it's less than ten years old. No self-respecting spirit would be caught dead in there."

Malcolm grimaced. With a great effort he forced himself up and over to the record player where he clumsily changed discs. Billie Holiday started singing "Miss Brown to You."

"A creative ghost."

"A painter."

"Is he good?"

"He doesn't have to be; it's just a question of joining the dots at this point, and using the right color. It is amazing what a relief it is for me to talk about my – our problem this way; to put everything down to a ghost. Praise be to alcohol!"

"Isn't that one of the classic lines the artist uses? 'Someone painted my picture for me. Someone guided my hand.' Your trouble is you're inspired, that's all, and you don't recognize the symptoms."

Mary frowned. "I haven't been inspired for months. That stuff in there is just plain work."

"Can you stop? Do something different for a while?"

Mary didn't have to respond. Malcolm was trying to be helpful. He knew as well as she that her show was imminent. She stared intensely into the fire.

"A holiday." She was scarcely audible at first but her voice grew more enthusiastic. "When was the last time you and I had a holiday together?"

"How can you ask?" said Malcolm wryly. "You a painter, me a university professor—every day is a holiday."

"June of 1974." Mary had been working it out on her fingers.

"Do you think our ghost just wants us to take a holiday?" said Malcolm.

"Malcolm! Of course, that's it!" Mary seemed genuinely elated. "A benevolent ghost forced to desperate means to get our attention."

"Any holiday for us would also be a holiday for the ghost," Malcolm reminded her.

"Precisely. It might do both of us a world of good, I mean us and the ghost."

"True, if he has put up with us for all these years he can probably put up with us for a few more. But right now he needs a break."

Mary looked at Malcolm, suddenly sad again. She had never been so moody as in the last couple of weeks.

"Mal, I don't want to have to go forever—move, I mean."

He kissed her. They fell into a prolonged embrace. With a certain amount of difficulty they helped each other undress.

It was raining again. The fire crackled. Their love-making wasn't all that successful, but it was something.

Any notion that their ghost was a benevolent one did not last the evening. The lights in the stairwell and in the hall flickered on and off. The fuse was found to be intact and the possibility of four bulbs going at once was too much of a coincidence, no matter what *Scientific American* might say to the contrary. The bedroom lights worked and so, by mutual consent, they agreed that some of the wiring must have been affected by the storm. Some. Despite being tired and by now a little hung over, Mary wasn't prepared to sleep and decided to read. But her book didn't make sense. She thought it was because she was drunk or simply not concentrating. It made sense to a degree and then all of a sudden it stopped making sense. Malcolm reminded her that such anomalies happened. The pagination was correct as was the type style; the prose style was the same as were the characters. There was something familiar about the setting, but the context was wrong ... and then it dawned on her. After comparing the two books she realized: six pages of *Memoirs of a Dutiful Daughter* were unaccountably taking the place of six pages in *The Prime of Life*. They had been interchanged. Malcolm had rolled over to go to sleep, and she hesitated before showing him. She pointed out the transfer without saying a word. He frowned but eventually had a suggestion. "Probably a signature out of place in the collating room." He knew it wasn't a signature, a signature was sixteen pages, but there was a kind of sense and it might just do until the morning. Mary didn't say so but she knew for sure his explanation was wrong. She had only finished *Memoirs of a Dutiful Daughter* three days earlier. It had been intact then.

They lay in the dark very still; waiting for the second shoe to drop; waiting for *something* to happen. They were miles apart. It was as if they had argued and gone to bed with the problem unresolved. They hadn't argued; everything had been good. They were going to go on a holiday together. Mary wanted to hold Malcolm or him to hold her, but she couldn't move. She wanted to talk to him, about anything but she didn't want to hear her voice in the dark. She didn't want him to suddenly say something. That would be far more frightening. He was awake. She lay there anticipating it – his voice coming at her out of the dark. Finally she couldn't stand the suspense.

"Why is everything the ghost does so small?"

"What do you mean?"

"He hasn't moved any rooms around or made the walls bleed. He doesn't fling open windows or slam doors. Nothing he does is really supernatural. Just small. The letters, my book."

Malcolm didn't speak. He was aware that his heart was beating painfully hard. He flicked on his bedside light. He spoke evenly and with a struggle managed, he felt, to keep any fear out of his own voice. "Because everything that has happened has been done by a human."

The statement wasn't reassuring. It was the bare statement of what they had known all along. Why did it sound so dreadful all of a sudden? Did Malcolm know more?

Mary's eyes were wide open, the muscles in her neck stood out. "What kind of human? Why? What have we done?" She paused but Malcolm knew she was going to go on. Her voice was already tremulous. He wasn't sure he wanted to hear what she might say.

"Sometimes I wonder about you, Malcolm; who you were before I met you, what you might have been. Have you really told me everything?"

"After all these years?"

"People change."

"Darling, you know everything that is important about me."

"How do I know that?"

Malcolm tried to inflect his voice with humor. "You don't

know. But I wasn't in the underworld if that's what you mean."

"No? But maybe you were in some kind of cult, the black arts, I don't know and maybe you still are. Or maybe you left after taking an oath and now they've come for you ..."

"Stop it!" He rolled over and looked down into her face. She backed off, her head sank into the pillow. She averted her face. Malcolm fell back onto his own pillow. He spoke very calmly. "Mary, you are going to talk yourself into a frenzy. Please don't do it."

She sat up in bed. "Tell me, Malcolm, I don't care, just tell me. Let me in on it–anything."

Malcolm sat up and grabbed her shoulders firmly in each hand. She was rigid with fear. The effects of the alcohol had gone, all the warm fuzziness was like a black pain in the back of his head. Mary's eyes searched for something in his eyes, looked through them as if looking through a mask for the face behind. He had seen her like this before. A look mixed with horror and incrimination. He found himself, against his will, trying to control his own expression, consciously to appear innocent of the implied accusations. She must see the concern and love he felt. Yet he felt that his face must by now look no more than a grotesque reflection of her own–the picture of fear. He couldn't talk, nothing he could say could possibly convince her that he was not whatever it was she thought he might be. The tension overcame him; he began to cry. It was not something he did often, but he couldn't stop himself. Mary's body shuddered and the grip on her let go. He could feel the tension leaving her. His own tears had been like a slap across the face. They embraced gingerly and lay back in the bed, this time without the slightest thought of love-making.

At some point they fell asleep. The light was left on until early in the morning when the sky was already red with dawn. The birds were singing joyfully–they had no memory of dawn; they sang gloriously of their redemption. A light rain fell.

10

I left the Sea Winds and its aging proprietor late last fall with the promise and the intention of returning this spring. I promised also to keep in touch, and to that end Miss Tinker did receive a postcard from St. Petersburg, Florida; an appropriate watering hole for a retired teacher, which is what she believes me to be. I have a front to keep up and postmarks are the stuff of the real world. How easy for the writer who can crisscross the borders of the world without so much as a passport.

Apart from that little jaunt I was never far away from Odd's End. I had only just had time to get to know the house let alone make any substantial steps towards making it my own when the idea occurred to me that I would return in the spring with the whole glorious summer before me.

The winter was spent predominantly in that most sedentary of active employment, research. Scholarship suits my temperament. Despite my years on the road I like best to stay in one place, and nobody stays in one place more effectively than the scholar. Social registers, archives, newspapers, whatever. Since Malcolm Close is a scholar, there was a thesis and various publications to be read, dry stuff in the main, but who knows to what end it might be turned; even the most objective scholar can be seen through his scholarship. And Mary Close being a painter, and one of some repute, has had her work reviewed, and was the subject of an "at home" profile in *Halifax* Magazine – a stroke of luck for me. Like any spy I had to familiarize myself with every aspect of life at Odd's End and vicinity: Mahone Bay, Lunenburg, little Raven's Bluff, and Steep Cove. There is no such thing as being overprepared. I had to know the place better than the inhabitants themselves. In any case, I enjoyed the image I was building, like any artist, and I could afford to be thorough for I had a whole winter to kill. A Canadian winter. A bitter east-coast variation on a theme. How nice it would have been to be curled in front of the fire at Odd's End. Later. All in good time.

My scholarship took me to libraries large and small and I cultivated the anonymous friendship of Zohra Harrt, the librarian in Lunenburg's single reading establishment, and Constance Pillbeam, her compeer in Mahone Bay. Anonymous due to disguises – an art I have found great use for.

There was detective work to be done apart from my scholarly endeavors. Unobtrusive observation. The Closes, he and she, whenever possible. I caught only an occasional glimpse of Mary in Lunenburg where she visited an antique store proprietor – that is to say, a young man. I could not ascertain the extent or nature of their relationship – that would have to wait until the spring and warm weather and more gossip at the Sea Winds but I was glad to see they spent so much time together. One could make so much out of others' affairs. There is also a companion in Malcolm's case. I say "companion" advisedly because all I witnessed between them was companionship. One must not jump to conclusions, but then who knows what companionship might blossom into? Malcolm was by far the easiest quarry. In a way, he came to me. He teaches in Halifax at King's College, whose halls I found a welcome respite from the blustery weather. Despite my crusty complexion and a bit too much color in my cheeks, I am not unprofessorial in appearance. It is, at least, my easiest disguise. Professors often look degenerate—not quite unkempt, but often unhealthy. I need only to adopt a lugubrious expression and a certain otherworldliness to seem quite at home at King's College. From reading carrels, in cafeteria line-ups, even in the lecture hall, I watched Malcolm Close. In these ways I built a comprehensive picture of the Closes.

Have you stopped to think just how much is known about you by others? It is amazing what a few phone calls under an assumed name and appropriate credentials can dig up. Most detective work is done over the phone these days. So much for the "gumshoe": "the cabbage-ear" is more to the point. Banks, department stores, and public services all provide vital information in dribs and drabs which flesh out the life and style of the quarry. I have to know the Closes intimately—their strengths and their weaknesses. People! How they interfere with my plans! If only the world would go away. But then I must admit I enjoy the challenge.

Many years ago when I wriggled through the basement window at The Crows back in Dayton I did so with great trepidation but then, once I was inside, it was my home again. It was all so familiar, so friendly; I was not the intruder, they were. My fears vanished then and have never returned. I always feel I belong when I am in a home—a strange admission for a self-imposed exile from society. The excitement is in the strategy. One cannot hope to map out the whole campaign in advance. One must keep a sharp eye and learn to react to each new situation. But first, observation, detection. Find out what makes a household tick and then warp the spring.

There is one wonderful quirk of human nature in my favor. Despite the fact that most people are to some degree paranoid, they seldom believe they are actually being taunted, followed, or otherwise pestered by someone else—a real someone. Not unless they are classically paranoid. A really sick person would be difficult to deal with. Most moderns of the post-Freudian age are inured to paranoia as a mere trick of the mind. Paradoxically, their capacity for paranoid fantasies is vast. The intellectual will seldom tumble to the fact that external forces *are* out to get him, assuming, of course, he has no reason to suspect as much. And most people don't really have any skeletons in their closet. The Closes don't – not yet.

So the whole thing can usually be accomplished without violence. The consequences of violence are too volatile. Control is lost and chaos takes over. The last thing I want is chaos. I want to live quietly, so people must be, how shall I say, disposed of quietly. I want to be alone.

I returned to Mahone Bay long before the tourists while the air was still cool and the rain sometimes turned to wet snow. But how refreshing it was and what a reception I received at the Sea Winds. I do believe Miss Tinker had other plans for me, but I had but one thing on my mind. Gossip was necessary to that end, and gossip there was. Although I was careful to divert any suspicion as to who or what I wanted to hear about, I heard about it anyway and savored every morsel like truffles, ahhhh truffles. It is the nature of superficial dialogue to swap anecdotes. For each story of mine – and I have thousands, real and fictitious – a tidbit of town tattle must be exchanged. In a week I was driving Miss Tinker's car to the grocery store, and inevitably its services were offered to me in my search throughout the country for a nice place to settle into my retirement. This was a bonus – a car was to prove most useful in the campaign. It attracted less attention too; in this country it was unusual to see an older man on a bicycle. Secretly I think that was why Miss Tinker had offered it to me. She was already attempting to tame me. Poor, silly old bat.

About this time, I found out about Kevin and Angela and their respective relationships with Mary and Malcolm. Both of the relationships were disappointingly harmless, but I could make do.

Kevin Brain is an old school chum of Mary's. He is a homosexual and lives with a musician friend named Tom above his antique store called Hope Springs Eternal, a large frame house just out of Lunenburg. His passion is glass, especially bottles. There is an entire shelf in the store of poison bottles; little skulls, coffins, snakes, all of glass. Having surveyed the shop, I beetled to the library to research glassware and returned an ardent amateur. I have been back several times and have made a couple of purchases. I bought Miss Tinker a piece of iridescent, marigold-colored carnival ware – a bonbon dish. It is precisely the kind of thing she likes. Kevin is a sociable fellow: slim, handsome, and quiet, but on the subject of antique glass he is voluble.

The tourist season had not really got into full swing and so he had time to chat. Often he closed up the shop and went to auctions. Mary was his sidekick on these ventures. They are very close. It is something I have seen before: it is even common. A friendship between opposite sexes and yet with none of the urgency or threat associated with such close ties. Kevin is "safe" and therefore Mary is comfortable. She can afford to be intimate without inspiring lust. If my understanding of human nature is all I believe it to be, Malcolm probably sanctions the relationship with Kevin and even likes Kevin, but he probably harbors the tiniest bit of jealousy too, and maybe a bit of resentment at the camaraderie that Kevin and Mary share. It is something that Malcolm can never know with his wife – an intimacy without those sticky carnal strings. Kevin has known Mary longer than Malcolm – he has that advantage. I knew at once that I could turn the situation to my advantage.

An incident occurred at the antique shop recently that provided me with some first-class information. I was discussing the relative merits of Beck's very early press-molded glass and that of the Imperial Company of Flint, Michigan, when Kevin suddenly whooped and flung his arms around a young woman who had snuck up on us using me as a screen – a dangerous occupation!

"I don't believe my eyes."

She was rather extraordinary, with huge eyes and long, pale blonde hair but that was obviously not what he had meant.

"Bliss."

I thought this an exaggeration, but he had not been describing his state of being; Bliss was her rather extraordinary name.

"Bliss Lund!"

"Kev."

I was quite left out in all the excitement and faded off into the woodwork listening all the while. They talked about the eight years over which they had lost contact. They talked of the old crowd of Pip and Ellie and Tom, Kevin's *amour*, and of Powys, his dog, who as if on cue began to bark furiously from the upstairs apartment. They talked about Bliss, who is an actress working in Toronto but now in Halifax for the season at the Neptune. And after much rapid-fire memory chasing, Kevin brought up the name of Mary Close.

"You must, must, meet her; you'll love her."

Bliss was pensive. "Was she always Mary Close?"

"No. She used to be Mary Draper."

"Dark hair, rich, a little crazy?"

Kevin laughed. "I'd almost forgotten. Not crazy – her painting yes, but not Mary. She's having a show at the gallery where Pip's work was exhibited."

"Spizziri?"

"The same; in June. In fact she's going to stay with Pip and I might accompany her, if I can get away."

Bliss was thinking. "Wasn't she living with some lanky bookworm?"

Kevin's face clouded for a moment, but he smiled again. "Close himself. A prof now; quite the success, speaking at

Harvard the week after Mary's show begins. That's why I might go along with her; as bodyguard."

And again their conversation deteriorated to laughter. Then Kevin was talking about Odd's End. With great animation he was describing it to Bliss.

I enjoy the relative solitude of my life but solitude is full of secrets and sometimes I wish to share those secrets if only for the excitement of astonishing one's listener. Suddenly I wanted to join in, to swing around and say, "I know Odd's End. I know more about it than you and more than the inhabitants know themselves."

"And now they think it's haunted because the forks are in the spoon rack and the spoons in the fork." They were laughing and for some reason I couldn't stand to hear them laugh. I wanted to scream; my heart was pounding and my vision clouded. The next thing I knew Kevin had sat me down on a bench and was mopping my forehead with a wet cloth. I could only assume I had said nothing for he was very kind. He suggested that I join him and Bliss for tea but I thanked him and refused. I apologized and acted old and confused. Mumbling something about going home for a nap, I left.

Angela Treadway is another story. Her relationship with Malcolm is friendly, but it is not an easy friendship nonetheless. There is frustration. I watched her once when Malcolm had left. Her eyes followed him for a full minute and all the while her fingers beat a nervous tattoo against her leg. Once he walked her to the lodgings she shares with another girl on Henry Street. A kiss that was meant for the cheek accidentally brushed his lips. Malcolm left looking quite disturbed. Conscience, I expect. Angela is not beautiful; her eyes are bright but without the keenness and depth of Mary's. She is, however, very pretty. Twenty-three, twenty-four, she smiles radiantly from under a mop of long red hair and she is a cheery soul: quick-witted and open. She is affectionate and hugs people, or grabs an arm, not in a silly

way; she is not stupid, only warm-blooded. And she is eminently embraceable; her body is rounded and soft. She
dresses simply yet stylishly in clothes that invariably reveal
provocative glimpses of thigh or breast. From the expression
on Malcolm's face, such glimpses are to his mixed delecta-
tion and dismay. On another occasion, in the park after
lunch, she slipped her arm around his waist in response to
some shared nonsense. When his long arm was thrown
around her shoulder his hand brushed her breast. Her
shiver was not one of distaste; he moved his hand only after
several seconds and the subtlest but by no means innocent
exploration.

11

"His name is Fielding."

Malcolm looked up inquiringly from his notes. Mary held a scrap of paper in both hands.

"Benjamin Fielding."

"Who is Benjamin Fielding?"

"Excuse me, *Doctor* Benjamin Fielding."

"Mary, for Christ's sake ... oh." Malcolm suddenly realized what she was saying; it irritated him, nonetheless, that she was being so cryptic. However, it was not the time to be critical.

"Kevin recommended him."

"I think you'll feel better for it."

Mary nodded her head up and down automatically, then perched on the arm of his chair.

"It's just the exhibition," he said soothingly.

"Come off it, Mal, it's not my first show."

Mary's hand was clammy on his. He tried not to fidget, to bother her. She was looking around the study.

"It's this house!" She looked squarely at him and her eyes were penetrating. "It's ganging up on us. Don't you feel it? Don't you notice what's happening?"

Malcolm looked concerned.

"Well, on me anyway," she murmured.

Malcolm was going to speak but decided better of it. She

studied him a moment longer and then with a sigh, she rose slowly to her feet.

"Anyway, he's a nice shrink, Kevin says."

Malcolm looked fleetingly at St. Michael. He had wanted to say something encouraging. She was shuffling out of the room, and he wanted to call out, "Good show, Zenobia. We'll lick the monster," but the words stuck in his throat.

He knew she was right. Something was going on. It was twisted, but in order not to alarm her more, he was determined to stay calm. It was precisely at such times that one must be sensible above all else; it was the only weapon they had. He did suspect her, and she knew it, and she suspected him, and he knew it, and both knew that the other knew. It was a marital paradox: first loved, first suspected. There were a complicated set of fears at work; fear for oneself and fear for one another, and mingled with the nameless fear and suspicion was an intense need to care for each other. Alongside the distrust was the realization that they had to trust each other. Like some organism suffering an eternal disorder, turning on itself, there was no escaping that responsibility. It could be licked – It! Just like a disease, it was invisible. The less that was invisible the better. Mary was high-strung; that had to be dealt with, and a doctor could deal with it better than he could. Half the problem seemed to be merely forgetfulness, understandable with a big show coming up. Forgetting she had put a wash in the dryer, forgetting she had already watered the plants, forgetting the last record she had listened to. The letters were something else again, but she was still overreacting. They could hold their ground against anything if they could be sensible; to Malcolm being sensible amounted to a religion.

12

With my research well-established, and comfortably ensconced again at the Sea Winds, I started my campaign at Odd's End.

And first on the list was the surprise party. It took a lot of running around to find the ingredients, and some things had to be made in advance, but it was carried off in grand style. Admittedly it was not a subtle gesture; much of my campaign will operate on a subconscious level. There was the need to break the inertia of routine life without raising the wrong *kind* of suspicions. The dinner party struck the right balance, I think, intimidating but certainly not heinous. Not wicked enough for a criminal and far too elaborate for a crank. An inspired mystery.

I watched the show from the woods behind the west wing. It was frustrating, the "Colin" is so much better hot and the order of service was all wrong. I would have liked to have heard what was said but bugging devices are costly toys and not really my style. I rely on my imagination. There are, after all, only so many responses a person can make in such a situation. They immediately suspected each other – I can only presume from long years of studying the beast. At one point they searched the house. The lights flickered on, one by one, and I could scarcely keep from laughing. They may have made phone calls, but not to the police; at least no squad car arrived. Odd's End is an isolated place: that is one of its most charming features. And how exactly does one phone the police in such a situation? "Help, help, I am being served a gourmet meal!" The phone calls were, no doubt, to likely suspects; everyone has a list on hand of likely suspects for any occasion.

The meal was a success even if very little was eaten. I suffered the insult calmly. More than a bugging device registering what was said, I would like a machine which could read their minds. Did they lie awake waiting for the telltale signs of poisoning? Did they sleep fitfully, hearing distantly the grandfather clock strike two and then two again and two all night on the hour? Did they notice it striking two, and, if so, were they surprised to find it telling the correct time in the morning? I only regret one thing – that I couldn't wash the dishes. I hate people who leave the dinner dishes overnight.

It was important not to follow such a coup with anything equally outrageous. The mystery would be greatly diminished in power if it were merely one in a series of startling events. People can become inured to startling events if they occur with any frequency. Timing is crucial; to do the right thing at the right time. A pool player setting up his shots. The water torture is what I have in mind. A persistent almost innocuous harassment. Not only must I maintain my own anonymity, but I must divert suspicion away from the notion of an external agent. This disharmony must appear to come from within the household.

Having served up the first course, so to speak, I let things cool down for a few days. Long enough for the whole episode to seem like a bad dream. Let them relax, lull the victim into a false sense of security. There was research still to do to use up my time and I must remain accountable to Miss Tinker at the Sea Winds. Keeping up a cover, spies call it.

After a few days I started making regular visits to Odd's End, to continue with my disruptive tactics. I started simply enough, affecting some small changes. Just mischief, really, to get the ball rolling. I filled a half-empty salt shaker and emptied most of the dish-washing liquid down the drain. I took the top off the toothpaste and loosened a fluorescent light bulb above the bathroom sink until it flickered. Comic relief—nothing reckless, nothing to inspire alarm. A calendar in the kitchen with appointments marked in a felt pen now had a couple of extra dates mysteriously circled and one page of Malcolm's most recent scholarly endeavor is now lost forever, burnt to a crisp in the fireplace. Is it too much to hope that he might find the charred remains? What might he think? Such things might well go unnoticed, but I have more up my sleeve.

Mary works at home in her studio which is tricky but then there is her antique-collecting friend. Now that the weather has cleared, she spends even more time with him, auction crawling, sometimes all over the province. And there is another card in my favor—Mary is an energetic soul. Like myself, she likes to walk and ride her bicycle. Despite the steep, unpaved hill from Odd's End she will, more often than not, bicycle to Steep Cove for groceries. That is a distance of four miles, leaving me two hours at the very least to myself. When she takes the truck I can be reasonably sure that she is going either to Lunenburg or Mahone Bay or on one of her antique plunders. On an average, I can expect half a day to myself when Mary leaves in the truck. I have determined a quite accurate schedule.

I liken my methods to the water torture. It is a tremendous game to see how much one can manipulate one's fellow man without his knowing it. You all do it, consciously or otherwise, especially husbands and wives. It is an existential dilemma: by one's very existence one interferes with the existence of others. There is a bright side to it—make a game of it! As quickly as I have gathered information concerning the Close family, I have devised some connivance to put it to use. Knowing that Mary is to be gone for a week with Malcolm to follow gave me a deadline.

One can undermine the peace and security of the domestic environment, but one must be devious. People tend to band together against a common enemy. In my campaign, I plan to make the Closes suspect not only each other but also the house itself. Devious. For instance, if I were to whisk away Malcolm's favorite reading lamp, he would notice. But if I were to gradually decrease the illuminative power of that lamp from one hundred to sixty to forty watts, would he notice that? Similarly, one cannot simply walk off with a person's avocado tree but to pluck off the leaves one by one . . .

Of course, this was not all I had in store. The occasional note from the desk of Malcolm Close. Anonymous notes from someone else. There is poetry in that redundancy. Needless to say, such notes could not be sent on Close letterhead or in Close envelopes, attractive though they may be in pale gray and cream. They must be on white bond, stuffed into drugstore envelopes, a package of which I secretly stored at the back of Malcolm's desk. How clever of Mary to find them.

And then there were the sunglasses, Angela's sunglasses. Anything would have done; a scarf, a discarded cigarette package, scented from being in her purse; anything. She left the glasses at her table one day after lunch at Filos; it only took a moment. How proud Mrs. Rapsey must have been to find them between the plush cushions of the couch before the fire; and prouder still to return them to Mary; expensive glasses, French.

Another little conceit depended on human curiosity. I had thought about the line in *The Prime of Life*. As soon as I had read it I had beetled to a dictionary to find out the meaning of *algolagnia* and *coprophagy*, so provocative was the sentence. I was willing to bet that only the dimmest sort of reader could resist looking up the words and I didn't think Mary was dim. She would ask Malcolm of course, but even though a scholar I am not sure he would know. Coprophagy perhaps, but algolagnia, probably not. There had been a concise dictionary in the bedroom but she would not find a definition there and so, curiosity piqued, off to the study and the faithful O.E.D. I can imagine her slipping from her bed, standing at the pedestal table in the middle of the night probably with nothing on, flipping through the venerable pages, and suddenly – a photo falls to the floor at her feet. A Polaroid snap, not a very good one. A picture of Angela? A picture of Malcolm and Angela together? Never! Simply a photograph of Malcolm, not really incriminating, standing in the park squinting into the sun and holding a clothing box from an exclusive women's boutique. There wasn't anybody else around, part of a leg retreating up the path and out of the frame. Angela wasn't in the picture; she had stopped for a drink at the water fountain and asked him to hold her packages. How remarkably foolish he looked squinting like that as if he were grinning awfully.

Once suspicion has reared its Hydra head it is a difficult monster to put down. Little incongruities, trifles, are blown out of all proportion. I leave things to trip over; little clues that allure, not point the finger. A steady drip, drip, drip.

On a pad in the kitchen I scribbled some erotic doodles. Tearing off the sheet their impression was left embossed on the following page. I move things around, only slightly, sometimes I have even helped with the chores. It was for all the world as if a third party were living in the house, but an invisible one. It is only after a considerable number of years, if ever, that a couple learns to live with each other's irritable habits. I have become the invisible vertex of a triangle with my own brand of calculated irritation.

After a while it didn't matter whether Mary was home or not. The house is large and I have established any number of escape routes and hiding places. It is simply a matter of not allowing myself to be cornered. Consequently, I have never ventured to stay in the house when they are both at home. It is very much Mary's house. Malcolm is only ever there in the evenings and on weekends and then Mary is usually at home too. He never has the chance to experience the house by himself – it seems a shame.

I have avoided risks except on one occasion. I took a chance, which, had I been discovered, could have ruined all my carefully worked-out plans. But then one must have one's excitement; it was irresistible. I happened to be upstairs when Mary came up to lie down. I hid in the dressing room, waiting. I was just about to slip out when I had the uncontrollable urge to see her. I could hear that she was snoring lightly. She lay in her underwear. Inches from her outstretched hand was her book. It was all done in a flash. When she awoke, her book would be open at the same page where she had left off, but it would be a different book; one she had not even started.

For all my stealth, I shudder to think of what might have happened. I have lived to curse such follies of curiosity; my plan depends on being invisible; seen I am nothing – another criminal. And then there is screaming and police and mayhem. It makes me angry and it's always a shame when I get angry. But what am I saying? It is all hypothetical. I am not caught. The gears are in motion; they will need priming from time to time, and there are contingency plans and alternative plans to meet whatever challenge they mete upon me. Mr. X, you devil!

And in between all this activity I still have found the time to enjoy myself, exploring the parkland that was once the Rood Estate. In the cool woods, the wintergreen and painted trillium are in bloom and along the forest edge by the beach, white lettuce and trailing arbutus – mayflower they call it here. The sun has shone for a week solid, burning the last chill of spring from the air and the ground, but the weather has changed quickly along the South Shore. Volant, one writer has called it, using the military term meaning organized for rapid movement. Clouds are banking high up over the sea and the wind is brisk. Storms are coming. It would be nice to spend these impending rainy days in front of the fire at Odd's End, but first things first. I must be careful not to appear too distracted in front of Miss Tinker.

Yesterday was Saturday; May is drawing rapidly to a close. I had hoped to be able to have the house to myself. Unfortunately, M and M had the same idea. I prepared to spend the day in quiet observation. I dug myself into a favorite bunker on the sea side of the dune with the courtyard before me and the grass swaying above my head. I was hidden but could not have had a better view of the "stage." If either of them came too close I could slip away soon enough. I settled down comfortably with the wind and the sun, just up, at my back. I had no idea that I was going to witness a first-rate performance of which I could take credit as the *auteur*. The fruits of all my labors were vividly displayed. I could not catch it all, but it was an argument. I caught the gist. Who would have suspected that easy-going Malcolm could have become so irritable. And Mary surprised me – so frail – she seemed a much stronger soul.

The storm passed. They walked with their arms about each other back to the house. The happy couple (almost). They had risen (for the time being) above meanness and suspicion. Loving devotion. I will have to step up my campaign against such formidable opponents. Mind you, they haven't solved the mystery. It is impossible for them to perceive it.

Three things struck me as significant about the squabble. One, they are both volatile when pushed far enough. Two, the mobility of young Malcolm's mind, or should I say the pliability? – his imagination is rather stultified, really. That is often true of people who think they are being imaginative but are actually very linear and limited in the range of response to the unusual. He makes no jumps in his thinking. Oh yes, and three, I was impressed by the anxiety in Mary's voice when she asked, "Do you really think it could be me?" There was a special pleading there. "Do you really think it could be me?" Perhaps, Mary Close, perhaps.

13

"Why don't we try Botticelli?"

"The game or the play?"

"Whatever happened to the artist?" interjected Mary sarcastically.

"The game or the play?" insisted Kevin.

Malcolm was suddenly animate. "They're virtually isotropic. The game is a play, the play is a game."

"I don't see why we should reduce my therapy to a game."

"Ah, but what a play, dear, what a play it would make." Kevin slipped his arm around her.

"*The Mousetrap!*" declaimed Malcolm from his chair. "The play's the thing, Zenobia, wherein we'll catch ..."

"My conscience is not my problem," Mary interrupted. She looked askance at the group, resting her gaze on Malcolm. "And I'm the one getting treatment? You are all major loonies!"

Tom, who had been sitting on the floor sorting out records to play, suddenly spun around with a mischievous grin. "What we need is an encounter group."

The others groaned, but Tom continued, twirling his moustache excitedly. "Don't knock it. Everyone drops their inhibitions, divulges awful secrets, tells irretrievable truths – it's a gas! I learned everything I know at encounter sessions."

Kevin winced. "Don't remind me."

"Maybe we could indulge in a fit of primal screaming, while we're at it," said Malcolm sarcastically.

"I'm going to primal scream in a moment." Mary's voice was raised. "This is not what Doctor Fielding had in mind. He thought it would be good to have some friends over ..."

"To exorcise the demons."

"No, Malcolm!"

Mary sat down with her arms crossed tightly. Kevin leaned over and kissed her on the top of the head.

"Now, now, sweetheart."

Malcolm smiled superciliously. "Just remember, dear, we're laughing at you not with you." It was supposed to be funny, any other time he had said it, it was funny, but no one was laughing.

"You've got it all wrong." Tom had left his duties as disc jockey and joined the group in front of the fire. "It's supposed to be done like this." He knelt on the floor in front of Kevin and, taking hold of his hand, he spoke with exaggerated sincerity.

"I love you, Kev, but I want to tell you that your spinach quiche is always runny."

"Oh, that kind of awful truth!"

Tom beamed. "Yeah, real consciousness-raising shit."

"My turn." Kevin looked around at each of the others as if trying to pick a likely candidate for his divulgence. His eyes fell on Mary and, taking her hand as Tom had done his, he spoke gently but firmly. "Mary, my dearest friend in the whole world except for this buffoon here, when are you going to destroy those red jeans? They make you look like a second-class tart."

Malcolm coughed to interrupt the laughter.

"Enough of this persiflage, runny quiche, and tarty jeans! Let's have a real down-and-out encounter."

"Mal, you're drunk."

"Good try, Mary, but that is merely fact; what we are

looking for I believe is a reflection on, or interpretation of, character which gives cause for annoyance or discomfort in others. You, for instance, have a crooked nose but that also is only fact and not an issue we can deal with at this time."

"You are being professorial!"

"That is also only fact ..."

"An obnoxious and insufferable professor!"

"Bravo, that's more like it."

Tom interrupted. "*Numero uno,* no family feuding, okay? Now, let us proceed. Malcolm, with all due respect and great affection, may I submit that you are from time to time a trifle stifling."

"How so?"

"Tedious. Take for instance right now, you were baiting Mary. True?"

Malcolm considered the idea. "Baiting is an ambiguous word. Do you mean I was setting a snare or tormenting like an animal worrying its prey?"

"Don't try to be so diabolic. You aren't really a monster at all."

Malcolm's face brightened. "I'm not? Thank you, Tom."

Kevin spoke. "This is ironic, you know, this game playing. We aren't talking about what's on our minds; we haven't done all evening."

"It is the nature of the parable to talk about everything else but what is on one's mind. There's a parable afoot," Malcolm intoned.

"Well, then let's not be parabolic. Can you say that, darling? – parabolic."

Malcolm nodded to his wife. "Parabolic."

For a moment nobody talked. The only sound was the logs crackling in the fireplace. Suddenly Tom clapped his hands.

"Well, that's over."

Everyone laughed and then the silence returned. Kevin at last spoke.

"When Tom and I first bought the store we got some crank letters, a few phone calls; quaint really: Get out, you fucking gearboxes! Things like that. You can't go to the police; they're liable to be worse. When you're gay, you learn to deal with it. Anyway, people gradually realize you're not a raging queen who is going to molest their children, and everything's copasetic."

Malcolm waited for him to go on and then a worried look came over his face.

"You don't still think I wrote those letters!"

"No."

"But that was what was on your mind?"

"I suppose so."

Malcolm was speechless with disbelief. "So just in case I had been, you have provided me with an opportunity to confess."

Kevin reddened. "No, that wasn't it, Mal. I was just bringing up what was on my mind. I didn't mean to insinuate that."

Malcolm looked at the others: Tom, leaning against the hearth; Mary, tracing a pattern on one of the pillows. "I get the feeling this evening wasn't planned to talk about Mary's problem but mine."

"Mal, cool down. That's not true at all."

Malcolm looked away.

"I really didn't mean anything, Mal."

Malcolm spoke in a measured tone. "I'm not one for showing my emotions. I'm sorry if you have ever doubted them. I like you both very much. I thought you knew that."

Kevin nodded. "Can I ask you something?"

"Not if it's where did I buy the envelopes!"

Kevin ignored the snare. "Do you ever wonder about Mary and me, about our friendship, I mean?"

Malcolm thought about it for a moment and then he grinned. "Does Tom?"

"Not me," chirped Tom. "A fag never loses his spots."

Malcolm looked at him quizzically. "Never?"

"So you do wonder!" Mary's eyes were wide with surprise.

Malcolm looked at Mary for a moment, as if considering the idea seriously, and then he shook his head. "I wonder about it, sure; but not whether you might be having an affair, if that's what you are getting at. Maybe I did, especially when I was first getting to know you. You still used to go on those overnight jaunts together. Sure it crossed my mind."

"How do you feel about it now?"

"After eight years of marriage?" Malcolm looked into his glass. He shook it and watched the ice cubes swirl around in the pale gold liquid. "I think I envy you in a way. I think . . . there is always something exotic about homosexuals that is strangely enviable, especially in their relationship to women. I suppose I get some kind of vicarious enjoyment out of your life style, I mean yours and Tom's. There now, is that enough of a confession?"

Tom raised his glass. "I think that's enough encountering for one night." There was a sigh of relief. "May I propose a toast?" Not waiting for a response, he hurried on. "In my native Wales we have a saying which is appropriate at such occasions: *Iechyd da i pawb*."

"Which means?"

"If the shoe fits, it's probably too expensive."

Mary laughed and the awkwardness of a moment earlier dissolved.

Malcolm with a certain amount of effort stood up. "I propose another toast," he said, "and when it is said and done I intend to do something I have always wanted to do; something dreadfully irrational."

Mary gasped and then snickered.

"Sounds kinky," said Tom, and Malcolm affected a glare.

"I want to smash my glass in the fire, and I want all of you to do the same."

Mary raised an eyebrow. "A very Reginald thing to do!"

"What is your toast to be?" asked Kevin.

"I hadn't got that far actually; only the format."

"May I presume the honor?"

"Be my guest."

Kevin raised his glass, solemnly. "To us and the mystery which brings us together."

The glasses smashed against the stone and wood, and pieces of them reflected in the flames. There was something cathartic about it, but even though Malcolm had initiated the ritual, he felt oddly uneasy now that it was done. He did not let on.

The next day, Malcolm visited Henry Street for the first time. The door was bright red; he hesitated for a moment and then knocked, three quick raps, half-hoping she would not be home. A voice called "Patience" from somewhere within, and in another minute he heard footsteps on uncarpeted stairs.

"Your handbag, mademoiselle." He bowed deeply.

Angela smiled and standing aside beckoned him in.

"I would forget my proverbial head if it weren't screwed on. Can you stay for coffee?"

"If you're making some."

"I am always making or on the verge of making coffee; you are as good an excuse as any." Angela went happily about the preparations while Malcolm sat almost gingerly at a tiny, round kitchen table. She looked different in jeans and a T-shirt and, her one concession to style, high spike heels. She turned and leaned on the counter. She was grinning and her eyes danced under her fringe of auburn curls.

"You didn't need an excuse, you know."

"Then you don't need your purse, I presume?"

"You could have left it in my box in the office." She was

teasing him but he was determined not to wriggle on the hook. He changed the subject.

"I did not think you even so much as owned a T-shirt."

"What you see before you is the other Angela Treadway, student on dwindling funds. My fancy look-alike, if you had ever noticed, has only three respectable dresses and does a lot of very clever mixing and matching to hide the fact."

"Did you really 'sleep on the beach at Nassau'?"

"Wouldn't you like to know!"

"Do you think women wear T-shirts with writing on them so that men will stare at their bosoms?"

Angela affected a frown and turned to attend to the kettle. When she turned back with the coffee things on a tray her expression had changed; it was thoughtful.

"What we were talking about at lunch; it's really bothering you, isn't it?"

Malcolm accepted with both hands a cup of coffee without handles, staring for a moment into the steaming black liquid. Angela continued.

"The troubles at home are really getting to you."

Malcolm still didn't speak.

"I suppose it is rather creepy."

"I suppose so," he finally responded.

"Is it Mary, do you think?"

Her frankness was somehow startling. He wavered. "She is seeing a shrink ... it's hard to say."

Angela waited, distractedly sipped her coffee, and then put her cup down. As she did her hand slid across the small table to Malcolm's hand.

"Talk about it if you want."

"I'm not sure if I want." He smiled sheepishly, foolishly, he expected. His heart was beating like crazy. "The fact is, she doesn't trust me."

"Should she?"

"Oh, Christ, don't you start!"

She squeezed his hand. "That's me, always with foot firmly planted in mouth." She smiled radiantly, Malcolm's tension subsided. He talked. He talked about the night before.

"I'm hopeless in those kinds of situations; I love being with people, I love any kind of social gathering, and heaven knows I love to natter, but the whole thing was so heavy. It was embarrassing. I got the feeling they were banding together against me."

"They think it's you?"

"No. I don't think they do, but that's not the point. They're an emotional lot, and this thing has brought them together in a way. They feel it."

"And you don't feel things ... it?"

"Sure I feel it, but they *feel* it. They misinterpret my inaction as indifference. I am curious at what's going on; I'm trying to see some kind of a pattern in it. There isn't any pattern."

"Doesn't that frighten you?"

"I suppose so but there is nothing I can do about it."

Angela looked at him closely. "Mostly you feel guilty as hell because you think it's Mary."

Again that frankness.

Suddenly she leaned across the table and kissed him. It was a gentle kiss, one that could be a token of friendship or something much more; it fell somewhere in between. Slowly Malcolm pulled his head away.

The front door opened and a cheerful voice called "Hello" down the hallway. Angela smiled and squeezed Malcolm's hand tightly. She nodded in some kind of tacit understanding.

"Karen, this is Malcolm Close."

The young woman shook his hand vigorously and told him she had heard much about him. He told her he had heard much about her which was a lie but seemed the appropriate response. The rest of the conversation was commonplace and Malcolm left shortly. Angela walked him to the door but to his relief did not kiss him again.

"Come again," she said softly.

He nodded vaguely.

When he arrived home it was late and Mary was already asleep. He lay awake, thinking about Angela; her parting "come again." He wasn't sure that he dared, and yet how comforting it would be to have someone to talk to. It was becoming harder and harder to talk to Mary.

She began to moan beside him. He watched her in the dark, catching snippets from her dream; displaced words, sentences. Hoping she would not awaken, he carefully sidled away and rolled over, but soon he felt her pulling at the bedclothes. The struggle increased as did her sleep talk; finally he felt her hand grab him by the arm. He had half-expected it but still it chilled him. He rolled back over and now she appeared for all the world to be awake, although he knew she wasn't really. Her eyes scrutinized him uncannily, like long, bright pins holding him to the dissecting table. Her face was tortured.

"For God's sake, Mary, wake up. It's only me. It's me, Malcolm!"

Breakfast was a quiet affair; both of them were tired and it was no use talking about it. And then Kevin phoned and Mary realized as she talked to him how desperately she did want to talk about it. To her delight, he was taking the day off and wondered if he might come over with the much-talked-about Bliss Lund. The exuberance of the reply must have startled him. He would be arriving at one.

Malcolm had decided to spend the day at home, ostensibly to mark papers, but he received the news with the same relief as his wife. Mary had to get some work done on her paintings; her deadline was rapidly approaching. But the thought of company released the pressure, so without finishing her breakfast she went to work, anxious to make the most of the morning.

Malcolm sat for a long time nursing his coffee, thinking of the previous night. The image of Mary's face was burned into his memory. It had happened before. Early in their marriage she had suffered a prolonged period of nightmares, or one recurring nightmare, in which Malcolm figured in one way or another. Her dreams had been as hideous as the hell in Heironymous Bosch's *Garden of Delights*. She had been possessed, and in her state Malcolm sometimes assumed a demonic identity. He remembered waking for no reason and finding her staring at him or sitting up in bed curled against the bedstead. It was just after they had moved to Odd's End. Neither of them was used to the isolation. It had been a trial for their relationship, and had brought them closer together, he suspected, in the long run. Now he wasn't so sure any more. In any case, visitors would be a relief. He looked forward to the arrival of Kevin and Bliss.

Mary, too, was thinking back. Had it been six years? She had refused to see a doctor then. Finally one night she had slept through it. Instead of waking she had struggled to stay asleep and let the nightmare run its course. The dream had burned itself out. It had been an exhausting experience. Malcolm had suffered. He was the villain of the piece. She didn't know why; there just had to be a villain. Somebody has to be the villain.

She had been nervous as a child. Nervous and imaginative. In art school she had been tempted into playing the role of the mad visionary – every art school has a few, an art school archetype. The rhetoric was all about living on the edge, burning oneself out, painting until you dropped or foamed at the mouth, and then using the foam in your work. Using yourself up! It had all been a lot of crap! A caricature of madness. Some artists did go off the deep end. Art books were full of their distorted faces, and she was old enough now to have seen it happen to people she knew. It was the "broad gesture," something heroic, but only in retrospect. When it was happening, it was a sad, pathetic thing. Gradually her desire to paint had become more important than her desire to be an artist – a subtle but important difference. And then the nightmares. It was as if she had tempted Providence with her art school madness and had been granted a glimpse of the real thing. She decided she couldn't afford the luxury of being mad. Not if she intended to paint – it required too much time. She had willed herself through it. No doctors, just she and Malcolm. Last night had been a replay. What would Fielding make of it? She would have to tell him about the earlier time and she had not wanted to. There was no connection in her mind. What was happening to them, to Odd's End, was not delusion.

She made herself work. The hum of the projector had never sounded so loud. It drowned out the sounds of the house. Was Malcolm still in the kitchen drinking his coffee? Was he thinking about her, about last night?

Another thought pressed itself upon her attention. She was aware of a growing antipathy towards her painting. It was not just the intrusion, or what she thought was an intrusion, of another hand, it was the desperate tedium of working in the dark. The paintings were excellent; she had little objectivity any more, but she knew them to be her best. But it was the idea that was interesting – the pleasure was for her academic at this point. The enjoyment of color and vigorous physical contact with the canvas, the sensual joy of painting – *that* was all missing. Now she was working out of professional pride; for the gallery, her friends, and the critics. To her dismay, she could summon up little excitement any more at putting the work on display. To watch people seeing her work had always thrilled her in the past. It was the reward for all those hours in solitude; when the inspiration was gone there was always the show to look forward to.

It was this damn method she had imposed on herself! Working in the dark, painting over a photographic image. Her mind was neutralized. Now she couldn't remember from day to day how much she had painted, how many of the dots she had joined. That after all was the only rational explanation for what was going on. She had no explanation for what else was going on at Odd's End and she knew she was repressing her thoughts about it. Bliss and Kevin were coming down – entertainment. She felt guilty even thinking about it. They were an excuse for her to leave her work. Only a few weeks earlier she could scarcely drag herself away.

They arrived at one-thirty. Kevin had driven to Halifax to pick up Bliss. They were punchy with hunger; neither of them had eaten any breakfast, but they were in high spirits. They seemed to exude a sense of holiday.

Upon introduction to Bliss, Malcolm launched enthusiastically into verse, much to Mary's surprise.

"The sun goes down and overall
These barren reaches by the tide
da da da da da glories fall,
I almost dream da dum dum bide
Until the coming of the tide."

Bliss joined in on the last line and the impromptu recitation ended in applause and peals of laughter. Mary was baffled.

"Bliss Carman, the pride of New Brunswick and Ms. Lund's namesake, I assume?"

Bliss confirmed the statement to Malcolm's obvious delight. The party was off to a rousing start.

Inside they launched into making lunch, drinking cheap white wine with ice cubes.

They never actually sat formally to eat. Before very long, everyone just started picking at the food as it was being prepared. The chatter was continuous and one at a time they would each take breaks from preparation and sit on the counter until they realized that nobody was cooking or fussing any more; that lunch was not only prepared but already eaten – simultaneously. Much of the talk was theater talk, gossip mostly, which Bliss dispensed with relish, and the others ate up. It was trashy, the way gossip ought to be, and terribly funny. Mary found her mind wandering; she had in a few hours relaxed incredibly. What strange beasts actors were. Because their lives were invariably hectic and neurotic, survivors learned how to relax whenever they could. The relaxed atmosphere Bliss had brought with her was almost palpable; one could eat it, thought Mary, and the taste was remarkably refreshing.

The woman was a born entertainer. She wasn't obnoxious and Mary noticed she rarely interrupted; but somehow she became the focus of all their attentions. Her sense of humor was infectious. Emotions ran the gamut across her open face. Mary found herself enthralled. Bliss was taking the lead in George F. Walker's *Power at the Crossroad*. Mary had seen it off Broadway and had talked for a week to Malcolm about it. Bliss's was a demanding part: funny, silly, and then strangely heart-wrenching. As Mary watched her visitor, she felt the part must have been written for her.

The day was like a holiday. The wine helped. The incidents of the past few weeks (was it really weeks?) seemed now like black slapstick. Lately alcohol had been the only thing that had helped, a not altogether encouraging sign. The previous night began to lose its pervasiveness; it was so much a matter of perspective. Isn't that what Malcolm kept harping about?

He seemed more relaxed as well. Lately his enthusiasm was tempered with a sharp edge. He was bantering again; Bliss was like a foil. He was smiling. Sometimes he would smile at Mary in a knowing way which she found patronizing; a "There, isn't this better than being crazy?" kind of smile. She smiled back, anyway. She would put up with him. He was putting up with her.

The party moved to the beach when the sun was hottest, and even though Mary had promised herself she would work, she allowed herself to be talked into joining the expedition. Everyone promised to prepare the evening meal and let her paint if she came with them. Normally Mary liked to be on the beach alone. When she and Malcolm went for a walk they were silent, sharing the belief that there is nothing you can say beside the sea. She had a favorite spot where she swam naked but most of the time she liked to explore tidal pools. She liked busy tidal pools more than busy beach parties but the company brought out the teen-ager in her. It had the same effect on Malcolm. They were seldom rowdy and most of their friends were altogether too "laid back." It was a wonderful change.

Mary managed an hour of painting late in the afternoon before Bliss interrupted her with a cocktail. They sat for a moment in the studio. The actress looked at the work in silence and Mary watched her face with interest. Bliss spoke frankly, she asked questions; and she looked, really looked, at the work.

"It's incredible, Mary, really. Kevin told me it was crazy but it's so much more."

If the statement had been calculated to win Mary's heart it could not have been more successful. Not crazy; she needed to hear that.

"Tell me about this one," Bliss asked.

Mary smiled and stood beside her, gazing at *Manshadow*; seeing it again the way she always did when someone else saw it.

"It's different from the others."

Mary nodded. "It was the first. There was a stranger on the beach down near the Indian Spit. I had been out on the spit photographing tidal pools and had watched him. He had not noticed me. He was a bird watcher, an older man. I could not make out his features from so far away, but he was bearded and had a telescope, which caught the sun from time to time. I noticed that first; the flashing of the telescope. But it was the shadows that intrigued me. In the shadows the telescope looked like a horn growing from the head."

"Did you ever see him again?"

Mary shook her head. "He was probably a vacationer who had wandered from the beach at Steep Cove. I took several photos; I enlarged one that had a particularly well-defined shadow. Then I got the idea to enlarge just the shadow, enormously large, larger than life. I built up this canvas and then treated it in photographic emulsion. I had never done anything like that before. It inspired the rest of the series."

Bliss touched the canvas, inches thick with layer upon layer of cheesecloth. Black modelling paste oozed from between the strips of bandage, looking remarkably like dried blood.

"It's more spontaneous than the others, isn't it?"

Again Mary nodded.

"More iconic."

Mary was beaming inside. Impulsively she hugged Bliss. It was the first feedback she had had on the work.

The next minute Malcolm was calling them for *hors d'oeuvres*. And Mary cleaned up, while Bliss still looked at the painting.

Just before they turned out the studio light, she turned to look one more time.

The party was a little worn out, and although it continued, it did so in a lower key. Almost breathlessly Mary had asked if Kevin and Bliss could stay the night. She could scarcely conceive of the day ending with them trooping off. They could stay. Malcolm could drive Bliss back to Halifax in time for an eleven o'clock rehearsal call. With that out of the way they settled down to an evening of a closer more intimate kind.

It was Bliss who brought up the mystery. It was inevitable that it should come up. Kevin had told her about it but she wanted to know more. Malcolm looked distraught for a minute as if the mere mention of their problem might start Mary off again. She took the inquiry calmly and even began the narrative of the more recent happenings. Bliss listened attentively, dragging deeply on her cigarette. Despite his trepidations, Malcolm joined in with the same kind of willingness with which one talks about a death in the family, when finally one can talk about it at all.

By midnight nobody showed any signs of retiring. Kevin suggested a midnight swim. Although not willing to join him in the water they all agreed to accompany him. It was, in any case, too cool to swim, but the air was surprisingly fine, and they walked along the shore. The tide was out, and they strolled along the fringe of the surf with pants rolled up and skirt hems tucked in at the waist.

Where the sand beach ended and the woods came to the very edge of the sea, there were great black boulders – a jagged but scalable wall. Climbing to the top, they could see across the bay the few winking lights of the port at its mouth. The conversation turned to legends of the South Shore – of ghost ships and privateers and pirates' gold. The stories, half of which were apocryphal, all seemed possible sitting in the moonlight on the rugged shore.

"That's what it's all about." Kevin looked triumphant. "Pirates' gold, and some half-crazed adventurer, who has spent all his life and a fortune to find it."

"Sounds like a Hardy Boys episode."

"Juvenile perhaps, but it happens from time to time."

"It is a kind of a solution." Mary looked at Malcolm, who shrugged his shoulders. It was a silly idea, but it was an idea.

"Why shouldn't it be filthy lucre? That at least *is* a motive."

"How about a secret naval base? If you want meaty juvenilia, that would be more up to date."

Mary began to laugh. She laughed harder and harder until she couldn't speak, until tears flowed down her cheeks. She finally sat down in the sand and pressed by the others shared the joke.

"The Parks Department, don't you see," she gasped. Nobody saw anything particularly funny about the Parks Department. "Ahhh," she said, finger pointing, eyes wide, "the decision has come from the top to develop Rood Provincial Park and they want our ten acres and Odd's End at all cost." She repeated the last statement with dark innuendo. "At all cost!"

Malcolm improvised a scene at the offices of the Ministry of Good Times. Bliss was suddenly a P.R. man, an "Amusement Expert" from the west.

"I can see it now. We re-enact the shooting of the Rood kid and the subsequent hanging/suicide every afternoon at four, followed by a clambake."

Kevin hunched up his shoulders and curled his lip – the archetypal hit man. "But first things first, eh, boss?"

It was a grotesque farce. But there were nightmare stories about the government screwing people out of land. Mary refused to consider it. Expropriation notices, interminable legal squabbles – that was governmental weaponry. If all else failed, bulldozers, but not naughty notes and gourmet dinners. What then?

They walked in silence for a while, savoring the calm of the moonlit beach. Above them the woods were filled with wind, a perpetual rushing sound, like a sea. If she closed her eyes the beach seemed like a narrow peninsula between two seas.

They were crossing the dunes with the house before them when Bliss finally broke the silent spell. Her voice was oddly mysterious, without trying to be.

"It's a very beautiful house. Not just splendid but perfect. The way it sits. The way it smells. When I came up for a towel this afternoon, the house was cool despite the sun being directly overhead. Not cold, mind you, but delightfully cool." She paused for a moment. "It's a dream house. I wonder what it is dreaming of."

Inside they settled down to brandy and a fire. Mary was

tired and, leaving the others, went to bed. Not many minutes later, Bliss poked her head through the door, to say good-night and to thank Mary again for a wonderful day. She walked in and sat on the edge of the bed. Mary noted how there was nothing bold about the gesture. It was not intrusive; it was done out of friendship, that was all.

Bliss was going to sleep in the "children's room" and something suddenly occurred to Mary. An impish look came over her face. Impulsively she climbed out of bed and led Bliss by the arm to the room. They moved the dolls from the bed by the armload. From the midst of the dolls and teddy bears, Mary found a favorite rag doll. She turned, beaming, and offered it to Bliss as a companion for the night. She blushed. It was a childish gesture, but Bliss accepted it as it was intended. Mary looked at the doll and suddenly her face clouded. She took it back again and stared at its face. She couldn't speak.

Bliss looked at her, at the doll, at Mary. Then she noticed the eyes: there was something about the eyes. Rag dolls had button eyes but these were almost real. They were real – but not real – photographs. One final look at Mary and she was sure. They were Mary's eyes.

Mary didn't tell Malcolm. She didn't know why. When he eventually came to bed she pretended to be asleep; and he, deciding she was pretending, blathered on about a conversation he and Kevin had been having; *The Winter's Tale* as apocalyptic vision. God, how he could go on, she thought. When he at last turned out the light she was afraid he might try to make love to her. That she couldn't face; despite a marvelous day, she was angry, she hadn't decided with whom.

The next morning Bliss said nothing about the doll; Mary appreciated her tact. Malcolm left with Bliss at nine-thirty. Mary promised she would come to see her in *Power at the Crossroad*. Kevin left a little while later; she didn't even mention the rag doll to him. As soon as he left, she ran back upstairs to look at it.

The eyes had been cut out of the photo that had accompanied the piece in *Halifax*. Anyone could have done it. She had bought five extra copies, which were in a small bookshelf in the bedroom. After only a brief hesitation, she went to look through them. The last copy was the one. How grotesque it was to look at the photo of herself without eyes; only some type and the corner of a Campari bottle showing through from the following page. She mustn't jump to conclusions. She must just watch and wait.

The previous day had been physically exhausting, and although she had eventually slept, she had lain awake for a long time. She felt drained, and the thought of painting was oppressive. She had, however, reached a decision. There would only be six canvases at the Spizziri. She could no longer work on *Temporary Quarters*. The mysterious passage was technically proficient but she was sure she had not painted it. The canvas was soiled for her. She looked it over and spoke out loud. "When I want an apprentice, I shall hire one myself." It was said to the world in general, and anyone else who might be listening. The walls had ears, did they? Then walls, take note.

She slid *Temporary Quarters* back into the storage shelves, and turned on the old radio, WABC, non-stop AM junk, but a pleasant change from the dulcet-toned announcers and deliberate programing of CBC FM. She had made up her mind not to be frightened. Give them enough cover noise and they could move all the furniture in the goddamned house!

14

The following day Mary drove to Wolfville to see Fielding. Although the day was overcast, even cool, the drive was pleasant; the cab of the truck seemed secure compared to the vagaries of home. When she arrived back at Odd's End at four, Malcolm was already there; the Fiat was driven half-way up the side of a low dune at the end of the road as if Malcolm had only remembered he was home at the last minute.

She peered at her face in the rear-view mirror, grimacing at the reflection; her eyes had the vacant stare of market fish, her complexion was like week-old bread, even her hair seemed lusterless and limp. The face that gazed morosely back at her from the mirror was not a face to be loved; pitied maybe. Shit! That was it, wasn't it, she thought. Pity poor mad Mary. She wasn't mad! Fielding had been convincing on that score, not merely patronizing; he had dismissed the idea. As she smiled grimly at her image, the anger from the previous day rose again and spilled into her cheeks. She would not be pitied; better loathed than pitied. With her mind made up on that bit of strategy, she hopped from the truck and strode across the courtyard.

Malcolm was lying on the bed fully clothed, reading. At first she wasn't sure he was listening to her. He was.

"Marriage counseling?"

"That isn't what I said; Fielding just wants to meet you that's all."

Malcolm clapped his book shut and sat up on the bed. There was a gleam in his eye.

"Well then, we'll give him a show, won't we; Reginald and Zenobia and the mystery at Odd's End."

"No show! No Reggie, no Zenobia. No nobody. Just you and me, Malcolm."

"Okay, okay, take it easy."

Mary calmed a bit; she knew she was overreacting. "That's part of the problem, Mal. Don't you see? We've been taking this thing too lightly."

Malcolm looked up at her. "Does Fielding think I'm crazy?"

Mary met his gaze squarely. "Maybe. I don't know. Are you?"

Malcolm frowned.

"He doesn't think I'm crazy, in case you're wondering. I hope that doesn't spoil your plans."

Malcolm looked startled. "What the hell does that mean?"

Mary wasn't sure she had meant to go this far, but she wasn't about to apologize. There was another agonizing silence.

"So we're taking this too lightly," Malcolm said at last. "Does Fielding have any suggestions? An exorcist perhaps."

"Malcolm, why won't you take this seriously." She was almost shouting.

"I do take it seriously! What do we do about it?"

"Well, for a start we could call the police."

"And show them what?" Malcolm's voice was as loud as his wife's. "What proof do we have?"

"Surely finding proof is their problem."

"There isn't so much as a footprint. I've looked."

"And I repeat, that's their problem."

Malcolm laughed derisively. "I can just see Gruber down

at Steep Cove. 'Sure, Mr. Close, we'll put a man on duty around the clock at Odd's End until this thing is sorted out!' Be logical. What can they do?"

Mary closed her eyes and tried to suppress an urge to scream or throw something. She managed, just barely, to lower her voice a notch but the anger was still there. She sat on the edge of the bed.

"Why are you so stubborn? You're fighting this. You keep going on about logic. What's happening here isn't logical; it's pathological. Fielding thinks these little abnormalities we are suffering could be the product of a psychotic. It's morbid. What will convince you of that? Do you have to find a ... a hand nailed to the door or something before you break down?"

"Call the police then! I don't care. I've got nothing to hide."

Mary looked at him steadily. "But I do. Is that it?"

Malcolm shrugged. "Fielding obviously doesn't think so. Why should I?"

"But you do, don't you?"

Malcolm's sigh was long and weary. "I don't know. I don't know what I think or feel."

It was almost a confession, or at least a concession. To get him to concede anything seemed like a minor victory, and Mary found her temper abating somewhat.

"Okay," she said. "As I see it, there are two problems: whatever is happening to the house is one; whatever is happening to us because of it is another. Fielding thinks we should work together. That's why he wants to see you."

"I haven't been exactly supportive, have I?"

Mary was touched, but all she could say was "No." She should have said more, apologized for being so high-strung, conceded some ground herself. The "No" seemed to hang in the air between them like a little buzzing neon sign. Malcolm looked at her furtively.

"Call the police. They'll come round, find nothing, and

suggest that we get an alarm system or a Doberman and that will be that."

"Well, why don't we?"

He looked hard at her this time. "Go right ahead. It's your money."

With that he left the room. Had he turned he would have seen her staring after him in hurt and frustrated disbelief.

She heard him clump down the stairs, and a moment later he appeared below the window in the courtyard. Obstinately he walked on, his hands deep in his pockets. He crossed the yard, clambered up the dune and down to the beach, never once looking back. His last comment burned in her ears: *It's your money.* That was calculated to annoy, to hurt. What had gone wrong? Somewhere along the line in the last few weeks his trust had turned subtly to support, and then the support had become patronizing and then condescending. Condescension had led to pity, and now, determined not to be pitied, she had made him angry. That's what had happened to trust; she didn't dare think what might have happened to love.

Malcolm had never intended things to become so desperate. He had meant to pour oil on troubled water and had ended up throwing a match into the oil. He knew he had not been as supportive as he should have been. Somehow it had all gotten out of hand. Perhaps, too, he had not acted responsibly, and for that he felt guilty. He had only meant to wait, to keep his mind open. Maybe Mary was right in accusing him of an unwholesome objectivity, maybe he was like the scientist taking notes as his mice died. But he couldn't see how getting emotional would help, nor would seeing her Dr. Fielding. He wasn't going to get trapped into baring his soul as Mary and Kevin seemed to so love doing. Now they wanted to drag him in too. No thank you. He was no psychopath.

With all this teeming in his mind he had found himself for the third time this week at the house with the red door on Henry Street. Angela was beyond the little maelstrom of his home life; she had scarcely met Mary and had never been to Odd's End. She found the mystery fascinating and amusing. She sympathized with him but for some reason was not drawn into the sordidness.

Again she greeted him affably, and in a few minutes he was in her living room, lying on the floor babbling while she squatted on a hassock beside him. And then suddenly she was on her feet, her hands on her hips.

"Why me, Lord?"

Malcolm looked up at her. Before he could say anything she spoke again.

"What does it take, Malcolm?"

Malcolm could have sworn that Mary had asked the same question of him only the day before. He was speechless.

"I don't want to talk with you right now. Do you realize that this is the fourth time you have sat here, drinking my wine, and done nothing but blather on about your damned house? If that's all you want, go find another ear to bend, preferably one with no feelings of its own." She stood in front of him, challenging him. "I can't go on like this, Malcolm."

He stared at her. "But, Angie, you know how I feel about you. You know I want you, but not now. I don't know if I can handle it now."

"If that means you aren't sure you'll be able to get it up, have no fear, I'll see to that." She raised one eyebrow.

Malcolm smirked. "You sound like a character from Ray Chandler. No, not Chandler, Jacqueline Susann—"

Angela's screams interrupted him. She threw her hands into the air and then before he could do anything she sat again on the hassock, grabbed his head between her hands and kissed him. Malcolm put his arms around her and pulled her to him. She slithered off the hassock to the floor beside him.

120

It would be so easy. Why fight it? How many times had he imagined this? But now he was resisting. Ever so slowly his grip on her slackened. Angela looked at him, first with disbelief and then with something verging on disgust. Gradually her hands slid from their grip on his head until they rested on his shoulders. She got slowly to her feet pushing her hair off her face. She crossed the room to the mantel and lit a cigarette.

Malcolm watched her in silence. He did want her, perhaps more than he dared think, and that scared him. Something else scared him much more: having to return to Odd's End afterwards. He knew he could never face Mary, it was hard enough already. For a moment he thought he wouldn't go home at all, but he knew he couldn't handle that, and he knew he couldn't leave Mary alone. As if in answer to his innermost thoughts Angela spoke.

"I know; this thing is out of hand. It's not the time, that much is written all over your face." She was nervously biting her lip.

Impulsively Malcolm spoke. "Sometime."

Angela laughed and butted her half-smoked cigarette.

"The expression is, some *other* time."

"No. I meant it; sometime, but not now."

Malcolm got to his feet. She crossed to him and took him firmly by the chin with one of her hands. He wasn't sure what she would do; her grip slackened and she rubbed his cheek, slowly.

"I don't know if I can stand it, the indecision. I guess when you started coming over here I assumed, no, I presumed it was just a matter of time."

Malcolm kissed her solemnly, without passion. She pulled away but not right away.

"Please, don't tease me, not now."

"Angela." His hands held her slim waist firmly. "I do want you. I want you very much. I have for a long time. You know that. In two weeks Mary is going away. Wait until then, I won't come round until then. I just can't now ..."

"And then?" There was disbelief in her voice and it spurred him on.

"No buts about it." He smiled.

Her eyes searched his face. With a long finger she traced the line of his lips. Gently he bit her finger.

"What else can I do?" she asked.

"You could always tempt home a sophomore."

"Don't think I haven't thought of that."

She leaned against his chest and he buried his head briefly in her red hair. His hands held her shoulders and the muscles were taut. She shivered slightly. When she looked up, the sparkle was back in her eyes but also a challenge.

"Malcolm Close, the next time you enter this house I'm not just taking your coat in the vestibule I'm taking everything right down to your socks and you won't get a stitch back until I'm good and satisfied. Is it a deal?"

The force of her intent shook him. It must have shown on his face because she suddenly burst out laughing. With both hands she grabbed the hair on either side of his head and shook him. Her grip was like iron.

"Now get out of here, before I change my mind."

He did with one last kiss, and like a fool he let his hand stray to her breast. She held it there briefly and then pushed it away. Again he was surprised at her strength.

Driving away he realized that his groin ached as it hadn't done since he was a teen-ager. "There are tides, Malcolm Close, in the affairs of men and then there are tidal waves!" he said aloud to himself.

15

Things are progressing smoothly but not for Malcolm and Mary Close. Their world is suddenly erratic, prone to sudden shifts in direction. It is erratic like one of those diseases, rheumatism or gout, which are not fixed but strike in one part of the body one day and a different part the next. I am always near at hand to prod at the painful area. I cannot always be sure what will happen next but I can imagine. For instance, Mary's doctor in Wolfville will probably insist on tranquilizers for her nerves; it is typical of modern treatment, pills. It makes things easier for the doctor and a lot easier for me, for there is nothing quite so easy to manipulate as a drowsy victim. Something to cut the edge of her keen senses. It is precisely the remedy I would have prescribed.

And Malcolm. His little visits to Angela's have become quite regular. X, you are a veritable matchmaker! It seems only fair; Mary has her psychologist and Malcolm his lover. His remedy is cheaper than his wife's medication, or at least I assume it is. But, of course, X is also a match-breaker and conditions are ripe for it. It must be done with finesse; Mary must discover Angela. I assume they have met at faculty parties or whatever. Malcolm probably even talks about her – or did, until their friendship suddenly blossomed. I must think of a way for Mary to find out about the affair or suspect it.

Suspicion! There is a pesticide made up of the ground bodies of the pest one wishes to destroy. The favorite haunt of the pest is dusted with the pesticide which will without fail contain a few carriers of some disease or other fatal to the species in question. The pesticide spreads the disease around – creates a localized epidemic. Suspicion is the oldest poison of all. Why waste money on poisoning someone when the poison is in themselves? Suspicion, dissension, havoc, and then . . . . But she suspects already: perhaps I shall have to be more blunt. Whom shall I choose to be the carrier of the disease? Whoever it is, I must decide soon. All this running around back and forth to Halifax; thank God for Miss Tinker's car. It cannot go on much longer; my patience grows thin. The way things are progressing I don't think it will last much longer – the waiting, I mean. I grow more confident day by day.

16

Life at Odd's End returned to normal for several days. There were no more anonymous letters, household objects seemed to stay put, and nothing was missing. Mary had been reassured by Doctor Fielding, and despite the tensions between her and Malcolm, she began to feel her old buoyant self returning to its senses. She couldn't help wondering if her more positive outlook was responsible for the return to normalcy, as if attitude could alter one's perceptions, or distort reality. She had always believed in a crazy kind of primitive animism: that a thought gave rise to action, words made flesh. But in the end she supposed there must be a rational explanation.

She phoned an alarm company in Halifax and set up an appointment for them to visit the house; that was a rational thing to do. But the other side of her wasn't sure any kind of alarm could catch the culprit. She tried to assess as clearly as possible the chances that it might be Malcolm after all, or might have been Malcolm, because for the present at least things were all right. She had never known him to be so changeable. Comic one moment, distant the next, and then the sudden flashes of unreasonable anger. Whatever crime was being committed showed signs of a nimble mind, witty and esoteric. All of which pointed to Malcolm. But some of the incidents incriminated him, and why, if it was him, should he do that, unless of course he was trying to incriminate her by showing her to be mad. It was too convoluted.

And then, just yesterday he had brought home an armload of brochures for a proposed vacation. They had talked all afternoon about where they might go; his enthusiasm reminded her of less complicated times. He spent the next day at home, and they dedicated it to the garden which had been neglected in the recent confusion. She joined him in planting, an occupation she had always found most soothing. They talked about the trip. New York, London, and Paris had been ruled out. This was to be a *real* vacation. Cultural centers meant afternoons in museums, galleries, and rare book stores, and evenings at the theater. They needed a rest. Lounging on some exotic isle, leisurely sightseeing, all the things they had never thought they could stand to do. Mary wondered if they were at last getting old. Just so she wouldn't feel too old, they decided on a compromise; somewhere both restful and culturally stimulating. They speculated on what it would be like to take it easy for a change—a boat tour perhaps. Maybe that was the perfect balance; lazing on the deck and intermittent flurries of activity when the boat docked. The Caribbean or maybe the Mediterranean. The planning brought them together again. Their love life, like the soft-bellied creature it was, had withdrawn into a hard shell when the trouble began. But at least over the last couple of days there was a guarded tenderness and an implicit faith in the "vacation" they were planning; that at some future time a month or so away love could be revived.

They were at a funny place in their lives, at an age when professionally everything was always "important." Mary's show could be a "big break." Malcolm was "finally getting some recognition." They were both competitors, it was true and no truer than now. As two, three, four days passed without incident, the entire episode of mysterious happenings began to seem like some kind of crisis in their relationship made manifest: a high-water mark, a warning. Secretly

Mary thought of the events as the handiwork of a benevolent, if devious, spirit. It was expected, she told herself, that life would have its little mysteries. If they happened to come in a bunch then that was how they must come. A mystery was not a mystery when it was solved, she told herself.

It was June the eighth. In three days the paintings would be crated up and driven to Halifax where they would be shipped off to Toronto. In two weeks the show would be hung a thousand miles from its conception and its painful delivery. What they would look like on white walls illuminated by track lighting and by that neutral gray luminosity that Hogtown called daylight was difficult to imagine.

Mary found she was looking forward to a visit with Pip almost more than her own exhibition. She had met Pip when she was doing a brief stint as instructor at Nova Scotia College of Art and Design. Pip was an amazing creature, a rare bird in the art world – a clown. A sage and a clown. Her performances, sometimes only minutes in length, were profoundly funny and unforgettable. She had promised some scatter-brain project to coincide with Mary's visit; something with feather capes, bicycle trainer wheels, and masks with inflatable lips. Whatever, it would be crazy and wonderful. Toronto did have that lunatic fringe; absurd and madcap, keeping the art world on its toes. Pip was a banana peel for dyed-in-the-wool "formalists" and "expressionists" and all the other "ists" plying their "isms" with turgid sincerity.

Mary often wondered whether hiding away on the coast had been the right decision. Why not be in the center where everything was happening? The center, right! Dealers who took fifty per cent and their patrons who bought for investment. That was the center at its heart. An "up-and-coming art star" could expect one or two pieces sold before the show opened, over the phone, sight unseen. Maybe Spizziri had already sold something of hers. So why should she worry what the damned things looked like? But there was no use being cynical. Spizziri was doing something that she couldn't do; he did it well, and she had to admit, in his oily way he was nice. She just wanted to paint, and when she painted well she wanted people to see the work, to find something in it that meant something to them. That took galleries and agents. Spizziri had spoken knowingly on his last call. "Feelers" from the Art Bank, "feelers" from at least two major public galleries. And even some tentative talks with the National Gallery in Ottawa about a show of East Coast painters. "They do have a mandate, dear," he had said in his most charming and knowledgeable way. What a racket! If it wasn't investment it was politics – espousing the cause of Regionalism. But she was doing it again. "Why not admit it, Mary Close, you would *love* to have something in the National." There, it was said.

Critically speaking, she expected *Street Noise* or *Temporary Quarters* would be judged more favorably than *Manshadow*, which was her sentimental favorite. But what was she saying! *Temporary Quarters* wasn't to be judged at all. She remembered with a shudder why it wasn't to go and yet her apprehension seemed suddenly misplaced. Her mood had shifted. The anguish, the suspicion, that was all past, at least for now. There was only a square foot of detail work left and maybe a few alterations in the broader passages: it could still be done. Just. If she painted all today, let the oil dry overnight, then painted Saturday and Sunday it could be ready. Why not? She realized with a rush of enthusiasm that she had anticipated this might happen. Why else had she not phoned Spizziri and told him there would only be six canvases? And why had she not told Ed, the cabinetmaker in Raven's Bluff, that she only needed six crates? She had hoped all along, subconsciously, that she would get it finished. And so she would. She slid the canvas out from the storage rack, puffing with the effort. It was six feet by eight feet and loaded down with pounds of paint, wax, and tar.

Even before it was all the way out she knew something

was wrong. The painting was finished. The small shattered faces of the children, the groups of shacks against the muddy dirty wash. It was all there. The oil was dry.

For a moment she couldn't think or do anything. Glancing at the other canvases about the room it occurred to her that they too may have been tampered with, but could she even tell? The only absolute proof she had was that *Temporary Quarters* had not been finished and now it was. Whatever, whoever, was meddling in her life was as fastidious in his work as she was in hers. He was cunning. He was playing with her. He, he, he – it had to be a he! This was an attack; she was being assaulted, psychologically raped. To have thrown paint at the canvases would have been less devastating. Blemishes could be cleaned up; she had learned that in art school. This was not graffiti, it was deranged. She was looking at her own work and questioning if it *was* her own work.

Suddenly the studio was oppressive. She couldn't stand the artificial light another minute. She wanted to tear down the godforsaken black scrim which shut out the sun. She pulled on one edge with both hands, yanking the heavy fabric. She threw herself at the task until one of the fasteners caught on its track and then she only yanked harder, ripping a corner of the material. Light flooded the room. It was glorious, but it wasn't enough. She threw open the sliding doors and screamed. She screamed a garbled threat at the woods. An indecipherable utterance of frustration and fear. She screamed again and again. She leaned her head against the glass but her anger would not let go. She was not finished.

Malcolm arrived home at five. Mary was in the living room, rocking in the rocker. Behind her Coltrane's saxophone roared against a cacophony of blaring horns and frenetic relentless drumming. Mary seemed almost not to notice. She just rocked. Malcolm stood and watched her from the dining room steps. She glanced at him then looked away. Her face was grim.

Seeing her Malcolm became even angrier. Everything had seemed to be righting itself, had seemed to be on an even keel. He had been caught unawares by the events of the day, but he was determined not to overreact. He was determined not to lose his temper but to be firm. It could not go on, the pranks – conscious or otherwise – had to stop! They would work it out together. He would see Fielding if that would help, but her pranks had to stop. Now he was challenged. He wondered for a moment whether it was already too late; whether she had already gone off the deep end. But she looked far too determined. If her eyes were unfocused they were not vacant. As if in answer to his worst fears, she stopped her incessant rocking and stared at him. She was biting her upper lip – it was the only movement in her whole body. She never once blinked. The record was exacerbating an already uncomfortable situation; abruptly Malcolm crossed the room and switched it off. He stood by the record player, staring at her back.

She did not turn. She didn't care how he interpreted the scene. Even beyond the fear of being manipulated was the outrage of being made a fool. Let him be angry, she was angry herself, and he was there so she would be angry with him.

Malcolm had not expected Mary to be waiting for *him*. He felt as if he had lost the upper hand. She had been drinking and smoking. He had not seen her smoke in two years. When he at last confronted her, she looked more than grim, she looked wretched. In a move that seemed too melodramatic, he simply pulled the note from his pocket and dropped it in her lap. There, it was done. Without any of the rehearsed fanfare. She took one look at the envelope and closed her eyes.

It seemed a long time before she opened them again. She sighed and, as if recovering from a trance, was suddenly animate again. She glanced at Malcolm who was sitting, expectantly, and then she opened it. In content it was like the others. Brief, two sentences, to the point. But it wasn't typed, nor was there even an attempt at anonymity. It was in Mary's handwriting and she had even signed it. Just an alarming little bit of filth for Angela to read when she got to school in the morning.

"Is this true?" she asked when she had read it.

Malcolm reddened. "Certainly not!"

She looked at the note again. Of course it *wasn't* her writing, really: it was a forgery, not even a particularly good one. It was too shaky, but it was recognizable, just. She couldn't resist it; she let out one outraged convulsive laugh.

"So, *I* am the culprit again! It makes sense. Oh, and of course this proves it." She looked at the note briefly. When she spoke again, the bitterness was more apparent. "It does happen; the domestic tragedy. Wife at home in the country. Goes mad, temporarily – never when hubby is around – hot and cold running mad. Sews a little chaos into an otherwise contented life, invents a lover for her husband. It makes so much sense, Malcolm. And we can't – *mustn't* – forget that there have been indications. Mary has had some close shaves with the loony bin; why even now she is under treatment."

Malcolm tried to interrupt, but she went on.

"There have been some startling assertions in the dead of night. Oh dear, we should have done something much earlier, years ago, *the first time*. Poor thing, we had to turn on the radio sometimes to see if the world was still on out there." With a start Mary realized she sounded crazy. Her voice was too big, not part of her any more. Still it went on.

"We should never have let it go on like that. Of course, you know it's cancerous, mental illness. A cancer; you can never yank it all out." She stopped and the voice flew away from her to fill the room. "Is that what you have come to tell me with that sullen and determined face?"

"If you think I'm having an affair with Angela, talk to me

about it. Don't go writing notes to her. That's what I came to talk about." Malcolm shoved his hands into his pockets and then immediately withdrew them again, as if that had been some kind of admission of guilt. He looked at last at Mary when she spoke. Her voice was under control again, just barely.

"This is not my handwriting!"

The statement startled him. He hadn't expected it. He had expected she might say she hadn't written the note but somehow to say it was not her handwriting was something else—more objective. He became confused for a moment. Meanwhile she crushed the letter in her fist. He thought she was going to throw it but she dropped it to the floor. Still he couldn't think of what to say. Certainly he had known that the writing was shaky, he had assumed it was the writing of a sick woman; the hand as disturbed as the mind. She was challenging him. She knew exactly what he was intimating, and yet she refused to believe it. She must have no comprehension of her other consciousness, if that was, in fact, what/who was responsible. It must be her! What other explanation could there possibly be? He couldn't help admiring her pluck. She wasn't going to "go quietly." He tried to talk reasonably, as he had planned, but did not get out more than a few words before she interrupted him.

"Don't talk to me in that tone of voice. I am not god-damned Zenobia! If I am sick it is only part-time. And I'm not sick at this moment, right? So don't treat me like I'm sick." She breathed in deeply and exhaled slowly and deliberately. She got up and walked over to the window. She didn't turn. "I don't know why I am so impatient. I *do* understand what you are saying. I am the only one who is at home all day, but something in me refuses to accept anything so preposterous. I have to believe Fielding. My nerves are shot. That's all. Besides I have the feeling that I would somehow know, if I was sick, I mean. Don't ask me how, but

I would know it. I don't feel sick at all. Doesn't that count for something?"

Malcolm nodded his head slowly. Of course it did.

"You don't understand," she threw back at him.

"I do, Mary . . . I'm trying to." He looked at her pleadingly. "All I want to do is find out for sure. Can Dr. Fielding find out for sure! You said yourself that you might be an Eve or a Sybil. I know that it isn't you, the real you, that has been doing these things. Are there tests?"

Now Mary was the one who was speechless. You cannot refute such an accusation. It is impossible to say, "I am not a schizophrenic." Impossible! To plead innocence is treated as the apology: "I didn't *mean* to do it." And even if she could convince him, which she thought she could, he would still have to know for sure now. She hated to admit that she was already losing ground. How could she know for sure herself—except for that feeling. The feeling that she was perfectly all right. She *was*!

"It's the only thing that explains all the contradictions. I mean that it was not done consciously but in some altered state. Nobody would deliberately incriminate himself, unless . . . unless maybe it was a way of crying out for help." He said this latter statement with difficulty.

"Or unless it was done by someone very devious indeed." She glared at him. "Who is to say that you aren't a . . . a Mr. Hyde after hours?"

Malcolm looked directly at her. "That was what I thought for a while." He stopped to let this seep in. Mary was caught off guard. It stunned her to think of Malcolm having such self-doubt. "Finally I asked my secretary and some of the people in the department."

"What did you ask them? Have I been a little gaga lately? Bill, have you seen my eyes rolling or froth at the corner of my lip? What kind of answers did you expect to get?"

Malcolm went on patiently.

"No. I just asked whether I had been at work when I thought I was at work, that's all. It's sixty miles to the college. I couldn't slip out between classes to execute the next move. Some of the things that have been done could not have been done unless the house was empty or unless one of us was not at home. Anyway, Anne MacCready keeps a log of who is in and who is out, and it checks out."

"Checks out against what?" But Mary didn't need an answer. She had understood what he meant. She was hurt and angry. She saw Mrs. Rapsey on Tuesdays and Kevin now and then but otherwise she was alone. Poor, old, mad Mary alone at Odd's End, day in day out. It was such an unkind accusation, a sad predicament.

Malcolm knew it was. He had wanted to be subtle, but when he thought about it that was somehow worse. Mary picked up the pack of cigarettes and threw it down again. Was it worth explaining that Bliss had left them and in her anxiety she had smoked a couple or should she just let Malcolm think they were residue from her "other" existence? Everything was suddenly incriminating. She was aware of giving up. When she spoke next, her voice was meek. A shadow of its former vehemence.

"I feel like the White King in *Through the Looking Glass* who tries to write down his feelings in his memorandum book. Alice, huge and invisible, stands behind him and manipulates his pencil; makes him say things he didn't mean to say."

Malcolm felt dreadful. He hadn't wanted victory, but he had one, a pyrrhic victory. Mary looked shattered.

"... And his brush," she said.

"And his brush?" Malcolm asked.

Mary smiled wanly, her voice ironic but no longer biting. "Yes, his brush. It seems that someone *has* been painting my paintings. He even finished one; didn't even give me the pleasure of varnishing it." She wanted to show him – but was it worth it?

"Can I show you?"

Malcolm nodded. With his untutored eye he knew he would not be able to tell any difference in the brushwork, but he did know that she wanted to show him something, include him in her dilemma and that was encouraging. Maybe there would be a clue; he wanted to do something to help.

He thought about the canvases; they were brilliant but they were schizophrenic in style and execution. Artists, he knew, were often people who could bring opposite ideas together—and manifest them visually; it was one of the wonders of the artist. Sometimes it didn't work. What would Fielding say about Mary's work?

Mary felt intensely vulnerable, but she also felt that there wasn't really all that much to lose. She half-hoped the paintings might hold an answer. Maybe if they examined the canvases something would come to light. She and Malcolm did not often talk about her work; not that he didn't care, he did, but their discussions usually revolved around meaning and interpretation—the intellectual rather than the physical reality of the work. She realized as they approached the studio that he seldom entered it; it was her world.

Like Malcolm she found herself thinking about the new series. She had always been aware of the "craziness" of them. It was their strongest feature, what made them tick. And maybe they had driven her wacko. Wacko—what a ridiculous word and yet it was the word she thought of as opposed to something more clinical. Wacko she could handle—the implications did not seem so severe.

Entering the room she had no idea what to expect. It was all like *The Picture of Dorian Gray*. Would the paintings have all aged in her absence?

She showed Malcolm *Temporary Quarters*. They looked at it in silence. Malcolm asked again about how they were painted. She explained. It occurred to her that nothing could be more incriminating than this. Nobody could sit in here and paint her paintings; it was impossibly daring. Mary realized with a shudder that the cards were stacked against her.

They studied the paintings for some time in silence, each thinking his own thoughts. And then they heard it; not loud but whatever it was they both heard and looked up simultaneously. Outside across the clearing a bush rustled. Even as they looked up, it was almost still. Everything else was still; there was no wind whatsoever. Something had passed by. The movement was too big for a squirrel or a bird. People said there were deer in the woods but they had never once seen one. The impression of the moving leaves had been brief but vivid. Mary suddenly noticed the sliding door was open just a fraction yet she had slammed it and locked it. She was sure of it.

They were being watched, or had been watched. The sensation of it was intense. Like an animal alerted, neither of them knew whether to attack or retreat. Like animals they did neither but waited.

An impossible idea occurred to Mary. She wished, later, that she had never thought of it, but it came over her, and she reacted to it, and then it was too late to change her mind. She turned to Malcolm and, pushing him forcefully with both hands, she yelled at him. "If you don't believe me you can go to hell!"

"Mary!"

"Don't Mary me, I'm sick to death of these accusations." With a violent kick she knocked over one of her little tables. Paint tins and jars full of brushes fell to the floor, clattering and smashing.

Malcolm looked at her aghast. She pushed him again and started for the door. He grabbed her arm and she shook him off. He grabbed her again and she screamed at him.

"Leave me alone!"

But this time Malcolm caught a queer look on her face, just a glimpse. Had she winked at him? The look vanished immediately. Again she tried to shove him out of the way.

136

She yelled at him over and over. It was terrifying. He could only think she had slipped into her other role, but it had happened so quickly, too quickly. He tried to grab her flailing arms and it was then that she slapped him. He reacted violently, slapping her back, harder than he had intended. She was hysterical and screamed at him.

"Get out! Get out of this house. It's my house, do you hear me? Get the hell out!"

There, it was done. She swung around and stomped out of the studio, leaving Malcolm standing there. She slammed the door shut behind her for good measure. If it was mad he wanted ....

Malcolm was stunned. In a moment he recovered; in her present state she might do anything. His cheek stung, and his shins were throbbing from her kicks. He raced after her but was in for a further shock. Halfway down the hall, she reached out and dragged him into the laundry room. Before he could do anything she threw her arms around him and pressed her lips to his ear. "Shhhhhhhh," was all she said.

She was out of breath and he couldn't tell if she was crying or laughing. It was neither. It was both. She stroked his cheek and apologized. Everything was too confusing. She congratulated him on a job well done. It had been a good performance. It had been a performance; the violent eruption had been staged. She had tried to signal him but she hadn't dared to stop; it had to be convincing.

"But why?"

"There was somebody out there, Mal."

"I thought so too but why the fight?"

"Mal, I don't think it's me, I can't seem to make you believe that. You haven't believed it all along. But if there was somebody out there and it's him, don't ask me why, but *if-it-is-him*, then he must be trying to get at me. He's got to have the chance!"

Breathlessly Mary explained her plan: not a plan really but an idea that grew as they discussed it. Malcolm wouldn't listen at first. It was ridiculous, it was dangerous. But Mary was desperate. And if it was just a trespasser, what then? Mary had made up her mind – the door had been locked, she was sure of that. If he was a trespasser then he was a trespasser who had entered their house. Malcolm had to believe her. It was a long shot, but Malcolm agreed to play along. It had to be soon. They couldn't afford to lose their audience before the performance was over.

The next scene was a difficult one. The farewell scene. Not Reginald and Zenobia, but Mary and Malcolm. The stage had changed to the courtyard. The very impulsiveness of Mary's action in the studio along with the fact that only she had been acting had given the first scene a compelling realness. (Malcolm's sore shins were proof.) Somehow Mary believed that the audience wanted more of the same. They had no proof he was there when they emerged from the west wing twenty minutes later; no proof that he had been there in the first place except a feeling they shared. They were clinging to that feeling, relying on instinct. If they were wrong, then the worst that might happen was that they would act out a little farce for the amusement of no one. It could be distinctly embarrassing but there was no one around to see them unless it was someone who had no right to be there.

They had both acted before in amateur productions but they were aware that what they had to do was not like any role they had ever played. It must not be acted! It must be real. They must become the characters they were portraying – become themselves – but themselves in a state of irreconcilable anger.

What frightened them both was how easy it was. There was an irresistible urge to be angry, furious with each other. The drama was cathartic, releasing all the pent-up suspicion and torment of the last few weeks. They fought in deadly earnest, and the more real their anger became, the more melodramatic it seemed. And the more melodramatic it seemed, the more desperately genuine it became. The zeal of the battle was like nothing so much as soap opera. Mary had been deathly afraid she might laugh because it was so silly, so embarrassing. But it soon was all too real to laugh. It was bad acting because they were real people and the drama was real.

Finally Malcolm threw his valise in the car and drove off. To her horror Mary did laugh, but her laugh was hysterical. She picked up a rake that was leaning against the shed wall and flung it after the car. She was alone.

17

Mary was used to being alone, but rarely by night. Malcolm had been arriving home late, but seldom much past seven o'clock. It was apparent now to anyone having witnessed the scene in the courtyard that Malcolm was, convincingly and dramatically, not at home; nor expected. Somehow it had seemed to her that this is what he wanted, the intruder: to have Mary all to himself without the possible appearance of her husband. It was a gruesome proposal but it was at long last something! By now, any action was better than no action. Malcolm had wanted nothing to do with it at first. Then, he had insisted on staying behind, but that was nonsense—Mary was the one who was being terrorized, and she must be the bait. Malcolm had only relented when she had taken down the old rifle. A friend had restored it and had even located a stash of brass-capped shells which it would fire. That had been four years ago. They had set up a target on the dunes. Mary had fared every bit as well as Malcolm and not badly at that. Her eye was good and her hand was steady; the rifle had quite a backfire but she had learned to anticipate it, correct for it. Her arms were strong. Whenever Philip had visited them they would get the rifle down and set up the target. He had not been around for almost a year but she had not forgotten how to fire the rifle. She had in any case found a certain enjoyment in keeping it clean and oiled. Never had she really thought of it as a weapon but merely as a valuable antique. When she had taken the rifle down, Malcolm had argued with her that she would never be able to fire it at a person. She was not prepared to argue ethics. Self-defense. She would not fire unless it was in self-defense. Somehow she had convinced him. Secretly she had been considering just what she would be tempted to do if she did meet up with the intruder. At close range she would fire very accurately, she assured Malcolm. Something in her eye further convinced him. She meant business.

Meanwhile, they had decided Malcolm would drive to Steep Cove to the RCMP station there. The RCMP was in charge of policing the bay area outside of the city. His contact with the division had been restricted to speeding tickets, several of them; but also, on the good side of the ledger was an association with Sergeant Gruber. He had run into the sergeant at the fish market in the Cove on two or three occasions and they had chatted. Malcolm hoped he was the same affable soul when on duty; he hoped he was on duty. He wasn't sure how to explain their plan to a complete stranger.

They had not dared to phone for they had no way of knowing whether the line was tapped. It seemed feasible; their intruder or prowler, whatever he was, had proved ubiquitous. They could only assume he was not omnipotent.

Malcolm had gathered the evidence together in an old valise—a rag-tag collection: a photograph, a rag doll, and a French existential autobiography. It wasn't going to be easy! He was all too aware that only two hours earlier, he had been reasonably certain that it was all Mary's doing. There was only that one palpable disturbance in the bushes to convince him otherwise.

Somehow he had to convince Gruber to set a trap; a stake-out. It was a crazy scheme but it was a scheme. He was taking positive action at last. Retaliating against a rustling bush, thought Malcolm, tilting at windmills.

Gruber greeted him with cordiality. The sergeant had seen the article in *Halifax* and was impressed. The Closes were local celebrities. Malcolm wondered what kind of a reputation they would have after tonight; but the warm greeting made his task a lot easier.

He apologized in advance for what he was afraid might sound a tall tale. Gruber waited patiently, apparently accustomed to nervous preambles. He listened to the story without raising an eyebrow. He nodded gravely from time to time but otherwise remained quiet. He questioned the efficacy and the safety of leaving Mary alone; however, he had the courtesy not to press the point. Malcolm was not in any mood for scolding, and in any case what had been done had been done. Gruber called one of his officers into the room; Corporal Bev Skimpole. Skimpole was a bony, hawk-faced man. Despite a dour countenance he listened to the sergeant's edited version of the story apparently without doubting its veracity or questioning its import. Malcolm began to feel a little better. He had avoided such a confrontation for so long. He had been stupid; this, after all, was what police were for, to deal with miscreants no matter what form they took. Malcolm realized with a start that he had worried all along that the crimes somehow reflected on him and Mary and he hated being dubiously regarded.

Basically the entire crime could be reduced to vandalism and breaking and entering. Malcolm noticed they didn't use any code numbers.

Both of the men were familiar with the house, having lived in the area for most of their lives. Skimpole said that he would need several men to surround it effectively, which was fine except that there weren't several men available. Constable Hew Bushy was enlisted, that was it. If there had been no further harassment by morning the officers would inspect the area and determine from there what to do next. Malcolm was informed that a real stakeout could be a long affair, but since there was no tangible evidence that the intruder was going to strike, they couldn't do much else. If it was merely a prankster, seeing the police would probably scare him off for good. That was if nothing happened tonight.

Malcolm had never driven ten miles with a police car trailing him and not been stopped. It was a night of new experiences. When they had left the station, he had tried to gauge the response of the officers to his story and the consequent stakeout. Skimpole was dispassionate; he gave the impression that he would respond the same way to a multiple murder as to a charge of littering–it was just a job. Hew Bushy, large and cheery, made a point of trying to make Malcolm feel at ease. The prospect of a night outside did not seem to move either of them one way or another. They had not talked much at the station, and after they parked their cars by the Manor and began the long trek down to the house they kept conversation to a minimum. Instructions were passed back and forth in whispers.

It was dusk. Malcolm couldn't remember the last time he had walked down the furrowed Park Road; not for years. How strange it was to be sneaking up on his own house. It was difficult to take it seriously: the hushed commands from Skimpole, queries on procedure, Bushy's reassurances. And Malcolm, the English scholar, silent for the most part in this little army.

They would reach the house before nightfall. He hoped something would happen to justify this hugger-mugger. It all seemed like an extraordinary game to him. Did policemen often feel they were playing at games–cops and robbers?

There was a path leading off the road half a mile from the house. It was an old logging path, now quite overgrown, that curved behind the house circling it until it disappeared into thick bush a couple of hundred yards from the northwest corner. Skimpole would take this back route while Bushy and Malcolm continued down the road. Nearer the house they would move into the brush where they would still be well-concealed from the house. Malcolm had drawn them a floor plan and map as best he could. It wasn't to scale but it showed all the entrances, which was the important thing. Three men, one untrained, could not hope to form a tight cordon. Skimpole would cover the back including the north exit from the studio; Malcolm would take a position just north of the stable with a view to the courtyard, and Bushy would watch the road and the front entranceway. By 9:10 they were in position. All that was left was to wait.

She was excited when she came right down to it. The gun was loaded and lay beside her where she was curled up in the big chair in the corner of the living room. It was a good tactical position; behind the potted palms she was not immediately visible. She was in a corner so she could not be surprised from either entrance to the room. Beside her stood the saints in their leaded-glass cages. There was no sun to light them now, but it was at least comforting to know that she could not be seen from outside. The windows were blind at night. She had gathered some supplies: a bowl of fruit and nuts and a large bottle of mineral water. She was going to read, not Simone de Beauvoir, but *The Thurber Carnival*, and she wasn't going to move until she had to. An hour passed before she really realized she had only read four pages of "The Lady on 142." All the time she was trying to read she was driving to Steep Cove in her mind. She climbed the hill from the house, gearing down and up around the interminable turns. She passed Rood Manor and turned out onto the Peninsula Road, and then she roared along that road as it banked up the side of the whale-backed hill and dipped down again to the sea. She tried to drive as Malcolm did, and when she arrived at the station she walked in his long strides. Despite her attempt to allow for the right length of time for each part of the route she had already arrived and returned three times in her mind. She decided to think of the reaction Malcolm's story might be receiving. Disbelief; reluctance to act; too little information; too few men; and, at last, begrudged assistance? No! This wouldn't do. She would have to rethink the conversation. She tried to imagine them rushing back to the rescue, Malcolm with the police, back to Odd's End. What else was there to think? She had no idea how such things were done; she could only think in terms of "the posse to the rescue."

Blood pounded in her head and flushed her cheeks. Someone had told her if you could hear your blood coursing through your veins without its being muffled by tissue and bone it would deafen you. Her head threatened to explode; she gave up on the book and picked up the rifle. It was already loaded, but she pulled back the breach and let the shell drop into her hand. She loaded it again and tried to unload it and shove in another cartridge. She couldn't really hope for two shots but it was worth trying. The first shot would "bring the troops," that was the hastily conceived plan. She tried to reload again and again – just in case. What she and Malcolm had seen or thought they had seen was human and not supernatural. She would not hesitate to test that humanity by firing at him if he came at her. She had never thought such a thought before. It went against everything she believed in. Another strange idea occurred to her: perhaps it was not such a good idea to kill the intruder even if she could. He was in essence her vindication, the proof that she was innocent, that she was not sick; but if she were to kill him she might never know. The man who had been outside today may have had nothing to do with the terrorizing of the house; a hobo maybe. She was getting muddleheaded. It was no use hypothesizing on what might happen.

Something had to happen, that was all, tonight. The drama that had begun in the studio and continued in the courtyard must not end yet. She couldn't be sure where reality ended and her fantasy took over. The noises in the house, for instance. She was astonished at how much noise the house made. It was settling into the night; the air was cooling, the wind changing directions, and the house was responding. Like her blood it was deafening.

And then she heard it. A light thud. It came from somewhere off in the other part of the house – upstairs or in the studio. It was different from the settling noises – not something knocked over, but something moved. It was 10:47. Malcolm must be there by now. Had the man been inside all along, or had he entered before Malcolm returned? She hoped the troops were in position and ready.

The second distinguishable noise didn't come for fifteen minutes but this time it was followed by a second similar sound. Just a soft thud but distinct from the noises of the house. This time she was sure it was not from upstairs, which meant it must be from the north end of the house, from the studio. The phantom painter; what he would do now that the paintings were finished she hated to think. Ten minutes passed without a sound and she became restless. Assuming that the police were outside and that the noise inside was the intruder it was her duty to give them the sign so that they could close the net. Finally there was another sound, this time a continuous one like something being dragged across the floor. She jumped from her seat and took a tentative step. She heard another sound and took another step; at this rate it would take her forever to get there. She was quite certain now the sound was from the studio. She was shaking with mingled fear and impatience. Also she was thrilled. This was what she had wanted; they had set a trap, and it was going to work. All she had to do was pull the string to trap the intruder yet she could barely move. Still another sound caught her off guard; she stumbled and

146

regained her balance clutching the rifle to her chest. It had been a sharper, more distinct noise. Finally she made it to the steps to the west wing. She peered around the corner. From here she could see through the west wing, past the staircase, down the corridor, to the studio door. It was closed. One further sound and she was sure it was from her studio that the various thuds and dragging sounds were emanating.

Crossing in front of the wide expanse of window in the west wing seemed impossible. What if there were more than one. What if the sound from the studio were a ploy to lure her into the open. She wheeled around. No one. How could there be? Malcolm and the police were outside by now. They had to be. And if they were, then they would be the ones to see her sneaking across the room with the rifle like Peter after his wolf. This thought gave her new confidence. The police would be able to close in on the studio before she made her move. This deduction seemed to make a lot of sense and she began slowly to cross the room, walking near the window where the floor wouldn't creak as much. She had taken off her shoes. Now she could hear all sorts of little noises coming from the end of the hall. It was not her imagination – cold comfort. Halfway across the room her vulnerability got the better of her. It was like being on a screen, naked. As quietly as she could, she managed to run the length of the floor until she was by the stairwell. She could no longer see down the hall. She had pressed herself flat against the wall. Had she been heard? What a fool she thought she had been, but she hadn't made a sound, she felt sure. She waited, scarcely daring to breathe.

This time the sound came as a mixed blessing. He was still there but had that been the studio door? A chill came over her. If it was, then he might be walking silently down the corridor this very minute towards her. She was in a corner less than two feet from the hall, he would appear in front of her, and she would not even have room to raise her rifle. He did not appear. The tension was unbearable. There were no sounds now for several minutes. He had lured her and now he was playing for time, making her suffer. What if it had been the other door? Then he was escaping this very minute while she stood by. She couldn't let that happen; it was more terrifying than any confrontation. She wouldn't wait any longer. She raced down the corridor, past the pantry, past the laundry room. Had he been in either she would have been trapped in the narrow hall. She didn't stop to consider. It was like sneaking home in hide-and-go-seek while "It" was still counting; games, children's games.

She threw open the door. The room was in darkness. She could not turn on the light with the rifle in her hands! She froze. She saw the shadow ten feet in front of her and then it was gone and then it was in the corner – another shadow. She fired and as she did she screamed for all she was worth. She ran back out of the room but behind her in the hall was a huge man coming towards her with a revolver in his hand. He almost filled the hallway. He had already raced by her before it penetrated that he was in uniform. She threw herself against the wall. The big man turned on the lights. She heard other voices; the sliding door was thrown open, and a minute later, the door from the shed was heaved against. Twice it was rammed and finally she heard it splinter. Malcolm rushed to her. She couldn't look, not yet. Instructions were yelled and one of the men pushed past them in the corridor. After a few moments her breathing began to even out although her heart was racing. This was no time to fall apart; perhaps they had got him, the shadow; but somehow she knew they hadn't.

By the time she and Malcolm re-entered the studio, the two men were back. She looked at them and sat down. Malcolm joined the men by the sliding doors. One of them was pointing at the painting *Manshadow* where it leaned against the wall. She couldn't at first understand; one of the men was behind the canvas digging at the wall with a pen knife. As he tipped the canvas forward she caught a quick glimpse of the hole. Not a bad shot really—she had shot it through the shadow of his head. How pathetic.

The men were conferring. She couldn't hear what was being said and she had the distinct impression she was not meant to. Behind them the curtains were partially open. They had been completely open this afternoon. She wanted to tell them but couldn't speak. The inside of her mouth was like chalk. The policeman with the bony face was talking to Malcolm and Malcolm was shaking his head, looking into the middle distance. She sat there waiting to be let in on the secret. It was like a bloody conspiracy. The big man, Bushy, came over to her. When he saw she was holding her throat with her mouth open he went without asking to her sink and, finding the cleanest glass he could amidst the paint pots, he got her some water.

"You've had quite a scare," he said, amiably smiling as he handed her the glass.

She gulped it down. "The curtains were open." That was all she said.

Skimpole looked at her and then at the curtains. The curtains had been closed and he had opened them enough to get through the door, he said. He was not refuting what she had said, but she couldn't help thinking that there was already a note of skepticism in his voice. Malcolm concurred with his wife that when he had left in the afternoon they had been wide open. Skimpole nodded but it didn't really change anything. There was no way of knowing who had closed them again or when.

Skimpole finally spoke. "He didn't come through the sliding doors. When I saw Mrs. Close crossing the open wing there I came back to wait. Since the hallway was pretty well jammed up with people it's pretty likely he didn't get out that way and when Mr. Close here came through the door from the shed he had to break it down, it being locked from inside. He was a bit late in getting here. But I don't think anybody could have gotten across the courtyard before we went out there."

That was it. A summary that seemed to imply only one thing. Mary felt a lump thicken in her throat. Why didn't he just say exactly what he was thinking? Something in her eyes must have said as much to him, for he continued.

"That's not to say there wasn't someone, Mrs. Close. It's just that he got away too damn fast for us."

She assumed this was said out of charity. He was standing there telling her this and meanwhile the shadow was getting away! Bushy enthusiastically jumped in at this point. If he was as skeptical as Skimpole his voice gave no hint of it.

"Did you get a good look at him, ma'am?"

Mary shook her head. "Not really. I thought there were two men. I saw one close up, not ten feet away but he, well, he seemed to vanish ... and then I saw the other ... I mean the shadow, that is, the painting ...."

Nobody spoke for a minute. Skimpole scratched his lean chin and looked around the room. Mary followed his gaze and noticed what she hadn't before. The paintings were all in different places.

"Everything has been moved around." As she looked again, it suddenly became clear to her. "Look," she said. "Malcolm, you stand by this canvas and you two come over here by the doorway." They followed her to the door. "I heard all kinds of noises from the studio before I came down. Look." She switched off the light. When everyone's eyes had adjusted she asked Malcolm to walk forward. "You see," she said triumphantly. As Malcolm advanced he seemingly vanished behind one of the large canvases which leaned against a corner of her fixed easel. It was not hard to see how the canvas acted as a screen, a tunnel, to the shed doorway.

The others could see it. Skimpole still scratched his chin. She wasn't finished. "And the shed door can be locked from inside and then slammed shut behind you as you leave." It made sense. Credibility was restored, but the look on Skimpole's face was more like tolerance than anything else. He nodded in agreement finally.

"We'll give the ground a good going over and in the morning we'll send some people over to check more closely for clues. If anyone was here there should be some trace. He moved fast though – damn fast."

It was the closest he had come to conceding that there might actually have been someone. Mary wondered if the others were thinking what *she* was thinking – *they* had botched it, *they* had let the bastard escape.

Bushy finally smiled and said, "Well, you've stopped *him*, at least," and he pointed over his shoulder at the painting. "He's not going anywhere." It was said kindly.

Skimpole, perhaps to atone for his earlier conclusion, wanted to check out the house. It was a long shot but they might be able to find something. Mary sensed he still didn't really believe there was anyone at all. He was looking suspiciously at the canvases. It was probably easy for him to believe that anyone who could make up these monstrosities could make up a lot more. He didn't say so.

It was the round-faced Hew Bushy who turned as they left. "If there is any more trouble, make sure you let us know." He said it with great sincerity.

Mary and Malcolm sat in the living room for a long time. Mary stretched out on the davenport and Malcolm sat at her feet rubbing them soothingly. Neither of them spoke. A silence had descended on the house the moment the men had left. The silence was pervasive. Not even the house sounds Mary had heard so deafeningly earlier were apparent any longer; she felt betrayed. She wished she had said more to the police. No, she hadn't seen the intruder, not enough to describe any features but she had seen a *moving* shadow. That at least was not illusion; she didn't care what anyone said.

Finally she went upstairs, but she couldn't sleep. She

curled up in the window seat in her room staring out into the dark, holding a cup of tea in her hands. She smiled weakly at Malcolm when he entered the bedroom. He sat down on the edge of the seat.

"I called Kevin. He says it would be fine for you to go over, tonight if you want. It's up to you."

She nodded yes. It had been Malcolm's idea for her to get away from the house for a while. She couldn't phone Kevin herself; it would mean explaining and she was tired of explaining.

"I'll drive you down."

"I think I had better go alone, I've done enough .... I'm sorry."

"Nonsense ...."

She hadn't the strength to argue. They gathered the barest necessities. Malcolm could bring another suitcase later. She didn't want to return again for a while.

It was a much quieter leave-taking than the one earlier in the evening. Had it really been the same evening? She had felt so hopeful, so brave then, now she was sad and empty. There was little to say; they drove to Lunenburg in silence.

Kevin had renovated the rooms above the store. With Tom away, there was lots of room, and there was Powys, Tom's sheepdog, for companionship, and, more than all of that, outside there was a little city, never entirely quiet and with the streetlights always burning.

18

So they have relented at last and called in outside forces. It was a close call but I turned it into my deftest stroke. I could smell a trap; in my career, I have become uncannily sensitive to such things. I also had made a point of checking out the local constabulary, a paltry lot, and of course I know the house better than its occupants do. Still, it was too close, requiring in the end an alert ear and a nimble foot.

None of it would have happened at all if I had not been overconfident. They almost saw me, that must never happen again. Patience is paying off but their impotence provokes me to rashness. I must not allow my eagerness to get the better of me.

I am provoked from all sides. My landlady at the Sea Winds is making life intolerable; I can only stand so much attention, and attention is presently heaped on me from that quarter. In order to justify my extensive use of her car, I have resorted to an elaborate ruse of house-hunting, in the legitimate sense. Deirdre, she insists I call her Deirdre, accompanies me occasionally on these jaunts. How she enjoys it! At first it seemed a wonderfully ironic parody of the real situation but it has become a tiresome exercise. We have looked at several properties. Deirdre suspects I am hard to please – if she only knew! She has no idea how far I have driven her car on the occasions I borrow it alone for I have disconnected the odometer. But I cannot afford to disconnect Miss Tinker's affections, not quite yet. It will break her little blue-rinsed heart when I leave. I must hold on until Odd's End is made ready for its new tenant; until it is empty at last.

They have called in outside forces. That raises the ante. The gambler in me changes the game. There is only one opponent now. Blackjack; with me as the dealer and Malcolm the lone player dealt his cards from a stacked deck.

There is one card I have been saving. I keep it up my sleeve. Perhaps the time has come to surreptitiously slip it to my unsuspecting rival.

19

Malcolm spent what was left of the night in Lunenburg with Mary. In the morning she drove him back to Odd's End, at least as far as the Manor, to pick up the Fiat so that she could keep the truck. Kevin had lots of errands to keep her occupied. Malcolm drove up to the college, he had a lot of essays to mark. He arrived home late in the afternoon and packed some clothes for Mary. He was on the road to Lunenburg in time for dinner at eight. Kevin had extended an open invitation to him to stay for as long as he wanted while Mary was recuperating, but Malcolm replied that it might be best to let Mary have some time to herself. He didn't really want to see anyone and he knew he owed Mary too much to let her down now. He couldn't help thinking that he was to blame for her present state. Nothing in her demeanor had indicated anything of the kind, but she clearly needed to be away, not only from the house but from him for a while. He needed to be away from her too. He could use the time to catch up on his paper which had suffered badly over the last little while. Besides, someone should be at the house. He felt keenly that one of them should be there even if only to water the plants. He had no ideas of seeing Angela. He had not been back to Henry Street since she had delivered her ultimatum. They were still friendly when they met, but there had been no further mention of their assignation.

Malcolm promised Mary he would see that Ed got the paintings crated up and delivered on time. *Manshadow* was going, bullet hole and all. Mary would probably still go to Toronto the following week as planned, and Malcolm had tentatively promised to get far enough ahead on his paper to fly out for the weekend of the opening if he could. Kevin had not been able to get his usual assistant for the summer and might not be able to go, but Pip would be there. Toronto was a perfect cure for mysteries. It was either the sanest city in the world or just the most boring. Anyway, it would be a start to their vacation together – the first stage. Their most recent idea was to go to Switzerland and bicycle in the mountains – invigorating and healthful – just what was needed. Meanwhile Mary would see Fielding again.

Malcolm was reserving judgement on the episode that had finally precipitated Mary's departure. He had not forgotten the noise in the bushes which had triggered the whole ludicrous game. There *had* been something: some kind of nexus he could not dismiss even if he could not explain it. He also had to admit that he had taken an interminable time getting to the shed door. It was only minutes really, he suspected, but if there had been an intruder, he was obviously crafty. Still everything seemed too unerringly clever. If there was a real someone, he was taking enormous risks.

Malcolm worked on his paper the next day, and although he got an early start it did not go well. It was humid and he was restless. All day he thought about being alone in the house; he was not used to it. Was this what Mary went through? Over a long period he felt sure it could have a profound effect on a person's stability. Malcolm was a gregarious soul; he could spend long stretches at a time lost in his work oblivious to his surroundings, but when he came up for air he liked people to be there. Alone at the house, when you took a break, you took it alone. It was hard to get used to. Maybe one was forced to invent other people for company. The thought made him uneasy.

He gave up after having written several paragraphs. It was late in the afternoon, the air was thick and hazy with heat. He decided to go out in the garden. Despite the heat he weeded – enjoying the distraction. Why were weeds so much hardier than vegetables? The tiny carrots were already choked with pigweed, lamb's-quarters, and some nefarious plant which looked remarkably like carrot. It was a painstaking job. The rain came at last without fanfare. He didn't quit right away but let it pour down on him. Inside he made a meal out of leftovers and sat on the steps leading to the courtyard, his plate in his lap, drinking a beer. Even with the rain the air was still close, and he realized with dismay they were in for the summer's first hot spell. The beer did not really refresh him, it only made him weary. Drinking beer alone invariably made him weary.

How often had he and Mary sat on the step drinking beer and watching a summer rainstorm. There was enough of an overhang from the second story that you could sit without feeling a drop of rain. It had become a kind of a ritual; they would applaud and discuss the storm's merits like a performance. Its scent, intensity, luminosity, that was one of Mary's terms; its ability to bluster. Mary had even put up a scoreboard in the kitchen. There was an afternoon, July 23, 1975, that had been their unanimous favorite; every other storm was measured against it.

He missed her already; he didn't really want her to be there but he missed her anyway and it had only been two days. Reluctantly he picked himself up and retreated inside; the storm wasn't much any more – a four or five at best.

He took a cold shower and threw himself once more at the teeth of "Structuralist Presumptions in Contemporary Literary Investigation." Of all times to have to deal with a major paper!

Gruber relieved him from his work, phoning shortly after eight o'clock. He had sent a man down to the house to search the grounds the previous day while Malcolm had been out;

they had submitted a report on their findings. It amounted to damn little. If the house had been under surveillance, the culprit had been careful not to leave a trace. They had hoped to find a favorite lookout or hiding place but had found nothing of the kind. Unfortunately, the sand dunes, which presented a fine view of the house and a natural blind, shift constantly, and they found no sign of occupation, only an occasional broken branch in the woods. In a wet patch, however, they had found one distinct footprint. To that effect they would need the impression of Malcolm's right shoe, the ones he had worn the night of the stakeout; and the impressions of the same from anybody who might have been legally on the property. The impression of the footprint they had found would be processed at headquarters in Halifax. It gave an indication of the man's weight and height because there had been another incomplete step and they could measure the stride. It was skimpy evidence, but it was worth investigating. It might at least validate the existence of a trespasser, and they could work from there.

There was something else, which Gruber brought up in an offhand manner, but Malcolm sensed an uneasiness behind his tone. Apparently on the night of the stakeout, Skimpole had investigated upstairs and had found markings on the windowsills. The marks were on the inside: someone had been trying to pry unlocked windows open from the inside! It had been most notable in the room which Skimpole had called the "children's room." Perhaps the windows were a little tight due to the humidity, Gruber suggested. There was no insinuation in the man's voice. Gruber pressed on with his report despite the silence at the other end of the line. Malcolm thanked him, distractedly. Gruber asked after Mary and responded sympathetically to the news of her retreat. He hoped her condition would not last long. The word "condition" Gruber had, not unkindly, imbued with unmistakable significance. Wishing Malcolm no further disturbances, he hung up.

In the children's room Malcolm felt the tiny chips and gouges with his finger. They were small and ineffectual, a pathetic gesture only recognizable because they were new. The bare wood stood out against the white paint of the sill. None of the windows was the least bit stuck despite Gruber's optimistic suggestion. Someone had been trying to get out – to escape. There was nothing outside; no ledge, only the ground twelve feet below.

To his surprise Malcolm felt sick. The implications were so desperate, so sad. He turned and looked at the room. It had always been a delightful miniature museum. The porcelain dolls in their muslin dresses, the tin cars and brightly painted drums and tops. And of course the doll's house, eighteenth century, German; four-storied and almost three feet high, each room balustered to prevent the delicate furniture from spilling out. And what elaborate furniture: chairs and tables, of course, but also paintings and tiny books, bound with real pages; chandeliers with real wax candles. In a bedroom hung a gilded birdcage and the bed was discreetly canopied in velvet. There was a rocking horse, two and a half inches high. In the parlor on a playing table, cards less than one-half inch square. In a passage room, sheets, napkins, and towels in bundles tied up with ribbon. The kitchen walls were covered with pewter plates and multifarious utensils. On the bottom floor, in the cellar, were beer and wine kegs, and in another room even a stall crowded with livestock. The details were breathtaking: a tiny wardrobe opened to reveal doll's clothes; the windows were made of latticed talc divided with real leaded squares. There were clocks everywhere and crucifixes. All in all, twelve pigeonhole rooms. Something made him examine it more closely. The whole thing was topsy-turvy. The neat little rooms were piled with furniture, hopelessly jumbled. The house had been ransacked. The scene was depraved!

Mary phoned later the same evening. He didn't dare mention the dolls' house. She sounded well if a little lackluster.

All he could think of to ask was how her visit with Fielding had gone. He sensed an uneasiness in her voice and she waited a moment before answering.

"Well, I'm not quite certifiable yet."

"Did he suggest any medication?"

"Mal, you know perfectly well I won't take drugs."

He began to argue with her, but she cut him off.

"Please, darling, don't start telling me what to do."

The line crackled for a moment. There was a faint conversation ghosting on their line. They both apologized at the same time and then laughed weakly.

"Maybe we'll try some hypnosis."

Malcolm picked up on this and talked enthusiastically about things he had heard concerning its benefits.

"Maybe he can teach me self-hypnosis techniques," Mary added.

He waited for her to ask him if he would visit Fielding with her, preparing to agree, but she didn't ask. He was relieved.

Their conversation stumbled on a little, and then they said good-bye.

Two more days passed without further incident. A man came from Detcon Alarms and bored Malcolm with electronic jargon for almost an hour before saying that they couldn't take on such a big job until later in June. Malcolm learned how to cope with the quiet and the gathering heat. He didn't feel any better about sleeping alone.

When he spoke with his wife, she sounded a bit more chipper or at least as if she was making an effort. She didn't bring up her treatment again and Malcolm resolved not to mention it until she did.

Hanging up after a good conversation, he felt suddenly as if the move must have been the best thing. He would rather hear her voice pleasant and relaxed over the phone and know she was in good hands than to have her around when she was nervous and frightened. She never asked him about the house when she phoned. He supposed the former attraction of being isolated from society, alone with just the sand and the sea and himself, had lost its charm for her. Malcolm didn't want to leave Odd's End; he hoped it would not come to that. He had occasionally wished they were closer to the city, especially in the winter. He missed not having any night life or being able to go to a movie on an impulse. In other ways, however, he had never known such peace. In the end, it had always been her house. Funny, she had said as much in their fight in the studio. She had said it for effect but it remained vivid in his mind. Maybe it had been meant for him after all: "This is my house."

As soon as she had seen Odd's End, she had wanted it passionately, and since she was the one who was to spend most of her time there they did not hesitate to take it. Had it proved too much for her? In her loneliness had she created imaginary friends *and enemies*; turned to her dolls for company, like a child? And had her childlike sanctuary become a prison so that in distracted moments she had chipped away at the windowsills – a kind of ritual of escape. The idea sent a chill down his back.

20

Five days after Mary's departure, things took an unexpected turn. Leafing through the rough draft of his manuscript, Malcolm found another note. It had been typed on his machine but it was quite different in content from the others. Where they had been vulgar this one seemed disconsolate, rather than an attack it was a confession:

What I have done is unforgivable.
You must only try to understand, to be charitable with me.
And yet, it is not charity I want or need. I have acted out of frustration. I want you to myself. To myself.

It was unsigned. If Mary had written it then it was as much as an apology. Perhaps there were moments when her alter ego was aware of what it was doing. And yet what could she mean, "I want you to myself?" Did she know how much Malcolm was seeing Angela? It made no sense. And then it suddenly hit him; something extraordinary. The smell. He recognized it immediately. The note was scented with L'Air du Temps, Angela's perfume.

Mary could have planted the note; perhaps she had remembered the scent from the times she had met Angela or maybe she had smelled it on Malcolm, or maybe it was coincidence – L'Air du Temps was not so rare. Intuitively

Malcolm did not believe she had done it. Intuition was not his strong point but his sense of reasoning was slipping away. Rational inquiry rejects magic as a solution. He began to wonder whether he had manufactured everything in his head. A diabolical magic seemed quite as rational as anything else at this point. But if it was magic it was a mundane, if loathsome, variety. Mary had said it – no bleeding walls! Maybe this was the way ghosts really worked, after all! Yes, perhaps ghosts operated this way.

To stop believing there was somebody, a *real* somebody behind it was to roll over and play dead – play right into the cat's paws. He only wished he could turn the tables. Act bored; ignore the clues, ignore the cat. That, for Malcolm, was impossible. The desire *to know* was too strong. His mind began to tick over again as he began to assess the facts in light of the new discovery. The present clue worked against an impartial evaluation. If there is one sense that rejects rationality, it is the sense of smell. That fragrance was linked to one person in Malcolm's world and one person only – Angela. As long as he held the note in his hand, his inquiry turned reluctantly but inevitably to Angela. He crushed it and threw it across the room – but the smell lingered on his hands.

She had never been to Odd's End. There had been a faculty party three years earlier, but she was not then at King's. Malcolm suddenly remembered, however, there was a map. It was an invitation to the party that Mary had drawn up with a comic illustration. It was still on the bulletin board beside Mrs. MacCready's desk among the postcards and cartoons from the *New Yorker*. That map could explain how Angela had found the house. Nothing half so simple explained the note sent to Angela in Mary's hand and yet .... Malcolm remembered back to when Angela had brought him the note. He had been shocked. He had comforted her, and for the better (or the worst) part of a day he had been upset with his wife. His allegiance had shifted. He had felt protective of Angela. Had Angela connived a way of getting his attention and his fullest sympathy, she could not have come up with a better method. Assuming that it was possible – and this required a considerable suspension of critical doubt – how did Angela stack up as the culprit?

She had her own car. Being an instructor, she only taught one class and conducted one seminar per week which gave her adequate time, time in which she was ostensibly working on her Ph.D. thesis. Malcolm opened the old valise and took out the photograph of himself standing in the park. Angela was not in the photograph but she had not had the opportunity to slip away and take this photo without him knowing it. He was sure of that. She had taken a drink at the fountain and, sensibly, handed him her clothing boxes. Had she led him to that particular fountain where she had a confederate hiding in the bushes? The boxes were the perfect incriminating evidence: Avant-Garde was chic and young, it was almost *more* incriminating than having the woman on his arm. He held the photograph more closely. It smelled of L'Air du Temps! It wasn't on his hands any more, it was the photograph. It hadn't been before, he was sure he would have recognized it. Damn it! Everything in the valise and the valise itself stank of the stuff. He slammed it shut. He was being played with. He was constructing a case against Angela as he had against Mary. Confederate in the park – it was ridiculous. The scent was fresh. How could she have got in the house anyway?

Malcolm's attention was distracted by a sound outside. A car had pulled up. It was an old, decrepit Plymouth. It stopped, let out its passenger and, turning laboriously, drove back up the hill, its engine knocking and pinging all the way. The passenger was Mrs. Rapsey.

She was late and apologized. She apologized again, and Malcolm realized that he had been staring at her. If she was made uncomfortable by this she didn't show it and bustled into the house. Without further ado she switched on the radio and prepared to wash the floors. Malcolm didn't leave. While she filled her pail and gathered her mop and broom, he watched her. He tried to imagine her pecking out a love note on his typewriter. It was an outrageous image. She stopped her work and turned to look at him. He was still staring. Quickly, he asked if everything was all right at home, meaning, was that why she had been late. Reassured that he was not angry, and taking his concern to be an invitation to chat, she launched into a rambling monologue about Frank, her husband, Carl, her son, the Plymouth, the chickens, the government, ragweed, and soaring prices – in no particular order. For the most part, Malcolm nodded yes or no, whichever seemed the most appropriate. At one point she interjected a question and caught him completely off guard, his mind was drifting far away. She had only asked why he was at home, and why Mary wasn't. For a moment he faltered and finally said he was finished for the year at the school, and Mary was away for a while. It seemed evasive to him as soon as it was uttered but it apparently was enough for Mrs. Rapsey. If she was curious to know more, she did not let on. She launched right back into her run-on sentence about life in Raven's Hill with all its ups and downs. There were a lot more of the latter.

Malcolm finally escaped. He found himself smiling. So, Mrs. Rapsey was the one who wanted him all to herself, was she? If Mrs. Rapsey had a *doppelgänger* he doubted whether it would use anything keener than a sledge hammer if it decided to go about wrecking a home. In the safety of his study he burst out laughing.

Perhaps it was the radio playing down east fiddle tunes or perhaps it was the vacuum cleaner; whatever it was, it had the effect of exorcising Malcolm of his urge to solve the mysterious happenings at Odd's End. He picked up the crumpled note saving Mrs. Rapsey the trouble and the questions it might elicit and put it away with the other "clues." The scent of perfume hung around him, but with the comforting and identifiable noises of the cleaning lady in the background Malcolm pushed ahead on his paper, taking the precaution to check his notes for further disturbances beforehand.

He was startled when some time later he turned to find Mrs. Rapsey standing behind him holding her broom like a rifle across her chest. For one horrifying moment he thought she . . .

"Yes, Mrs. Rapsey, what can I do for you?"

"I was wondering should I bother with the front room?" Malcolm looked at the door. He didn't know anything about the front room or the arrangements about its cleaning while it was not used. From the way she had asked the question, he decided she didn't really want to bother with it so he suggested as much.

She nodded. "Mrs. Close be home next week?"

"Yes, maybe she will."

Mrs. Rapsey left finally at about four. The wounded Plymouth gathered her up and farted its way up the hill. Exit suspect number three.

The paper had been going well and Malcolm took a break to garden. Before long he was bathed in sweat and decided to take a swim. He gathered his bathing suit, but once he was on the beach, he decided to skinny dip, one of the luxuries of isolation. He plunged into the waves and surfed back into the shore. The party with Kevin and Bliss was the only other time he had been in the water that year. He wasn't much of an outdoor man but he loved to splash around. The water was invigorating, icy; so much so that he could only stay in a few minutes at a time and then he would rush out to lie on the hot sand. When he was dry he would race into the cool water again. This went on for an hour. Finally he lay down to dry off before going up to the house. He felt delightfully exhausted – sensual – the hot sun and the pounding waves; the wind washing the heat over him. He could feel each tiny bead of water, every fiber in his body responded.

He felt as though every cubic millimeter of his flesh

could talk. Stimulated and simultaneously relaxed – the mind drugged by the sea and the sun. The life of the flesh – the world ruled by Eros, but there was one thing missing, and without even trying to stop himself, Malcolm found himself thinking of Angela.

Angela, not his friend and colleague, but voluptuous Angela. The note had disturbed him; the perfume disturbed him more. Now she was disturbing him in a way he had not allowed her to in a long time. *If* the note was from her, then she was not in love with him, she was desperately, psychopathically infatuated. Such an idea was awesome – a terrifying responsibility, but not here in the sun with his body tuned and keen. Angela, the erotic fantasy. He had imagined her in bed, but now infinitely more desirable was the thought of her here, naked beside him. The idea possessed him, playing over him like the hot fingers of the sun, the tickling wind. The vision grew more lurid. His body was aroused, his muscles were taut, his pulse was huge. Not an adequate lover now, but a monumental, a brilliant lover. He would match her desperate needs with a vigorous performance and she would respond like an animal. She crouched over him, her breasts hanging above his face, her red hair in his eyes like the sun. The vision was animal entirely. In his fantasies, women always responded like grateful pets, panting and begging for more. Malcolm imagined convincing Angela through the force of his love to give up her persecution in return for a night together now and then. In his fantasy she was happy with whatever she could get.

Later he sat with a beer on the steps. He prickled all over with a new sunburn; he had lain on the beach too long. The sun was already behind him, somewhere, setting over Fundy. In an hour he was expected in Lunenburg for dinner. He planned to stay the night and would drive directly to Halifax the next day.

He didn't feel guilty about his daydream. One learns to live with fantasy, he had told himself, the way one learns to live with a real person. But the throbbing vision of Angela had stayed with him as he had left the shore. He thought of phoning her. He wasn't going to. By the time he had reached the house the dream had dissipated. He hadn't ever thought much about infidelity, one way or another, until he met Angela. If the idea was titillating, it was also full of dread. He did not think of himself as having the *savoir-faire* to conduct an extramarital relationship without a great deal of anguish. He was too damn Anglo-Saxon for his own good, or was he just too moral in a half-assed kind of way? And yet how easy it was to have sexual fantasies and how very easy it was to alleviate them. A simple and mechanical gesture – the body stirred briefly into action, taken in hand, literally, and so relieved. And then afterwards, no real regrets. The mystery he had found himself caught in had captured his imagination like a sexual fantasy. An idea, a solution, would insinuate its way into his mind, startling him the way a sexual fantasy did. The solutions never seemed real and yet were briefly compelling and his sense of reasoning had been, so far, little more than mental masturbation. The solutions came quickly, too quickly, and were unsatisfactory. He was too busy to play detective or was he just afraid – afraid of what he might find out if he looked too closely into the lives around him or, worse yet, afraid of the conclusions the mystery had so far driven him to about those lives. All the same ideas impressed themselves upon him constantly, working away in his subconscious if not springing into his conscious.

The fantasy about Angela had been appealing not because it was erotic, but because it was diabolical. He could not imagine actually loving anyone who resorted to such lengths but somewhere in his libido lurked a primitive Malcolm who could. And not so buried was an ego that cheered the hulk on. It is enticing to fancy oneself wanted, needed.

Sitting now with the sun almost down, showered and shaved, and smelling of shampoo, aftershave, deodorant, and freshly laundered clothes – the hulk was vanquished. The libido safely clothed. He felt altogether too cultured for anything so seamy. The archetypal battle for good and evil, Beauty and Beast; ultimately one – an identity. Jekyll and Hyde – the same man. There were times when he had imagined the tormentor, the trespasser, the intruder, the joker – whatever he was – was actually the devil himself. The range and the subtlety of his torment was cruel and crueler still in its insinuation. But it was cruelest in that it was uncalled for. What grudge could anyone have against them that could invoke such invidious cruelty? He thought again; what grudge could any *one* person have? He stopped with his bottle raised to his lips. Unless there were more than one.

Not a group but an unconscious collaboration. Persons each with entirely different motives for wanting to upset the Close household. Malcolm put down his bottle gingerly as if afraid that a sudden noise might jar this new notion from his brain. He walked calmly back to his study, although his mind was racing ahead. He needed paper and a pen. He needed to make a list, to map out the sequence of events with this new theory still buzzing around in his head, revisiting his earlier suspicions, rearranging them as quickly as he exploded them. No, not a group because that meant a conspiracy and that was precisely what it was not. He sat at his desk, and as if his pen were thinking for him, he ruled a line down the center of a sheet of loose-leaf. On one side of this ledger he wrote MARY on the other side he wrote ANGELA.

His first entry was under his wife's name – *the banquet*. As soon as he had written it, he knew he would need another sheet which he labeled MOTIVES. He numbered the banquet "1" and on his motives page he hastily summarized: *bored, upset with work, too often alone, determines to make hubby sit up and take notice*.

He sat back and looked at this footnote. It was a marvelous idea, not really malicious and certainly attention-getting. For a few days it had been a matter of mutual concern, underline *mutual*. She had probably meant to tell him but had enjoyed the lark and been carried away. Finally when Malcolm began to joke about it, she had interpreted his levity as indifference and decided to play on. He entered a "2" and circled it. This also was under Mary's name and beside it he wrote *any number of little perversities*. It had a nice ring to it and why bother listing them. None of them really wicked, perhaps not exactly good-housekeeping but easily classifiable as practical jokes. And that was all it was meant to be: an attempt to get his attention. Enter suspect number two. Under her name he entered *sunglasses*, after all she was the most reasonable person to have planted them there. He had told her all about the mysterious banquet and all the other incidents as they occurred. She had a car and she had the time and she was clever. None of which was really motive, only opportunity, but the motive was quickly obvious and he entered it on his second sheet of paper. *Love.* He had thought about it earlier and suppressed the idea, passing it off as fantasy. She was very much in love with him. He had always wanted to sleep with her but she wanted more, much more. Angela saw in the disturbances a chance to disrupt Malcolm's marriage and to be there for the rebound. He remembered her frustration at their last meeting. He remembered her strong grip on his hand.

The theory was outrageous but no longer as outrageous as it had been to imagine one person. If two people were guilty, they were each only half as guilty; that, of course, was not how the law would see it but the law was not going to see it. It was a family matter. He went on to list all the little crimes guessing on which side of the ledger they fell. Poor Mary; once her innocent enough little subterfuge backfired it was too much to take and too late to apologize. How confused she must have become. And that's when the spring slipped. He suspected it was easy for someone with Mary's active imagination to believe someone else was painting her paintings, or even that they were painting themselves. The machine had a

170

life of its own, that's what she would think; her plot was breeding tiny plots. That was the way her mind would work.

Angela's letter to herself was a *tour de force*. She must have found a letter from Mary in the drawer and traced it or whatever. As the list grew, all the entries seemed to fall naturally on the right side of the ledger. Mary must have withdrawn from the unconscious contest early in the campaign. With increasing alarm, he realized how the little crimes grew more and more unpleasant.

Malcolm stopped again. He would need another page for listing ambiguities and unanswerable questions. Where, for instance, did Angela Treadway learn to pick a lock? Who exactly took the picture in the park (Angela's roommate Karen?), and who wrote the letters to Tom and Kevin? It couldn't have been Mary unless she was unaware of what she was doing. And there were more questions; on the night of the stakeout, was it Angela in the studio? Impossible!

He threw down his pencil; he had gnawed off the end. A fictional detective could have made it work, but then in a fiction, all the crimes and clues would have been tailored to fit; the puzzle would suddenly appear to fall into place. His own puzzle was full of holes. Looking at his watch he realized he was late. One more go at it, the idea wasn't so bad. Maybe there were more clues he hadn't seen. What, for instance, if Mary had sent Angela a note in the first place that Angela had never shown him? God knows there may have been hundreds of notes. For that matter what if Mary and Angela *had* conspired? New end to a suspense thriller: they all did it! That was unthinkable or at least unmanageable. With a sigh, Malcolm gave up, for the present in any case. A moment later, he was slamming the Fiat door shut. He revved up the car and turned up the radio full blast.

The evening in Lunenburg was a pleasant one. Tom had been released from his engagement at the Pines for a couple of days due to a convention there at which his services were not required, and he had been helping Kevin and Mary rearrange the shop. By the time Malcolm arrived, the other three were hungry and thirsty and in a mood to celebrate a hard day's work. No one had any energy so beer was picked up and pizza was ordered. Later they went to a film, a dreadful suspense film at the drive-in.

Back at the apartment afterwards, they talked and drank until quite late. Kevin mentioned a movie in passing that so intrigued Malcolm that Kevin and Tom were forced between them to remember the whole story. It had been a box-office failure called *They Might Be Giants*. George C. Scott was an eccentric millionaire who believed himself to be Sherlock Holmes. His powers of ratiocination were as profound as those of his namesake but for Scott everything was a "case" and behind every "case" lurked Moriarty. Clues were everywhere to be found; scratched on any wall, in any trash can. All it took to make something a clue was to believe it was. He enlisted the support of Joanne Woodward, who became his Doctor Watson, and a faithful band of followers, who like Scott, saw all of life as a mystery with Moriarty always near at hand.

Malcolm thought of the theory he had concocted earlier in the day. Little crimes everywhere, and yet what clues were there? He lay awake for a long time after Mary had fallen asleep beside him; this was suspect number one? All of a sudden he felt strangely out of control as if he were being swallowed up by the mystery which pervaded Odd's End. Moriarty was behind it. He fell asleep thinking of Moriarty.

21

Angela was not at the faculty meeting the next day. Term
was long over, and as a part-time instructor she was not
required to attend. Still, she usually did; she had the week
before. Malcolm couldn't help wondering if it was merely
coincidence that she was away.

After the meeting, he phoned her house. Karen answered
and he could tell that something was wrong. At first Karen
didn't want to say anything but finally she spoke up. Angela
had not come home the night before. As far as Karen knew
Angela did not have a boyfriend who she was on "overnight" terms with, but then these things could happen
rapidly. Yes, Malcolm supposed, they could. He thanked her
and hung up.

Angela was not at home the next day either when he
called. Curiouser and curiouser. After leaving the office,
Malcolm dropped in at Henry Street. Karen was glad to see
him and invited him in. In twenty-four hours she had
become noticeably more worried. Angela might on occasion
be away for a night without telling her but it was not like her
to be away for two nights without phoning. Karen was obviously perturbed about something else, and without much
coaxing she admitted to having phoned Angela's parents in
New Brunswick, thinking Angela might have gone there for
a visit. Without meaning to, she had alarmed them and in

trying to reassure them had made matters worse. She was alarming Malcolm as well, but he didn't say so. A detective would have foreseen this; it would not have occurred to Malcolm in a million years, but how neatly it fit into his theory. He dreaded to think where she would next show up.

He left Henry Street with Karen's promise that she would contact him if and when she heard from her roommate. There was one other thing, she called out after him. Angela had not taken her toothbrush.

Malcolm dropped by the school again and asked around. No one remembered Angela's mentioning that she was going away. There were so many possible answers to her disappearance; Malcolm wasn't sure which one worried him most.

Again he spent the evening at Hope Springs Eternal. Kevin and Tom were away, and Malcolm found himself only half-looking forward to an evening alone with Mary. In two days his bizarre little theory, despite its inconsistencies, had grabbed him and taken root in his imagination. Angela's disappearance had somehow made it all seem feasible, although he could not exactly explain why. He knew that he wanted to stay at Odd's End in case she showed up. He no longer desired her, but neither was he frightened. He would be able to handle it somehow or other. She wanted him alive, didn't she?

Mary seemed much better and without really thinking he asked about her therapy. She became evasive, and Malcolm found himself irritated. Both were determined not to go through another of the tiffs that had characterized Mary's last week or two at Odd's End, and so the conversation became progressively more awkward. Mary tried to be cheerful, Malcolm ended up sulking. He decided to watch television and Mary went to wash the dishes. As he stared distractedly at the television, his mind wandered elsewhere. Suddenly Mary was back in the room.

"Shall I move home again?"

Malcolm looked up at her with surprise. "I'm not sure . . . ."

"I'm not sure either, but I will. It's good here, so relaxing working in the shop, I'm sure I'm a lot stronger."

Why couldn't he speak? Even if she had been the one who had started all the nonsense at home, she wanted to come back now; it might be her way of asking forgiveness. She wanted to come home and start over. But Angela might show up! He was sure of it and Mary mustn't be there; who could tell what she might do.

"Why don't you stay here until you go to Toronto?" he suggested.

"I suppose I could, but don't you go liking being alone." The scolding was affectionate, she patted his hand and went back into the kitchen. Had she been able to read his face as he agonized over what to say to her?

He came up behind her at the sink and put his arms around her.

"I'm sorry," he said into her ear.

She smiled and rubbed her cheek against his.

"It's just my paper. I haven't got much done."

He glanced at her to see if his excuse had passed muster. She looked as though she wanted to believe him.

The next day Gruber phoned him at Odd's End to say the shoeprint had been neither Malcolm's, Kevin's, nor Tom's. As slim as this line of investigation seemed – one full footstep and part of a second – how much more tenable it was than Malcolm's theories, his masturbatory detection. From those footsteps, they could build a man, a phantom, six foot one or two and maybe one hundred and ninety pounds. Gruber wanted to send someone down to the house if Malcolm was going to be there. The house would be checked out more thoroughly and a full statement would be taken. Malcolm decided to say as little as possible about Angela.

There was nothing linking her absence to the incidents at Odd's End. He would wait and see.

Corporal Skimpole was assigned to the job. He arrived at two o'clock and went right to work while Malcolm typed away in the study.

Malcolm shouldn't have been surprised when the corporal found a Polaroid camera. He shouldn't have been surprised that it had been wrapped up in paint rags and stowed in the back of a cupboard in the studio. After all that was how the envelopes had been found – hidden in the back of a drawer. He remembered the day in the garden when Mary had produced them. She had been frightened, frightened of him, of what he might do. Skimpole said nothing, he would make his suspicions known in appropriate officialese in his report. To that end, he took a long and thorough statement from Malcolm. Ostensibly it was the same camera that had been used to take the picture in the park. Malcolm explained about the picture. It was obvious immediately to the officer that Angela would have to be contacted. Malcolm said nothing about her absence. No other clues could be found in the house but the corporal asked if he might take the valise and its contents. Malcolm handed it over with relief.

Karen phoned at five. Angela had written her, a simple note really:

Dear Karen,

You are no doubt wondering what has become of your roommate. Sorry to have left so abruptly. Needed to be alone for a while and so I haven't told a soul. Just needed to think things through by myself. Sorry if it has caused you any grief. See you soon.

Yours, Angela.

Karen bubbled on enthusiastically. She was a little annoyed but nonetheless relieved. The next day she had been going to phone the police. She was glad she wouldn't have to. Malcolm listened and waited. The letter was post-marked from Mahone Bay. Karen asked whether that wasn't quite near where Malcolm lived and he said it was. He added that she might have just been passing through. Karen could not hide what she was thinking. Malcolm could almost hear her wink over the phone. From his first meeting with her, he felt she was assuming the role of go-between. He didn't imagine Angela had told her all that much but Karen implied she had been told everything. Whatever that was. Karen had somehow decided that the letter was for Mal-colm's ears, and she seemed to say, It's okay. I know what's up. She sloughed off Malcolm's suggestion that Angela had just been passing through. Karen, he decided, was really quite intolerable. He couldn't help sounding irritated when he finally interrupted her. There was one other thing he had to know: was the letter typed? To his surprise it wasn't and Karen was sure it was Angela's handwriting. People didn't usually take their typewriters when they were getting away to mull things over, did they? she asked. Malcolm supposed they did not. He thanked Karen shortly and hung up.

Why had Angela not phoned? Why always silent commu-nications? She may have been passing through Mahone Bay or she may be waiting there. It was a small place; was he meant to go and look for her? He would do no such thing. He would wait.

That night Malcolm dropped off some more clothes for Mary but decided not to stay; he had so much work to do. He was only gone from the house for two hours, but when he arrived home there was yet another note propped against his typewriter and it was in a woman's hand:

Dearest,
I have behaved abominably. You will understand in time. It's still too early to show myself ... when Mary's gone. Try to be patient with me and please don't hate me. You will understand, I know you will. I love you.

There was no signature, nor any heading for that matter, but he knew it had to be from her. The woman was obviously mad. He had been right; his theory had been right, yet he could scarcely believe it. He held the letter closer for inspection. Again his senses were bombarded by perfume. The writing was not a forgery, he felt sure. He had no writing of Angela's to compare it with, but it was not mechanical in the way that the letter from Mary had been. Why the cloak and dagger? Surely she couldn't expect to torment him into loving her. She had succeeded in getting Mary out of the house, but now she was using the same tactics on him! Malcolm shivered to think of his fantasy of a few days earlier. This was sordid; Fielding had been right; it was psychopathic. Angela must be helped. Malcolm fell back in his chair. He stared at St. Michael's worn, sad face, at the dragon's anemic fangs. She could be here right now. He felt simultaneously repulsed and thrilled.

He should phone the police. He had a moral responsibility, even a legal responsibility. To withhold information when they were investigating a case was criminal itself. But he had a responsibility to Angela, too. And surely the height or depth of *ne pas savoir faire* was to have the police conduct one's extramarital affairs! When he came to think of it, plainly and simply he was embarrassed. It now seemed likely that he had dragged the authorities in to view a little dirty laundry. No doubt they were used to it. Gruber would be understanding enough, but Malcolm didn't wish to imagine Skimpole's face when he was informed. It was all so convoluted. No, it was downright kinky. He had to deal with it himself. He would tell the police as soon as Angela had contacted him in person. He had to be sure. Having come to that decision he rose quietly from his desk and went to explore the house.

The brass bell above the door rang noisily. Mary looked up at the man who had entered the store and smiled. Then she went back to marking prices on an assortment of knick-knacks displayed on the counter before her. Again for the hundredth time she thought how soothing it was to work at such a job, how pleasant and varied each little task seemed from painting. She knew it couldn't last but it made for a good vacation. Suddenly she was aroused from her musing, aware of an immediate presence. The man who had entered the shop only a minute ago was standing before her across the tall glass counter. She had not heard his approach. She started and the man smiled at her surprise. His voice was mellifluous.

"Is Mr. Brain about?"

"He is busy at the moment. May I help?"

She wished Kevin were there. She wasn't very good with customers, especially ones who crept up on her. The man did not answer her question immediately. Then he smiled again and shook his head. Not knowing what else to do she smiled weakly and went back to work. The man did not move, however, and after a moment she looked up. His head was cocked to one side and he had been staring at her.

"Forgive my impertinence but are you not a painter?"

Mary nodded blankly.

"Yes." The man scratched his bearded chin. "Mary Close." He said her name slowly and deliberately. "A very good painter, I might add."

Mary was a bit surprised, but since the article had appeared in *Halifax* an unlikely assortment of people had recognized her on the street or when she was shopping. She blushed and thanked him.

"I have seen your work in Ialanthe Gallery." The man pointed a long finger into the air and began to declaim stentoriously: "Broad throbbing gestural sweeps with swallow-like passages of venous tracery!"

Then the astonishing fellow laughed robustly. Before she could say anything, he shook his head. "No, my dear, it is not coincidence; it is cribbed from Devon Kutter's review in *Artscanada*."

Verbatim, she thought, and as if he had read her thoughts he pointed dramatically at his head.

"The photographic mind, Mrs. Close, the photographic mind."

More than ever, Mary wished Kevin would hurry up.

"May I inquire as to the direction of your recent work? I assume that this" – he took in the whole shop with a broad sweep of his hand – "is a sidelight, a mere bagatelle."

Mary was not sure whether he really wanted an answer or not; in any case she found it hard to talk about her work. The man, to her dismay, was waiting.

"Well, I . . . it is much the same, stylistically." The man nodded enthusiastically like a teacher waiting for his student to spew forth answers by rote. He encouraged her to continue.

"I am trying some new techniques and experimenting with . . . more contrived color . . ." It was difficult to go on. The man nodded his head still more vigorously, impatiently, she thought, and his brow was furrowed deeply. "I . . . am trying to get more surface . . . ." Suddenly she couldn't look at him any more and she dropped her eyes to the shoe box of knickknacks she had been marking. She felt distinctly foolish. She noticed the man's hands on the counter resting lightly on the glass like those of a pianist. What kind of a man was he? He spoke intelligently but in an antiquated manner. His face was tanned and weathered like a laborer's but his fingers, though strong, were slender, and the skin was not tough.

Now the man began to talk about her work, and as if he realized his hands were on display, he began to gesticulate in a theatrical manner. In fact, his whole manner was too theatrical, overblown, unreal. She did not look up except briefly to nod at statements that seemed as if they required acknowledgement. Mostly it didn't matter whether she was there or not, for the man seemed almost in a trance. He was theorizing, not talking, telling her about her own work but not really about her work. He spoke only in generalizations. She found that although she was distinctly conscious of the man's presence, she was only listening with half an ear. She watched his hands. They were clean but showed slight stains. When he finally stopped his diatribe she asked him whether he was a painter.

Surprisingly he clasped his hands to his chest instantaneously. Then he smiled a close-lipped smile.

"A Sunday painter only, Mrs. Close."

"You are very knowledgeable for a Sunday painter," she said, trying to even out her voice.

"Ah, but I am only a dilettante, nonetheless."

In fact, thought Mary, he didn't talk like a painter at all. He was too articulate. Now she noticed that her question seemed to have thrown the man off stride. His expression had lost its sureness.

Just then a noise on the steps attracted their attention, and they turned to see Kevin enter the shop from the apartment. And not a minute too soon, she thought. When she looked at the man again she could not believe her eyes. He had changed entirely. His cheeks had lost their ruddiness and for a large man he seemed small and somehow older than she had thought at first. To her horror, Kevin invited the man to tea, but he politely refused. He picked up one of the recently marked objects before him on the counter, a silver coffee spoon; noting the price, he paid for it with exact change. In another moment, he had shuffled out the door.

Mary did not realize until he was out of sight down the street how tense she had been. Kevin noticed and slipped his arm around her shoulder.

"Had a lively little time with the old gent, did you?"

She shuddered. "I almost died when you invited him to stay."

Kevin laughed. "It's the only way to get him to leave. It

happens every time; likes to chatter for a while and then, *poof*, he's gone. Strange old bird."

Mary awoke with a start. The room was dark; it was the middle of night. She had been having a dream. Over and over again, she had painted the same dark canvas. Then on the canvas an image appeared slowly and out of it came two hands, long stained fingers which grabbed at her own hands. The painting laughed horribly and she knew it was the man in the store, laughing over and over and grabbing at her hands.

22

The next few days did not pass comfortably for Malcolm Close. There was no more substantial evidence to either back up or disprove his theory and so it festered. He looked for clues every day everywhere. He didn't go to the college. When he drove into Lunenburg he would scour the house upon his return. Had his chair been in precisely that position when he left? Hadn't the telephone book been under the phone? One morning he stared at the kitchen curtains not sure whether he recognized them or whether he had just never noticed them before.

The house was full of a thousand little mutabilities. The mystery that had been planted in his mind pervaded his perception. Feeling he knew the source of the mysteries did not change their mysteriousness – for they were still unexplained. The house was seething with mystery. In a much subtler fashion the house was being turned topsy-turvy just like the doll's house. Not violently demanding attention, but insistently, challenging his attention.

A house was supposed to be an extension of oneself, noticeable only in the same way a person notices his own limbs, from time to time. It should be loved, certainly, and respected and insured, but otherwise taken for granted. One couldn't afford to be constantly questioning a home any more than one could always be questioning oneself. Your home was supposed to be on your side! A stronghold against the chaos of the world at large. Chaos seemed to be seeping into Odd's End, and Malcolm could not find the leak. He recalled a recently separated friend who had taken a tiny walk-up apartment which he spoke of affectionately. At last, he would say, I have peace. Peace, it seemed, meant that a magazine left open at a particular page would be open there the next day, the next week or forever, as you so desired. That was the way it was supposed to be at home: nothing altered unless you altered it yourself.

He thought of Mary with her acute perception. How little time it had taken to overthrow her. This mutability. It had to do with a sense of place. A sense of place was like the under-pinning to a sense of self. Once the one was stripped away, the familiar rendered unfamiliar from day to day, the other, the sense of self, became shaky. Home was like the psychic foundation.

On another occasion he thought of a childhood book his mother had read him. It was about little tricksters who are held responsible for all the household odds and ends which go missing. *The Borrowers*. What fiendish relative of the Borrowers had come to Odd's End? He thought he knew. It was as if she was already living there. Not visiting but *living* there. Not content to steal, only to rearrange, the house and his life. Living with him like an invisible harpy. It was a macabre courtship. But it was also tantalizing, Angela living with him in his house invisibly.

Somehow amid the flux he sensed all around him his paper took its final shape. He had only the tedious proce-dure of rechecking his sources and making out footnotes and a comprehensive bibliography. He saw Mary only once dur-ing the week. The chance that he might finish in time to join her in Toronto made the temporary separation seem not so bad. But he knew he didn't dare leave until he had made contact with Angela; God only knew what she might do in her present condition; and so Malcolm let Mary believe he would join her on the Monday following the opening, hoping that Angela would make a move by then. Since he couldn't travel with her, Mary decided to leave on Thursday. Malcolm hoped that this would give Angela an extra day. He had no idea how closely she was following their movements but he suspected she would find out about Mary's early departure since she knew so much else. And she would respond quickly. The waiting was getting to him.

Corporal Skimpole was back in touch with Malcolm. Without his saying so, Malcolm could tell the officer was annoyed at not having been told on his earlier visit of Angela's disappearance. They now wanted her for questioning. Malcolm could imagine the innuendo in Karen's voice as she read Angela's letter to the police. Meanwhile he was going to keep silent about the latest letter; he wasn't even sure why. He explained his relationship with Angela to Skimpole and from the gleam in the policeman's hawk eye, Malcolm felt sure the officer had come to a similar conclusion as he had himself about Angela's plans. Still Malcolm wanted to play it his way.

Bliss phoned on Tuesday to speak to Mary. She responded dramatically when Malcolm told her of Mary's incarceration. It was a stupid choice of words; Malcolm used it to try to make the affair seem less serious, but it had exactly the opposite result. Then when he started to explain what had happened, she cut him off, anxious to talk to Mary herself. Malcolm was irritated by the call; Bliss had not been rude but she had dismissed him.

Mary was in Kevin's shop when Bliss phoned her. Bliss wasted no time getting to the crux of the matter, and Mary found herself opening up as she hadn't, not even to Kevin, since she left her home. She could see Bliss listening, smoking her cigarette carefully. She told Bliss everything that had happened, and Bliss, in her dramatic way, made each morsel of information seem important. When Mary casually mentioned the man who had visited the shop and turned up again in her nightmare, Bliss pushed Mary to describe him in detail, as if she might know him, though of course she didn't.

"Had you ever seen him before?"

"No," answered Mary immediately and then paused. "No, I'm sure I haven't," she added more slowly.

There was a pause, and then Bliss spoke with her curious urgency. "Are you sure?"

"Bliss, what are you getting at? Do you know something you aren't saying?"

"I don't *know* anything, Mary, and I wouldn't hold back on you if my life depended on it, but I'm sure *you* must know something."

Mary found herself caught up in Bliss's urgent inquiry as if by desire alone an answer could be wrung from her. But the answer was still No. They talked a little while longer. A future date was set for a luncheon, and the strange phone call ended.

It was an hour later when the phone in the store rang again and Mary jumped. She had been deep in thought ever since Bliss had phoned.

"Mary."

"Bliss, is it you again?"

"I can't get this idea out of my head."

"What idea? Are you all right? You sound terrible."

"I'm fine, I'm sorry to be troubling you."

"Bliss, darling, you aren't troubling me. What's the matter?"

"I can't get it out of my head ... you have never seen the man in the store before?"

There was another unbearable silence. Later Mary couldn't remember if it was Bliss who said it or herself. It was like a small explosion in her brain not spoken at all, not made of words, only a series of images:

The man on the Indian Spit.
The birdwatcher.
Manshadow.

On the Wednesday before her departure, Malcolm had
planned to spend the night with Mary at the shop and drive
her to Halifax in the morning. At dinner he found her
strangely out of sorts. She seemed to try too hard to keep the
conversation bright though she looked anything but bright.
She seemed anxious, and Malcolm wondered if there had
been a relapse. She insisted that it was the exhibition. Now
that it was upon her she was frightened. It was a reasonable
excuse, but Malcolm still felt she was holding out on him.
Kevin was oddly silent throughout the evening.

The next morning, Malcolm was shocked when Mary suggested that he need not drive her to the airport. Kevin was to
pick up a piece of furniture in the city and he could easily
drop her off. Again she was insistent. Now Malcolm was
sure there was something she was not telling him, but he
could see in her eyes that she had no intention of letting him
know what. It was not, he thought, a calculated stab, but it
might just as well have been. He was being given a second
chance; he had no other choice but to trust her. He had no
idea what was going on.

Their parting in mid-morning was a quiet, dreary affair
swathed in a mystery Mary was not prepared to share. By
Monday everything would be fine, she promised. Malcolm
nodded. He hoped so.

When the phone rang an hour and a half later at Odd's End
Malcolm shot into the air from his seat. It must be Angela
and yet he was incapable of believing she could respond so
quickly to Mary's departure. He must have expressed every
bit of his mingled terror and excitement when he said hello

because the voice at the other end of the line laughed as soon as she spoke. It was Mary. She was at the airport. Kevin had left. She had only phoned to reiterate her love. That was all. No explanation for her secrecy was forthcoming. Trust me, she said. He had no other choice.

How odd it was talking to her like that while she waited at the airport alone. It was as if they were not husband and wife but only good friends. It was sad, somehow.

The idea dogged him all day, until his sadness had become an honest-to-God funk. Mary had always been the moody one, but since she had gone he felt he had become increasingly moody himself, running the entire gamut of emotions; an emotional yoyo. The idea that at any moment Angela might phone him only made matters worse.

The day dragged by. A haze covered the sun, the heat gathered around him only adding to his discomfort. Somehow he managed to keep to the task at hand: checking his sources, writing footnotes – tedious stuff for a tedious day. But the anticipation built hour by hour. At five he made a tall gin and tonic with paper-thin slices of lime. He walked down to the beach holding the glass in both hands feeling the cool spread from his palms through his body. The sea was leaden and gray without highlights. A storm must be gathering somewhere up the coast behind the thick curtain of heat. The birds were quiet.

He didn't feel like eating, he had eaten little all day, but eventually he could stay away from the house no longer. He made himself another drink. He decided to listen to the stereo, something to lift him from his funk, something up-tempo, but he settled on Billie Holiday instead; sultry and blue. He fell into a chair to sit and wait. He was prepared to languish away the evening waiting.

When his eyelids started to fall he assumed he was tired. When he attempted to go upstairs he knew he was drunk. As soon as he climbed into bed, however, he knew he wasn't going to sleep. The air was close around him. The bedroom, usually so airy, was like a tinderbox. He was too tired to do anything about it. When he shut his eyes the heat became like a presence in the room, and he opened them immediately. He would drift off, and then he would remember and fight his way back to consciousness.

He was alone. She had him to herself – drunk. Of course she would make her entrance by night. He would wake and find her naked beside him or like a dead weight on top of him. The thought sent shivers down his back. The erotic dream was over; the confrontation would be anything but erotic. It would be like this weather, wet and heavy.

At three o'clock he gave up all pretence of sleep. He would do an all-nighter, the way he used to in school, with a pot of coffee on the stove and all the lights on. Around five the sun began to rise, or at least the fog outside became a brighter shade of gray – pretty really – opalescent. The birds began their morning song and Malcolm wearily reconsidered the delights of sleep. In the bedroom there was just the hint of a cool breeze. He opened the windows full and propping himself with pillows sat in the window seat. He had seen Mary sleep there sometimes. The image, however, was more comfortable than the reality. A light rain began to fall. He fell asleep, anyway, his head against the rain-splattered sash.

It was the phone. He had no idea how long it had been ringing. He uncurled himself from a tangle of damp pillows and blindly stumbled into the hall. It was Anne MacCready. There were, she said, quite a number of letters for him at the college including one from Harvard that was probably about the conference. She had thought it might be important. Malcolm waited, not sure whether a question had been asked or not. Should she send them down to him? Even as he replied that she needn't bother he knew it was not the reason she had phoned. Malcolm at last woke up. Mrs. MacCready had heard that Angela was missing. Malcolm explained that not to be the case but before he could finish Mrs. MacCready, refusing to be thwarted from her story,

189

proceeded. They had found her car. It was hidden in the woods off a farm road near Duckworth. The Halifax police had phoned Mrs. MacCready only that morning. They wanted to speak to any members of the department who might be able to give information as to Angela's whereabouts. They had not, as yet, set a date for these interviews but she was phoning everyone in advance to tell them. Malcolm thanked her for the warning. Apparently the police were to be at the college that afternoon to examine Angela's office. His astonishment as this news filtered through his consciousness woke Malcolm fully. Asking when exactly the police were to be there, he told his secretary that he wished to speak to them and would drive down.

"Good," Mrs. MacCready said. "You can pick up your mail while you're at it." The statement obviously pleased her sense of propriety, after all that was why she had phoned him in the first place.

He was going to add that he had information for them but he decided to wait, one last procrastination. How relieved he would be to unburden himself. He showered and changed, then drove through a steady drizzle and clinging fog which stretched from Odd's End all the way up the coast to Halifax.

The scene at the offices of the Department of English was unusual, to say the least, for a Friday in June. Everyone was there. Everyone except Billings, who was in England on sabbatical, and Angela. Mrs. MacCready had phoned them all, and they had all decided to drop round to pick up their mail; mail that could have waited until Monday, or, for that matter, until September.

When Malcolm arrived they were milling around in the common room. Anne MacCready and Connie Tippet, another secretary, had made coffee. Dr. Seigal, the head of the department, was circulating in a pale blue leisure suit, the closest he ever got to informality, anxious to make his staff comfortable. Despite his audible attempts to accomplish this, no one was paying much attention to him; nobody seemed particularly uncomfortable and the conversation was about gardens and cottages not about Angela's disappearance. Sorrel was in his jeans, Farrughan was in tennis whites; a sportive-looking turnout if one considered the reason for the gathering.

As soon as Malcolm entered, however, the topic of conversation turned to Angela. There were so few details known to them that there was little to say about the case except to initiate each new arrival. Most of them had not known Angela outside the department but her friendship with Malcolm, while never broadcast, had found a place in departmental gossip. Malcolm sensed, as he waited, that he was, in their eyes at least, the star witness. He was treated accordingly.

Each of them had already talked to the police officer, Detective Inspector Penny. They had had very little information to offer: Bill Farrughan and his wife had had Angela for supper the week before, on the Monday, and Bill had given her a lift home afterwards. Otherwise no one had seen her since the week previous to that. The detective inspector was presently ensconced in Malcolm's office, Mrs. MacCready hoped he didn't mind; meanwhile two other men were examining Angela's office. The mention of the detective brought knowing winks from the initiates without further comment. The excitement was palpable and even juvenile, Malcolm thought, considering the ages of the faculty. Malcolm had to admit to himself, however, that had he not been so personally entrenched in the case, he would probably have acted much the same way. He felt quite different. Surrounded by his colleagues, Malcolm felt exactly as he had when he was waiting to stand for his Ph.D. oral examination. It had been an ordeal he had hoped never to relive.

Driving through the rain on the way to the college he had thought how liberating it would be to dispense with his responsibility. No matter how embarrassing the truth might appear, he had behaved irresponsibly in not telling all the facts to the RCMP. Perhaps it had been Skimpole's manner but he was inclined to believe it was mostly just his own reluctance to make the police privy to what seemed a sordid affair. And then there was his theory – his precious theory. Despite all the anguish it entailed, mostly for himself, he had wanted to prove his theory correct. Not because he wished any ill to Angela, or Mary for that matter, but just to prove something, to have his chance to be the detective, half-seer, announcing the truth to a startled crowd of suspects, each of whom is guilty of one indiscretion or another, an accessory after or before the fact, but only one of whom is the murderer. It was the detective-as-St.-Peter syndrome; a scene from fiction. Of course there hadn't been a murder, thank God; in fiction there would have to be. He knew he could no longer suppress evidence no matter what it meant. He was tired from an awkward night, and from the awkward month in which his critical powers had been under pressure and had proved wanting; yes, it was like an oral exam but with an invisible voice among his examiners, a voice he could pin no background to and therefore was incapable of answering appropriately. He had never been so irresolute; blowing hot and cold – who had said that, Angela or Mary? – it made no difference, it was true. He was not prone to vacillation. He was a clear thinker, a scholar, and he had attempted to marshal his facts like a scholar but they would not stay still. The facts of this mystery were not committed to the page like the facts of his scholarly research. He would stick to that safe world of investigating literary interpretation when this was over. When this was over.

Malcolm was suddenly aware that he was being talked to.

"Wait until you see the note, Mal," said big Bill Farrughan.

"Right up your proverbial alley." This from Tod Coombs.

"There is a note?"

"Yes – saucy bit of fluff," said Coombs enthusiastically,

his thick Yorkshire accent scarcely dented by his years at Oxford. "Fluff to me, but to you it will probably be Prose." The capital *P* was audible. Coombs had never read anything past Spenser. It was a departmental joke that he considered Henry James *avant-garde*.

"Rhona thinks it's Burgess," said Farrughan. "Salty stuff. The man tends to be a bit onanistic but there is no denying his inventiveness."

Malcolm tapped Rhona Mulhany on the shoulder. "The note?" was all he said.

"Yes, wonderful touch, makes it all like a fiction. I hope it has nothing to do with anything, of course; it's actually quite menacing!" Her whole mood had switched mid-sentence from the scholar to the concerned woman. The note required literary evaluation, it was something Malcolm found himself doing with circulars which came through the mail, fixing the grammar. It was a professional handicap. Rhona continued.

"The good detective asked each of us to guess at the possible meaning. Superficially the meaning is transparent enough but in regards to Angela's disappearance, possible kidnapping ... well, it could be horrific, really." Her mood again shifted. "I think it's Burgess, possibly *MF*; it's more your line."

"I don't think you should worry about the content of the note." It was the ever bubbly Tod Coombs. "It is fictive, preposterous, clueless, except for the fact that it is literate. It appears to be smut but it is literate to the nth degree. That's the clue. That's what I told Penny." Coombs was smug, secure in his opinion. Not having seen the note, Malcolm could only guess, but his guesses were tempered by a surfeit of anonymous notes. He wondered if he would recognize the style. Now Dr. Seigal had joined the circle.

"And you assume, Tod, that meaning is implied not by the content, nor the structure, nor even its grammar, but by its very literateness?" Seigal had an exclamatory manner of speech which made everything he said sound final, even when an answer was expected. Tod Coombs nodded, Rhona said, "Of course, Ken," and Bill Farrughan smiled mysteriously at Malcolm and walked off. Malcolm was left alone with the head, a formidable character even in his blue leisure suit. His thick eyebrow was cocked; he was waiting for a response.

"The clue is that Angela's kidnapper, if there is one, is also a scholar and wants everyone to know it," said Malcolm.

"Context over syntax," said Seigal triumphantly. He closed his eyes dramatically then suddenly opened them again. "What do you mean, Professor Close, by saying *If there is a kidnapper?*"

Malcolm had no desire to share his enlightened situation with Seigal. "Let us hope, Ken, that it is something other than kidnapping."

Seigal was too smart not to recognize the statement as a gloss, but Malcolm was rescued from explaining himself by a woman come to lead him to the inspector. He explained to her that he knew the way. It was meant in good humor and was taken so. The woman was short and sturdy, not in police uniform but rather in a red pants suit, altogether too red for such a muggy day. Her figure was not at all bad but she had a way of walking briskly – "on patrol," he thought – which rendered the hot red not in the least way sensual. He was surprised when she took up a position across from him at his desk and busily organized her notes.

"Professor Malcolm Close," she said checking a list, "I am Detective Inspector Harriet Penny." She smiled briefly and immediately resumed the organization of her notes. It was not in any way a coy gesture but, he suspected, allowed him the opportunity to regain his composure. In her position, she must be used to eliciting surprise. He recalled the knowing winks in the common room – adolescent indeed; professors on their "hols."

Something else caught his attention and crowded every other thought from his mind. The infamous note lay on the desk folded neatly, sitting on its envelope. Had anyone in the common room recognized the stationery's source? He could not remember having ever sent a letter to any of his colleagues on his letterhead. This note was.

"What shall I call you ... Professor, are you all right?"

The question was genuine without ulterior motive. He must have looked dreadful that moment.

"I'm afraid I didn't sleep too well, the weather and all."

"Thank you for driving up. It certainly helps speed up the due processes." She was about to say something else, and Malcolm interrupted, guessing what she was going to say.

"Malcolm would be fine, or Mr. Close. Doctor or Professor always makes me nervous." It was a statement calculated to ease tension – his own.

"I must say your colleagues have been helpful, an enthusiastic bunch. I hadn't hoped to get the preliminaries over quite so quickly." Malcolm doubted they had been of much help except that they could all be dismissed from the investigation.

"Ah, the note," she said, startling Malcolm. He had been trying not to look at it but obviously without success. Her voice was pleasant if brisk, peppermint scented and Irish, Newfoundland Irish.

"Yes, everyone was talking about it; a riddle of some kind?"

"Perhaps. See what you can make of it, the others were prepared to write essays." She was cheerful and, when she smiled, quite pretty. Her chin was weak but her face was ruddy and uncomplicated with the one concession to make-up of eye liner too heavily applied.

The letterhead had been snipped off the page making the note square. It was typed. He would destroy that typewriter, he promised himself. He read.

Meeting her at last
eye to eye, very good to very good, Ay ay.

The soul of a sailor leapt in his pants, settled in his pocket –
wet-snouted, spaniel, playful wagging
Grrrarkkgwaggwark!
She hiccupped into her porcelain-white hand.

Malcolm looked up at the inspector who raised her eyebrow quizzically.

He paid for several drinks too many. Going for walkies,
old chum, wag, wag . . .
   Little giggles, drop of gin, a pearl on the parted lip. To
the sea boy – kiss it off son.
   At his house. White goosebumpled arm under blue serge
arm – kisses planted in yellow hair – a crop of giggles, head
buried in yellow hair – much giggling, much diddling
fore-fore-play, ten for diddling and in the end, at the end,
of the end . . .

Malcolm looked expressionlessly at the inspector. He said
nothing.
   "What is the verdict, doctor?"
   Malcolm sighed deeply. "I know the source."
   "That ties you with, uh, Professor Mulhany."
   "No, I'm afraid I win." It seemed a dramatic way to begin
his narrative. "It isn't Burgess, although there are stylistic
similarities. It's by a Canadian, Trevor Hill, a talented writer,
from a book called *A Heard of Scandal*. The book is not well-
known, not well enough known, but I suppose you don't
really want a critical appraisal."
   "Is the author from the Maritimes?"
   "No, and he isn't a suspect. He lives on the west coast and
is, I believe, crippled."
   "You know a lot about him, Mr. Close."
   Malcolm sighed again. "I ought to. All three of his novels
are sitting on my desk at home – quotations from them dot a
paper I am presently preparing." He paused and chewed on

his lip. "You needn't suspect Mr. Hill. He does not, to my knowledge, have ready access to my typewriter."

The statement got the stir Malcolm had expected it would. It was no use waiting for the inevitable questions that must follow.

"The paper and the envelope are also mine, my wife's and mine. However, I didn't send this letter." Malcolm realized with a shock the base implication he had made and quickly added, "And I am sure it was not sent by my wife."

"The letter wasn't sent Mr. Close, it was found by the car with several other articles that might have fallen from a handbag."

Malcolm could not resist a cynical laugh. "Might have," he murmured. Inspector Penny looked at him gravely, summing up his response. Her own response was canny.

"Only *might have*, Mr. Close. It might have been set up, perhaps by Miss Treadway, as a decoy, which is what you suppose. Why?"

Malcolm was silent for a moment. There were any number of reasons why—where to begin. Before he could, Harriet Penny asked another question.

"Do you know Miss Treadway's whereabouts, Mr. Close?"

"No. I wish I did."

"By the way, Mr. Close, you are not obliged to say anything unless you wish to do so, but whatever you do say will be taken down in writing and may be given in evidence."

Malcolm smiled. "You really have to say that?"

The woman smiled back at him. "The courts like to hear that we did."

Malcolm nodded.

"You haven't seen or heard from her?"

Malcolm sighed again, his head was aching even at the thought of what he had to say. Stick to the facts. Just the facts which refer to Angela for the time being.

He told the inspector of the two most recent notes and

then produced them from his canvas shoulder bag. Inspector Penny dug into her briefcase and took out two letters; the one from Angela to Karen and another, presumably an example of Angela's handwriting from some earlier time. She compared them closely, the three of them.

"Are they the same hand?" Malcolm couldn't resist asking.

Penny had laid the notes aside. "Ostensibly. However, I'm not a specialist. The notes to you and Karen Armstrong might have been written under duress. Mr. Close, please excuse the indelicacy of this next question, but was there an affair between you and Miss Treadway?"

"No. At least it never became an affair. We were good friends; we flirted, but it was not consummated."

"Was there a breakup, then?"

Malcolm hesitated. "Not a breakup, but ... a lot of procrastination on my part." It was a stupid answer only begging the question. Penny seemed to be waiting for elucidation. "There had been ... occurrences at Odd's End, my home that is, which ... mitigated against it; an affair, that is."

"Occurrences?"

Malcolm began to tell the rest of the story, the one he had told the RCMP. He had already signed a statement concerning the happenings at Odd's End. He told this to the inspector. She was interested and wrote several things in her notebook. When she was finished, she spoke again.

"Miss Treadway's car was found near Duckworth and reported from the Steep Cove precinct. Somebody down there is bound to notice the name. I'll get back to them." She was not only interested she was pleased. Malcolm had good reason to be pleased too: the fact he had reported the case already helped to acquit him. With a chill, he realized that he was probably the chief suspect at this point.

She wanted to hear about the occurrences at Odd's End. When Malcolm was finished, she paused a moment, sucking on her pen.

"You seem to believe Miss Treadway is responsible for this elaborate and protracted assault?"

The question was asked without prejudice one way or the other but it was a question, demanding at least an answer of yes or no. How could he say no when for over a week he had been thinking yes? And yet, he did not want to say yes.

He had rejected the idea of Angela's being kidnapped, which had been his very first thought, because he didn't want to think of her being brutalized in any way. When the letters in her hand had appeared he had been able to dismiss the idea wholesale. Ironically, it was easier to think of her as a devious psychopath than to imagine her at the hands of one. It dawned on him just how much he had suppressed the idea of her being in trouble.

"I'm afraid I have believed her responsible," he finally answered.

"But you don't now?"

"I don't know ... I just don't know."

"Nobody else we have talked to thought Miss Treadway in any way imbalanced."

"No. I'm sure that is the case, I mean, I had never thought of her as imbalanced myself." He wanted to say more, to confess, but Inspector Penny was not a priest, he was sure she didn't really care how guilty and stupid he felt. His head ached, and he was beginning to feel sick. He didn't expect the next line of questioning.

"You say your wife has suffered a minor breakdown due to the incidents of harassment?"

Malcolm nodded.

"And she is living in Lunenburg for the time being?"

"Actually, as of yesterday she is in Toronto ... on business."

Penny looked through her notes. "Business? I thought she was an artist?"

"She is – it's art business. She has an exhibition opening."

The inspector acknowledged her *faux pas* with a smile and proceeded.

"When did she move to Lunenburg?"

"The ninth."

The inspector nodded her head abstractedly and tapped her notebook with the end of her pen. The last person who had seen Angela had been Bill Farrughan on the ninth, the day of the stakeout. Penny's expression gave nothing away but Malcolm began to wonder what she was thinking.

"I can give you her number in Toronto."

The inspector looked up from her contemplation. "I don't think that will be necessary at the moment. I'll call you if we wish to contact her. I'd like to come down to Odd's End, perhaps tomorrow, if you don't mind."

Malcolm nodded his assent. The interview was over. Penny reiterated that she would contact Sergeant Gruber. The anonymous footprint might prove helpful. Various footprints around the car had been cast. There might be a correspondence.

Malcolm tried to organize his thoughts as he drove home. Duckworth was five miles from Mahone Bay. It was only across the bay from Odd's End, fifteen miles by road; not more than two miles by boat. Still he couldn't imagine it any more; he wasn't going to try. All he could think about now was Mary. Paper or not, career or not, he wanted to be with her and as soon as possible. He was tired, hungry, and more depressed than he could remember ever having been. He did not relish the thought of spending the night at Odd's End alone.

23

As Malcolm passed through Raven's Bluff an hour after his interview, the sun broke through the clouds, low on the horizon. The Park Road would already be bathed in long dancing shadows pointing down towards the sea. The wind had picked up. It had blown the fog away, and black clouds had scudded in from the sea to take its place. Malcolm was driving fast. He swerved off the Peninsula Road, short-cutting across the overgrown shoulder and into the rutted driveway of the Manor. He geared down only to correct his spin and then geared up again. The Fiat was swallowed in a leafy twilight. The darkness was like a wall forcing him to slow down once more and put on his lights. In the clearing he sped up rounding Rood Manor. Its stone face was lit up momentarily by the eerie light that precedes a storm, blinding like the reflection of fire on copper flashing. Malcolm veered east and headed the car down into the tunnel of trees, more like a chute when he was driving fast, which led to Odd's End. Here and there the same metallic light pierced the gloom, but as he dropped into the woods it grew darker and darker for he was on the nether side of the sunset with the great arched back of the peninsula between it and him.

He was not twenty yards into the turn when the car suddenly fell forward to the left, and was sent careening up the mossy bank and down again before he could regain control. A flat tire. He was about to raise his fist in defiance against whichever god was piling up the odds against him when he noticed the glass. His enemy was neither infernal nor supernal – no bleeding walls, only little things, always little subtle things. The shards of glass were not all that little; he would have seen them if only he hadn't been driving so fast. They were sharp and there were enough of them to stop a tractor trailer. By swerving up the bank he had missed much of the glass and only had one flat. Malcolm sat for a moment before getting out to survey the damage. His inclination was to roll the car home, but it was almost a mile and he knew it would ruin the wheel. Reluctantly he climbed out of the lame and listing car. The left rear tire had also picked up a jagged shard. Malcolm had no idea how deeply the glass was buried. He left it in the tire for the time being. In a sudden rage, he kicked at the broken glass and bottles. He kicked them right and left into the woods, swearing with every kick. Once that was over he settled down to change the flat.

The darkness was settling in. He was tired and nervous, and the job took nearly half an hour. Fully ten minutes of that time were spent looking over his shoulder, up and down and across the narrow roadway. The wind disturbed the woods, displacing branches, gusting suddenly so that brief armies crashed invisibly through the shrouded, blue-green dark.

Malcolm drove slowly. He had been tempted to back up and spend the night in Mahone Bay, guessing that other treacheries awaited him. But he didn't know how long his rear tire would hold out. It wasn't more than a few hundred yards before he was certain the weight of the car was shifting. Checking he found that the glass had been dislodged; the tire was leaking slowly. There was no choice but to proceed to the house.

The yard light was on. He saw it flickering from halfway

up the hill. He had not turned it on. For a moment, without thinking, he hoped it was Mary. He imagined it would turn out to be no one at all. He didn't expect Angela any more; he didn't know what to expect. He slowed the car to a crawl. It was a well-laid trap. He supposed he could turn and drive back but not until he reached the bottom of the road. His best bet was to proceed to the house and phone the police, assuming he still had a phone. He waited with the engine running at the mouth of the courtyard. Out of the woods it was not as dark. The moon appeared fleetingly through breaks in the regiment of black clouds trooping up the bay.

Finally he climbed from the car. He found some stones and put them in his canvas bag which he twisted around his fist. It was something. There were still tools leaning against the shed, and taking a hoe he approached the French doors. The wind whirled around the courtyard making and unmaking spiral trails of sand. All the curtains of the second floor fluttered and lashed out from their black lairs like long white tongues. The windows were all wide open; he couldn't remember if he had left them open. The door was locked as he had left it. Cautiously he opened the door. Inside he listened. He stood still, listening, looking around him, behind into the courtyard. Nothing. A full-scale search was in order but there was something he wanted to do first. He wanted to phone Mary. First Mary and then the police. His last conversation with his wife from the airport had been unsatisfactory. There was a lot to tell her. It could wait but he didn't want to wait. He phoned from the kitchen where there were no walls. He put the hoe down only long enough to dial. The phone rang five times. Finally it was answered by a breathless voice.

"Pip? Malcolm here." Pause. "No, I just got in, why? No, I won't be there—Monday maybe, Pip...she isn't? Yes. I guess so. She didn't? No. No, I didn't take her to the airport, Kevin did. Pip, have her phone me as soon as you see her.

Get her to phone from the airport okay? Yes. Yes, *that* soon. Bye for now, yes, yes. Same from me ..."

Pip had been phoning all day. No Mary. She hadn't even phoned to change her plans. Even if she had missed her flight Thursday morning, there had been flights since. Malcolm had only just put down the receiver when the noisy bedroom alarm went off, startling him. He listened. His heart stopped until it finally ran down. He would not go up; he would phone the police. Then another idea occurred to him. He phoned Kevin, no answer; maybe he had gone to Digby to see Tom. Hell, he could be anywhere. Malcolm threw down the receiver. Irresistibly an idea insinuated itself into his mind, lodging in his brain. The plot was rearranged but strengthened by the latest facts. Both the lead characters were inexplicably missing. One of them had lied about her whereabouts. And Kevin, he had been so odd, almost sullen, the night before yesterday; he had not wanted to look at Malcolm. What had they cooked up? Supposing it had started the way he thought it had, and then Mary had got Kevin to help her, and together they had captured Angela and cooked up the stakeout as a means of getting Mary away from Odd's End. The idea raced through his thoughts growing fantastic. Doctor Fielding had said she wasn't sick, but who was Doctor Fielding? A friend of Kevin's, Kevin's doctor, Malcolm had never met him, how did he know Fielding even existed? Trust her, she had said. "Trust me." It was the last thing she had said to him.

Malcolm suddenly grabbed the phone again and dialed information. The phone rang and rang and while it did he looked round him finally resting his gaze on the staircase. "Hello ... yes, a Doctor Benjamin Fielding in Wolfville. Well then, his office number, please, yes, and that too. Thank you. Thank you." At least he existed. Malcolm phoned one of three numbers. It was the Acadia University switchboard but it was only a security guard and he could not be put through to the office. The guard reminded him it was late; Malcolm thanked him for the reminder and hung up. The second number was the university clinic.

"I'm sorry, Dr. Fielding is not on call. Will you speak to Dr. Shreyer? .... No, I'm sorry I cannot divulge that information .... Are you sure you won't talk to Dr. Shreyer?"

Dead end. There was one more number. As he expected it was the answering service. He hung up without saying anything and a moment later phoned them back.

"Hello, oh damn – excuse me – this is Dr. Shreyer at the clinic. I'm on call with one of Ben's patients and I really ought to consult with him. I wasn't sure if this was his home or office number. Listen ... I know, dear, I know .... Get him to phone me at this number .... Immediately. Thanks."

He hung up and waited. His eyes darted around the room resting again on the staircase. There was no sound but someone had set off his alarm.

"Dr. Fielding? Hello, this is Malcolm Close, Mary's husband. I've used rather a cheap subterfuge to reach you .... Yes, yes, it is urgent. Mary has disappeared. Well, no ... not exactly .... Yes, of course I've phoned the police, but I was wondering if there was anything she might have said which would explain .... No, of course you can't divulge .... Yes, yes ... but I am her husband, sir .... Only three times! Yes ... no, no I'm sure .... Nothing much wrong ... nerves. Thank you, doctor."

Malcolm hung up in a daze. She had only seen him three times. Not once since she moved from Odd's End. Malcolm was suddenly light-headed. She had lied to him; about that and her trip. What was going on? He had the horrible feeling he was going to faint. He couldn't remember when he had last eaten. He leaned against the counter, his face bathed in sweat. He must get a grip on himself, his mind was running away with itself. He found some cold beef and some cheese in the fridge but gagged on it. His throat was like sandpaper. He settled for an orange. He threw each peel across the kitchen at the sink.

He phoned the police. Gruber was not on duty, neither was Skimpole; they had been on the day shift for a week now. The man on desk duty knew nothing about the case; Malcolm tried to explain the situation sticking to what was salient. Without going into it, without listing the details, it sounded rather petty. Littering, albeit with glass; illegal switching on of yard light! No broken windows, no looting. Malcolm didn't want to say he hadn't checked, but he knew anyway. The officer, to his credit, did not take the report lightly, and when Malcolm explained that it was probably related to the disappearance of Angela Treadway he became genuinely concerned. He had a circular about Angela in front of him. The link was tenuous at this point but Malcolm didn't care as long as it got results. The officer agreed to send someone round, but it might be up to an hour. It was Friday and they had their hands full. What more could he say? All Malcolm knew was that he had an overwhelming sense that something was going to happen. Tonight. It had all been staged for tonight. He started to phone Gruber at home but didn't carry through with it. An hour. An hour at most, the officer had said. He gripped the hoe tightly. He would have to wait it out.

The wind had picked up considerably. It wouldn't be long before it began to rain. Malcolm remembered the rifle. He made his way carefully through the house switching on the lights, alert for the tiniest sound. He carried the hoe across his chest – how did you hit someone with a hoe? It didn't matter, it was something. To his dismay it was going to have to do – the rifle was gone. As he looked above the lintel in the front room, he felt the same dizziness he had felt earlier when he had phoned Pip. He checked the drawer in the study where the shells were kept. They too were gone.

A door slammed upstairs. He stood stock-still. It slammed

again and a third time. There was no rhythm to it. It could be the wind, after all the windows were wide open. But when the wind closed a door, it stayed closed, at least when it was closed with the force with which the door had slammed. First the alarm, now the door. Someone wanted him upstairs. Malcolm ran back to the kitchen and gathered the sharpest knife he could find in the drawer. He made for the stairs and then stopped. The walls of the staircase were smeared with blood. No, he realized, not blood, thank God – lipstick – slashes of it like headless arrows leading up the stairs. The hall was drenched with the smell of L'Air du Temps. Malcolm's heart was in his throat. He should wait, downstairs; an hour the officer had said. Somehow he knew that were he to retreat now the slamming would only continue. He began slowly to climb the stairs. The red arrows continued on the upstairs walls until they reached the entrance to the master bedroom. The door was open and at rest. Malcolm stood on the threshold. Immediately the wind met him. The room was cold. He switched on the light and gasped. The room – every wall and each open window – was smeared with lipstick graffiti. The mirrored closet doors, the chess board, the trunk, the framed pictures, the commode – every surface held a message.

Malcolm screamed, *"Come out! Come out!"* There was no reply, not the slightest noise to give away a presence. Nothing. Holding the knife ready he threw open the closets, watching his own reflection on the mirrored surfaces fly out of his vision as he did. He hurled the clothes apart and took great handfuls which he threw on the floor. Nothing. He raced around the upper story like a madman. Each room was empty. In a frenzy he opened closets and chests and cupboards and finally even the drawers, in his search. Nothing, nothing, nothing. The only way out was down the stairs and nothing had slipped by him, nothing human. A flurry of rain spattered against a window, startling him. He tried to calm himself. He made his way back to the master bedroom.

It was from there that the sense of danger came. He brandished the knife, sweeping it before him in the air – already fighting an invisible opponent.

The writing across the walls was not graffiti, not merely graffiti. It was quotations from Trevor Hill's *A Heard of Scandal*. Malcolm did not want to read it. But it was compelling. Slapped across the walls was the writing of a minor author whom he was championing. He had read the book several times but it had never seemed so awesomely powerful and so depraved. It was no longer literature; it was no longer safe. You couldn't stop when you felt like it or shut it out. They were not random quotations; they were all taken from the drunken love scene between the protagonist, Gob, and Maystamp, a girl he met in a bar. The same scene that had been quoted in the letter found in Angela's car. It was a love scene transformed into an angry red rape the author had never intended:

> The porcelain hand blurred and waved o'er heads, he and she wrestling 'gainst walls, 'gainst bleary heads, 'gainst time and the furniture ....

> ... kisses for yellow hair, kisses for brown roots, kisses for responsive lips, responsive skin, responsive, twice responsive tits ....

> Whirlygig, and well he did and well she jigged in the tumbling room. Clothes every which way with minds of their own clothes – fleas from a dead mutt – mustn't say that, chum. Not dead yet, old spunker. Bark old spaniel yelp ....

> Up to his neck, up to his red neck in flesh, Lord love me.

Everywhere the scene was re-enacted. Almost the entire chapter but without its humorous beginning and its almost tender finale.

There was only one part not from the love scene. It was scrawled across the bed sheets; the next to the last scene from the book:

All around the unknown seeking refuge from the unknown. Closet it, boy ....

And now another door began to slam, downstairs. Once, twice, again and again. This time it was not the wind: the slams were like funereal drum beats. Malcolm closed his eyes. The drum beat. He gripped the knife. His anger rose, his cheeks were flaming with heat, but he didn't move. Suddenly he began to run, hurling himself down the stairs and screaming. Yelling like a warrior, tapping whatever savage power he had in him. The doors into his study were closed; he kicked them open. He kicked at the doors leading into the front room but they wouldn't budge. He tried the handle; it was not locked. He pushed with his foot. Something blocked the way. Again he pushed; slowly it edged aside. With all his might he heaved the doors open. A chair clattered across the floor. That was all, a chair. The room was empty. Everything was the same as it had been only a few minutes earlier except for the door to the storage closet which was open now. Again Malcolm stopped. The only sound came from bursts of rain against the diamond windows and his own gasping breath. There was nowhere to hide but the closet. He watched it carefully, his back against the wall, not wanting to go any farther. There was not a breath of movement from the closet. The closet.

"... Closet it, boy ...."

The plan was devilish: slam the doors; make him read the messages—he won't resist. He must read everything and read *into* everything. Then call him again; slam the doors like a drum, he'll come, screaming his head off. Leave the door open, he won't resist.

Malcolm realized he was gripping the knife so tightly his

fingernails were digging into his palm. His knuckles were white. He approached the dark, little storage room. He leaned for a moment on the table in the center of the floor. Still no sound except the plitting of the rain on glass and behind that the wind and the muffled sea. There was a smell figured against the mustiness of the room and the camphor of mothballs in the closet. He reached into the storage room and pulled the string that turned on the bare light bulb. The room was hot from being closed up for weeks. He stepped inside. The smell, warm and faintly putrid, met him; he was closing in. He separated scarves and gloves on the shelf. Nothing. He moved farther into the room, towards the sagging coat rack lined with heavy coats and winter clothes in gray plastic bags. He glanced down at the cardboard shoebox below the coat rack. He looked again. Amidst the galoshes and snow boots was one tiny, ivory foot. Malcolm grew weak, his legs threatened to fall from under him, and desperately he reached out to the coat rack for support. It gave way immediately under his weight. The coats sagged to the floor but one of the plastic bags heaved forward and fell towards him. Around the hanger were knotted strands of red hair. Angela! Malcolm fell back against the closet wall and the door behind him slammed shut. He screamed hideously, writhing against the wall as if the bundle lying now before him were a snake. He wanted to throw up; he wanted to hide. He should move and yet his muscles would not, his mind was frozen with horror. He could not take his eyes from the sack with its pathetic pale legs but he had to. The danger was outside. He lunged for the door. It would not give at first. He felt nauseated and his heart like it would burst. He threw all his weight at the door. This time it gave.

Later he could not clearly recall the sequence that followed. It all happened at once. All he could be sure of was that the first thing he saw as the door flew open was Mary, her features exaggerated, almost deformed by fear. At her shoulder she held the Snyder-Enfield, cocked, ready to fire. She turned to him as he burst from the closet, and for a moment only she aimed the rifle at him. There was a flurry of action in that split second. A vase was hurled at Mary's head. She ducked and then a third figure, a man in a black coat appeared from the corner where she had held him at bay and hurtled past her into the study. She fired and the figure fell on one knee but immediately picked himself up again and bolted for the living room. The man stumbled again, this time over Kevin, who had jumped out from behind the door. Kevin was no match for him; the man was burly and threw him off. He disappeared around the corner into the west wing. Mary tried to reload and Kevin jumped to his feet to follow. The entire scene could not have lasted a minute. Mary tore after the man. Malcolm unlatched the huge front door. The intruder would leave through the first exit he came to, the French doors. Malcolm might be able to cut him off as he cut across the courtyard. He grasped his knife. There was a real target now. Before he had taken three strides into the dark, however, he was leveled by a crushing tackle. He swung out like a madman with the knife. It connected and the grip on him loosened. The knife fell from his hand with the impact.

"Dear God, it's you!" bawled a huge voice. Its owner rolled off Malcolm clutching his hand which was bleeding badly. It was Hew Bushy. A figure dashed past them limping. The policeman, despite his wound, was on his feet again and chasing the figure. He drew a revolver as he ran. Malcolm was badly winded and crawled to his feet. Kevin flew past him without a word, his usually gentle face distorted with rage. Mary followed. Seeing Malcolm bent over, she stopped. Through clenched teeth he told her he was all right, and she followed the others, the heavy rifle held like a flag.

Malcolm began to follow but suddenly stopped. With a burst of adrenalin he raced back for the car. The Fiat roared.

He passed Mary without even slowing. He held his hand on the horn and Kevin jumped from his path. A hundred yards later the lumbering figure of Hew Bushy was forced out of the way. Around the next turn he saw the intruder. Without losing a stride, the figure turned and clambered up the steep grassy embankment into the woods. Malcolm pulled to a stop, yanked the emergency brake and left the car idling. He almost fell out the door and in a second was crashing into the woods behind the man. Bushy followed and then Kevin too. Bushy took charge, pulling out his flashlight and signalling the others to spread out. He had them stop to listen. Only the wind and the rain. But the man couldn't possibly be out of earshot! He must be hiding. No one spoke. They had come about twenty yards into the woods. Bushy began to edge slowly back towards the road. Malcolm couldn't believe he was giving up – the man must be near – he'd have to make a move. He did. Bushy's guess had been correct. There was a brief clatter, the Fiat's door closed, and the car again roared to life, spitting out mud and grass on Bushy as the officer burst from the woods.

A shot rang out, and the back window of the Fiat exploded. The car kept on going. Mary had not been twenty feet from the car when the man had made his exit. Bushy was running up the hill already. It had been lucky Mary hadn't shot him. The car squealed around a bend in the road and Bushy followed. He knelt to the ground and fired his pistol two-handed. The car stuttered and for one moment they thought it was stopped, but the engine caught again, and it was off.

Bushy was on his feet again. They were about halfway up the hill. His car was at the top by the Manor. The Fiat had been leaning, he had noticed, and his last shot had hit something, perhaps the driver. There was a chance of catching him if he could just get to the car. Malcolm ran after him. He did not see Mary collapse into Kevin's arms.

The stranger, secure in his start, had visited the police car just long enough to slash a tire and, more important, pull out the radio cable. As the officer arrived at the clearing he was in time to see the lights swing onto the Peninsula Road. He would risk it. It broke the rules, but it might be the only chance. He jumped into the squad car despite its slashed tire and with the siren screaming took off. Malcolm appeared in time to see his car turn onto the Peninsula Road. He watched the lights until they had gone, the squad car hiccupping after the wounded Fiat in a pathetic chase.

Once again it was quiet. Somewhere behind him were Mary and Kevin. There was nothing left to do but join them.

The rain was falling again. The wind had dropped, and the still trees were like a canopy, an arched, dark hallway closing him off from the elements. The darkness held little fear, not any more. His legs were like jelly, his stomach ached from Bushy's tackle, and painful blisters had formed on his right hand where he had grasped the kitchen knife. It now lay on the wet sand, on the road at the bottom of the hill. So much else waited at the bottom of the hill. His legs gave way beneath him momentarily. He steadied himself. In the dark immediately ahead of him were two figures. The smaller of them, seeing him, moved towards him, one step and then two steps, tentatively. It cried out his name, and when he answered, the figure ran and threw her arms around him. He responded gratefully and for a moment he had the strength to hold her tightly, very tightly until finally his arms ached and fell away in the same jelly-like state as his legs. He felt drugged. He was not sure he could talk. Kevin was there and all of them embraced, huddled silently.

Malcolm knew he should rush to the house and phone the RCMP but he doubted that his legs were up to it. The luminous hands of his watch indicated 10:15, he had phoned at 9:35. How quickly it had all happened – an incredible unbroken rush of events. He found himself thinking it through but stopped himself. He shook his head. To think it through would mean having to think about those white legs falling from their gray package and that hank of red hair. He tried to convince himself it had not been Angela, but he knew it had. He shuddered and immediately the arms around his waist tightened their hold. Mary. She was alive. She had probably saved his life. Less than an hour ago he had half-suspected her again ... that at least was over. The mistrust, the awful not knowing. There was a lot he didn't know but that much was over.

When they emerged from the woods, the rain was falling lightly. It was cool against their faces and their scraped arms. The front door had swung wide open but they did not enter by it. Kevin pulled it shut and they walked around to the west wing through the courtyard.

Mary put on coffee. Malcolm phoned the RCMP. A squad car was on its way, the duty officer informed him confidently. Without any discernible expression in his voice Malcolm related the events of the last forty-five minutes. His narration was concise, emotionless. The officer wasted no time. He left the phone to put out an all points bulletin on the Fiat. He then returned to Malcolm who was waiting patiently. Malcolm suggested the man contact Detective Inspector Penny of the Halifax Police Department. Someone would be sent to attend to the body.

The grim reality was forced in on Malcolm. No, he explained, he had not touched her. Her – Angela, not her – a corpse. He felt dizzy again as he remembered the lunging gray puppet with legs as limp as cloth. He hung up and racing to the sink vomited again and again.

The squad car arrived shortly thereafter and then there was no avoiding the front room. To Malcolm it felt as if the room had a pulse, as if it were still beating furiously from the recent action. He pointed to the body, repeating that he had neither touched nor moved it; that was how it had fallen, pulling the rack and all the clothes with it. The putrescence was stronger now, since the fall. The officer sent out on a routine vandalism case was not prepared for this. He left everything as it was and seemed as anxious as the others to get out of the room. He phoned headquarters to make a report and then took statements from each of them. It would be the first of many repetitions of the story each of them would give that night.

Between the delays, Mary told Malcolm how she and the others had come to arrive when they did. She started from the beginning, it was obviously not going to be a short wait for the due processes of the law to take place.

Several things had helped to convince her ultimately that the fleeting shadow in the studio had not been a hallucination or her imagination. She had thought again and again of that night, about the set up in the studio, staged as it was with an alleyway behind the large canvas and the easel to the shed door. She had tried to reconstruct the incident, remembering as best she could just how long a time had elapsed before Malcolm had broken through the door. An idea had occurred to her, and so, one morning the previous week when she knew Malcolm was out, she had returned with Kevin to Odd's End. She had felt like a burglar herself, sneaking around, but she found what she wanted – or nearly. In the shed, there was a series of shelves three feet wide piled primarily with paint tins and lumber. One of the lower shelves had been recently disturbed – not much – the dust was streaked and the cobwebs that covered the shelf were broken or new. It was just barely possible that the escaping figure had heard Malcolm coming and had thrown himself into the shelf, judging that the racket from inside would cover any noise he made. As soon as Malcolm passed, he could have escaped into the barn and hidden in the loft, or for that matter, he could have continued through the barn to the dunes. He would just have had time before the men had searched. It was inconclusive but nonetheless confirmed Mary in her determination.

"I couldn't tell you, darling. I couldn't tell you I had stopped seeing Fielding either. He was convinced I was not sick but you wouldn't believe it." The next moment she was crying. Malcolm tried to comfort her but he had little strength, his whole body felt numb. In a moment she regained her composure, enough to continue her story.

She told him of the visitor to the antique shop and her vivid dream.

"The last thing I saw in my dream were the man's hands reaching out at me. I woke up and put on the light. I noticed my own hands. I looked at my dirty fingernails and remembered how the man's fingernails had been dirty like mine. It was that that had convinced me he was a painter. But the black under my fingernails was tar. It takes ages to get it out. Painters' fingernails are often dirty *but not with tar*! I sat for a moment trembling and then I woke Kevin and told him. The more we thought about the man the more ominous he seemed. I immediately assumed he had followed me there, to the shop, that he was probably out on the street that minute waiting. You had told me that there had been no further incidents here. What else could I think? I could hardly sleep. Whenever I thought of what the man had got away with so far, the limits he was willing to go, I was sure he would try anything."

Mary paused and drained her coffee in one long gulp. It had cooled down during her narrative. Kevin took her cup without asking and filled it.

"Why don't you stop now, Mary," said Malcolm reaching out and taking her hand but she was off again. The sobbing had stopped; she was determined to get it all out.

"Bliss called Tuesday . . . ." She remembered the conversation vividly and related it to him.

"For the first time I began to understand. I couldn't imagine what the man's plans might be but they included getting me out of the house and out of the way. I remembered he asked me when I had another show coming up. I told him, and he nodded as if he already knew. It didn't surprise me since it is advertised in arts circulars, but when I thought about it, it was easy to read into that nod. I wondered if he was waiting until I left to make his move. I didn't know what he planned, but I did know my going would only make it easier for him. I decided not to go. I also decided to do some spying of my own.

"I watched the house most of yesterday from the woods. It was stupid; if he had been there I could have been trapped, but I was sure he would not expect someone to be playing his own game. In the shop, he had struck me as arrogant, impossibly arrogant."

Malcolm suddenly went pale. He could feel the blood draining from his face and a dizziness enveloping him.

"You could have been killed," he whispered.

There was no reply.

"I was playing games, and you could have been killed, and Angela ... was ...." He looked down at his hands which were shaking.

Kevin got up and poured him a shot of brandy, which he gulped gratefully.

"I'm sorry, Mary. What happened next?"

She looked at him worriedly, and he patted her hand to assure her he was all right.

"Well," she began, "this morning after you left I saw him. From where I was in the woods, I could see clearly through the west wing. Suddenly he appeared out of nowhere. He was just standing, all of a sudden, in the dune grass directly in front of the courtyard. He seemed to materialize from the sand. I was very scared." She laughed nervously. "I couldn't help thinking he could see me clear through the house the way I could see him. His appearance in the dunes had been so dramatic that I began to fear he was more than human. It was horrible. I didn't dare move. He walked so securely, so proudly – I couldn't believe it. He was again like an overblown actor, or a pantomimist really – the house-proud landowner. I half-expected him to give orders to an imaginary chauffeur or kick an imaginary dog. The pantomime ended when he had to pick the lock but even that he did with exaggerated panache.

"He was inside about an hour, upstairs mostly. When he left he switched on the yard light. I watched him cross the dunes, evidently he had finished for the time being. I waited a long time, and then I slipped around the house to the beach. By then he was far down the shore heading north to the mainland. I was sure he was not coming back until later. Why else had he turned on the yard light? I slipped in the house long enough to get the rifle. I thought about going upstairs, but I was afraid he might come back. I felt more like a burglar than ever, afraid *he* would catch *me* there in my own house! I almost wanted to chase after him and shoot him then and get it over with, but I knew I would never catch him. His performance had been so complete, his pretence of ownership utterly convincing."

Malcolm seemed almost not to have heard; his mind was elsewhere. "I wonder how long she was here." He looked at each of the others, not expecting an answer. "How long was she in this house, dead?"

"If I had known, I would have phoned the police immediately." Mary spoke almost apologetically.

Kevin suddenly broke in. "I begged her to go to the cops, Mal."

"I couldn't. Not after everything else," Mary replied.

"After everything else you should have ..."

"Stop it!" Malcolm interrupted Kevin.

Kevin blustered. "I didn't mean ... I wasn't blaming ...."

Mary spoke gently. "I know, Kev."

"I'm the one who is to blame," said Malcolm. "I should have gone to the police weeks ago ..."

Mary interrupted him. Her voice was firm. "This is not the time for recrimination. We all made mistakes!" She paused to let this statement sink in and then, as if there had been no break, she continued with her story, determined to finish.

"Kevin saw Constable Bushy outside the Sea Shanty

Drive-In when we were already on our way here tonight. I didn't want to stop; I was afraid of making a fool of myself. Kevin insisted."

"I was driving!" said Kevin.

"He had been kind to me. It seemed like fate that we should see him. I think he was more worried about me and the rifle than anything else; we were taking the law into our own hands. I guess I got mad."

Again Kevin interjected, almost smiling. "Her exact words were 'I'll kill the bastard.'"

"That's when Bushy decided to come. He radioed head-quarters to say he was checking out a case of vandalism up the coast; he didn't mention Odd's End. He followed us out in the cruiser and then we walked down, cutting off the road up at the old logging track and hiding in the wood down behind the west wing; that way we would be able to see him if he came up from the dunes the way he had earlier. Actually he arrived from the road, he seemed in a hurry."

"I'm not surprised," said Malcolm dryly. "He had a lot of surprises to prepare for me."

"It's strange now that I think about it," Mary continued. "I was almost glad to see him. When he finally entered the house it was the first time that I actually believed it. I'd seen him before, but until someone else saw him too I wasn't entirely sure. I wanted to nab him right away but Bushy saw too many escape routes. The thought of losing him was enough to keep me patient. Bushy was annoyed that he wasn't close enough to the car to radio headquarters for support but it would have taken too long to reach it so we were stuck. Then you arrived, Malcolm, only minutes later, which complicated the plan. We could only wait. It was an excruciating time. Finally you went upstairs where we knew he was and were ready to make a move until we saw the man leaving by the spare room window. He dropped from the ledge and shinnied around the corner of the house so that he could fall onto the living room roof. He crossed the roof and dropped to the ground by the study. Had he climbed off the roof in the back of the house, Bushy could have arrested him there and then, but now he was out of sight. Bushy, rather than following him and risking being seen or heard, took off the other way around the house, around the stable. After a minute, we saw you come downstairs and run screaming through the house. A moment later the man crossed the courtyard and entered behind you. I couldn't stand the thought of his being behind you, following you, and Bushy had not yet appeared around from the other side, so we rushed around and in. The rest you know."

The story was at last over, and there was an uneasiness between them: Malcolm, Mary, and Kevin. For one thing, the man had got away. Bushy was chasing him somewhere along the peninsula, but there had been no report yet, and they suspected the worst.

All of them felt something that they didn't want to put into words. What might have happened! How tenuous the web of clues that had at last convinced Mary to act the way she had – coincidence mostly. What if the man had not shown up at the shop? Why had he showed up at all? Bliss's intuition, Mary spying – what if none of these things had happened? What had the intruder planned for Malcolm? What if – that was what was unspoken between them – what if?

Reports arrived throughout the night and into the morning as did various parties of officialdom. Forensic specialists and photographers from Halifax examined the front room, a doctor examined the body. Malcolm was asked to identify it – her – it. It was Angela. Her neck was blue with hideous bruises.

Inspector Penny arrived after midnight. She conferred with the team of investigators, and then passed on what information she could to the waiting trio. The death had been due to strangulation. There were remarkably few fingerprints on the body or in the vicinity of it, and none was very clear. They had found in a pocket a message typed on Malcolm's typewriter and signed with his signature or its double. It asked Angela to meet him in the park near her home. The letter apologized for such a clandestine meeting but said it was urgent. There was no time or date. It must have been waiting for her on her door or maybe in her mailbox at school. In any case the implication was that she was to respond immediately. It didn't take long for Malcolm to realize what the man had planned for him! Eventually the police would end up at Odd's End, clues would pop up here and there until finally they found the body. Even if Malcolm phoned in himself, he would still be under suspicion. The entire story about the mysterious intruder would be questioned; it would all appear either as an elaborate plot or as if the murder was the result of temporary insanity, perhaps brought about by guilt – the awful end result of a weekend assignation with the wife safely out of town. Temporary insanity – he might have gotten off with manslaughter.

Penny could tell what Malcolm was thinking. She had been brought up to date on the events of the evening and informed him that handwriting analysts would be able to detect whether the signature was a fraud. If it had been traced from an original rather than copied then their best bet would be to locate the original, since no two signatures by an individual are ever the same. There was a chance the man used something from the desk drawer since it would be handy. They inspected the checks, contracts and documents that bore likely matches to the signature and Malcolm signed them over to the detective's safekeeping.

The Fiat was found in Mahone Bay at eleven o'clock. The rear tire was shredded, and the front of the driver's seat was drenched with blood; Mary had obviously hit the man in the back of the leg. There were also small traces of blood on the head rest, perhaps from Hew Bushy's shot. But for all that, the man was not located. It was not until after one that further news was forthcoming. A Miss Deirdre Tinker had phoned in reporting a robbery. She ran a tourist lodge, the Sea Winds. The money had been taken from her money drawer, as she called it. She had always kept some of her cash there. The lock had been forced. Incidentally, her car was gone too. Strangely, she didn't seem to link the two events, or wish to, at least. The car, she assured them, had been lent to one of her regular clientele, Mr. Nice, he called himself. When had he "borrowed" the car? Shortly after eleven. She had thought it odd that he wanted to borrow the car so late. He had looked a little peaked. But she had respected his privacy and asked no more. She had been in her sitting room upstairs and had gone down for a lemonade – and that was when she had found the drawer open. The window in the study also seemed to have been pried open. With some difficulty the officer had got Miss Tinker to let him look in Mr. Nice's room. His luggage was gone and on the bed they found badly stained pants and socks, soaked in blood. Peaked, she had said! He must have lost a pint of blood in the Fiat alone. The man must be made of steel.

By four-thirty Angela's body was finally removed from Odd's End. With it went all but one of the policemen, an RCMP officer who had been left in case the stranger returned. Nobody could really imagine he would return, but then a month ago the Closes would not have been able to imagine such a man existed. As one of the policemen put it, he was persistent.

There was nothing left to do but try to sleep; filled with coffee and waiting for the phone, there seemed little hope. The matter of where to sleep also posed a problem. There was really no room in the house that didn't hold a reminder of the man. His presence was pervasive. The master bedroom was out, so was the spare bedroom – that was the room Mary had seen him escape from. The second floor was out. In the end, they pulled mattresses into the living room, and cut the edge of the coffee with generous doses of brandy. The three of them fell asleep together like children.

Information trickled in over the next few days, the bulk of it far from satisfying. No Mr. Nice, for one thing. He had not returned to Odd's End, nor had he returned Miss Tinker's car. They did find it at last at the airport outside Halifax but not until Monday evening. He had broken every cordon but then he had had two hours headstart. He must have gone straight from Mahone Bay to the airport. A description circulated to ticket offices had elicited that a man, possibly the suspect, had booked a flight to England on the Saturday British Airways flight. The ticket had been one-way. A money changer also felt he remembered a man fitting the description. The exchange minus the airfare added up roughly to the amount stolen from Miss Tinker. There was little to be found in his room at the Sea Winds except one very important item. In the garbage pail was a canceled check of Malcolm's. There was nothing of Mary's to account for the letter which had been copied, but the signature on the check corresponded exactly with the one at the bottom of the letter to Angela. It was enough to get Malcolm off the hook.

Mary found in her studio the photograph that had been the model for *Manshadow*. It didn't provide much information: the face was concealed by the telescope and the picture was in high contrast. Life at Odd's End had been temporarily shattered and all that remained in the way of tangible evidence of the culprit was a shadowy photograph. Mr. Nice indeed! Like everything else, his name, assumed, no doubt, had been well researched. Malcolm read from the *O.E.D. Nice* – foolish, senseless, wanton, lascivious, extravagant, flaunting, strange, rare, uncommon ... difficult to please ... nice!

From time to time they made new discoveries: traces of

their oppressor. The moon of the grandfather clock had been scratched so that his sanguine face appeared to grimace. Also the Cornell sculptured box had been tampered with. The tin stars were all there but the one empty pigeonhole had been changed – the stars had been moved. Each discovery was fascinating but still tinged with terror.

What baffled them most was attempting to find a motive short of sheer unmitigated evil. What could he have hoped to gain? If he had wanted the house for himself, he must surely have known that to drive them away would not guarantee him the property. Miss Tinker had told the police that Mr. Nice had been looking for a place to retire, he had said to her that money was no consideration.

Reports from state police in Maine seemed to shed some light on the case. The reports were further substantiated by an FBI investigation of a series of crimes that stretched throughout New England. The cases pointed to a similar *modus operandi*: houses broken into and lived in, sometimes with tragic consequences for the inhabitants. In one instance in Maine, a family of three were trussed up and shoved in the attic. When the police found them they had been dead for a week, but in the kitchen there was a warm pot of coffee and the remains of a freshly abandoned breakfast! If a trail could be established for these strange and wanton acts of violence it ran north along the eastern seaboard; and it had ended the previous fall, coinciding with Mr. Nice's arrival at the Sea Winds.

He had been a model guest at the Sea Winds and then had taken almost a thousand dollars. He had stolen nothing from Odd's End.

The Closes did not go on vacation after all – not right away at least. Mary did not go to Toronto and Malcolm canceled his speaking engagement at Harvard. He did send the paper, which was finished anyway; it was reportedly well received. Mary's show sold well and *Manshadow* was purchased by the Art Bank. This pleased her immensely because it meant that the piece would spend most of its time locked away in a factory building in Ottawa. She didn't want to see it any more. She joked to her friends about painting nothing but flowers and seascapes, maybe Peggy's Cove too. For a while she didn't paint anything.

Pip felt she had been cruelly robbed of a visit which she had been enthusiastically looking forward to and so she came to Nova Scotia for two weeks and stayed at Odd's End. Bliss also visited, and they went to see her in *Power at the Crossroad*. Mary went several times. The two of them became fast friends. The house was alive with comings and goings. Interior decorators were hired, and the house given more than a new coat of paint. A ritualistic cleansing was in order; as were dead-bolt locks and an alarm system. The Closes were determined to stay on. It was a duty somehow. They loved the house and refused to have it wrestled from them. It was like a little triumph over Chaos. Almost. They had not forgotten Angela. The inquest confirmed that death had been due to strangulation; there had been no sexual abuse. She had been nothing more than a decoy. It was a senseless and hideous crime. The Closes set up a trust fund to provide a scholarship in Angela's name for a student studying the humanities; it seemed a pitiful gesture, but it was something. Malcolm suffered a bad time over her death. Not right away, not at the inquest or at the funeral, but weeks later. His whole inside seemed to cave in, what had been grief at her loss, became a gnawing hole within. The wound was still painful, when school began again in the fall.

One day, near the end of June, a rather frail and greatly agitated lady showed up at Odd's End. Miss Deirdre Tinker. She felt an accessory before the fact and could scarcely be comforted. She was eventually consoled, however, with tea laced with gin.

And finally in July they heard from him again, Mr. Nice. Just a postcard from Edinburgh, a city he liked and was thinking of moving to, or so the postcard said. He thanked them for the visit to Odd's End, praising the tranquility of the place and begging them to visit him once he had settled down. Just like any other postcard but like no other postcard! There was no signature, but the handwriting had to be his own, but who could tell? The police took the card, for what it was worth.

In August, on Mary's birthday, there was a surprise for them. Not a party, which would have been highly inappropriate, but a dog. Powys had sired a litter, and Kevin was given choice of litter, which he presented to Mary. The Closes were now a family. They hoped the puppy would grow quickly. They named him after Kevin's store – Hope.

Epilogue

Stupid X! What foolish Vanity! Everything so well conceived and carried out with patience and mastery and then the little voice ... that demanding little voice of pride. Oh the compelling need to see the fruits of one's labors. I am content enough to work away in my anonymity and then the little voice wants to cry out – Me!

First the trip to the shop; that was to see Mary's eyes; I had promised myself I would see her eyes, and beautiful quick eyes they were too. And then the slamming doors, unnecessary really, I needn't have even come back. Just one little peek, that was all I wanted – a chance to see *his* eyes when he found my little present. Well, what is done is done. They took a long time to break but they did at last; they always do, you know. And now the house is mine. I'll not stay there. Why? Do you ask why? How boring! How little you have understood. A man cannot own his home. It is a lesson I have learned well, didn't I say that? I'm sure I did. Now that Odd's End is mine I am free to go on and leave it. A house is, in the end, all in one's head. The papers are signed in blood. No mortgages. No interest. No insurance.

Anyway, there were things wrong with Odd's End I hadn't noticed at first. Silly little things really. I grew annoyed with the order of the books in the study. It's petty I know, but it was less than perfection. And all those windows in the west wing – a veritable fish bowl! And there was that smell in the front room, I couldn't live with such a smell and chrysanthemums!

I have no time for renovation. Renovation is like housekeeping, all cosmetic really. I don't believe in beauty that is only skin deep. It belies real character. Here there is character.

I feel quite different about Great Britain this time around. I suppose my spell in the New World helped me to appreciate the essence of character all over again. There are houses here with real character, character revealed by age. The makeup has peeled with time showing a true face underneath. Some of the most wonderful examples are well off the beaten track, which is good in some ways, I do like my privacy. But then I walk with quite a limp in my other leg now, apart from my trick knee. Still I am full of enthusiasm.

Old England to New England and now New Scotland to Old Scotland. It makes sense. It is a sign. I always pay the closest attention to signs. Where to exactly? Somewhere near the sea, I do love the sea, but somewhere sheltered from the wind . . . .